MISS CHISUM

A COLORFUL 19TH CENTURY TEXAN ROMANCE

By

Russ E A Brown

Copyright ©2019

FOREWORD

The days of the Old West are the most romanticized in all of America's history; in books, songs, TV shows and most especially in the movies.

In countless Westerns the heroes and villains of the era were immortalized as rugged larger-than-life characters; against a backdrop of the stunning beauty of the western States, and dramatically orchestrated musical scores.

In truth, not everything was as black and white as the movies might have you believe. Join me to explore my vision of the westward migration of the Wild Frontier, through the eyes of a very complicated Texan family.

CHAPTER 1

EUGIE THOMAS

On an oppressively hot afternoon in Denton County, North Texas, in early August 1970, 84-year-old Eugie Thomas was sitting on her veranda swing chair, attempting to stay cool in the shade, with her electric fan on full blast, casually observing three Rhode Island Reds, fighting over a recently deceased rat. She looked out towards the Grapevine Reservoir, thinking a swim might have been invigorating, if she was a mite younger.

Eugie quietly reflected on what had been a tough few years, punctuated by her brother John-Emory dying in '68, her sister Alice in '69, and then to compound her grief, she had just buried another sister, Virgie. But despite her losses she remained upbeat about the world, counted her blessings, and loved her uncomplicated routine life.

She also loved to keep up with world affairs; her daily afternoon treat was to read the Fort Worth Star-Telegram newspaper, which her husband, McKinley, ritually left for her after coming home for lunch.

The day's international headlines were a mix of racial and Cold War paranoia, with both the French and Russian nuclear tests competing for column-inches with a story about the release from prison of the Black Panther leader, Huey Newton, a man for whom Eugie had very mixed feelings, as an ambassador for her race. The news might not have been the brightest, but then she turned over to the entertainment page, and a big smile radiated from her wrinkled face.

The rumble of a V8 engine distracted her from her reading, its sound emanating from a bright red muscle car heading up the road, leaving a trail of terracotta dust in its wake. It pulled up outside the homestead, amid scattering chickens, giving Sam, Eugie's ginger tomcat, the opportunity to resolve the rodent debacle.

She didn't know the car, but deduced from the Confederate bumper sticker that it probably wasn't owned by a Northerner. A man stepped out, stretched his tall, wiry frame and approached the house.

He walked into the shade of the veranda and took off his sunglasses. She recognized him as Daniel Johnson, one of her favorite seasonal white truck drivers, he wore a deep tan, which suited him well. She looked deeper into his handsome face; his expression was uncharacteristically serious.

"Hello Danny, nice new car, crop dusting clearly pays better than we do, how was your trip?"

He tipped his head and respectfully took off his straw Stetson, "It went well, and thank you, Mrs. Thomas. I just came by to say I was sorry to hear about your sister, and for missing her funeral. She was a fine lady, always very kind to me when I was a boy".

At 41 years old, Danny had retained the calculated speech of a North Texan country boy, but his accent had clearly been softened by prolonged worldly travel.

Eugie nodded and answered pragmatically, "That she was, but it was her time, she was 90. She had a mostly wonderful life, and I'm sure she's enjoying an even more wonderful afterlife with Bob, Meady and the rest of the family.

"Anyways, it's about time you called me Eugie, you've known me since you were a baby. 'Mrs. Thomas' is saved for the bureaucrats... and McKinley, when he's mad with me," she qualified with a wink.

"Yes, Mrs. Thomas... I mean..."

Eugie raised her hand to interrupt him, and stabbed at the cinema listings in the newspaper, "You like cowboy films, would you mind taking an old lady to see John Wayne... if that would be okay with your girl?" she added with a chuckle.

Surprised, but honored to be asked, Danny replied with country-born composure, ignoring the beheaded rat Sam had deposited on his boot, "It would be a pleasure mam, and there is no girl to trouble about at the moment, are you free tomorrow evening?"

"Pick me up at seven... and you can keep that," she added with a grin, pointing at his bloodied boot.

There were few things that Danny enjoyed more than a good Western, but he was surprised to discover that Eugie Thomas was a fan of the genre.

For him they did not come much better than those starring John Wayne. He had really enjoyed True Grit the previous year, a rare evening out with his father to celebrate his fortieth birthday, and was glad to see that Wayne had finally been honored with an Oscar. His personal favorite was 'The Searchers', which he had seen in the very same movie theatre in the 1950s. He even forgave the director, John Ford, for trying to convince the world that the mesas and buttes of Monument Valley, on the Arizona-Utah border, were in Texas.

The movie Eugie wanted to see was also about a Texan, a very significant one, albeit that he was born in Tennessee, and spent his later days ranching by the Pecos River in New Mexico, trying not to lose his herd during the notorious Lincoln County War. A man by the name of Chisum, John Simpson Chisum, though he was regularly confused with another trail-blazing contemporary, Jesse Chisholm.

Danny arrived punctually, suited and booted in his freshly washed and polished, pride and joy, a 1966 Dodge Charger Fastback, to escort a very smartly dressed Eugie to the theatre.

The tall cowboy, and his diminutive, elderly companion were an incongruous looking pairing coming into town in such a sporty vehicle, but Danny's long respect for Eugie's family, and the confidence he had in his reputation for being able to 'look after himself' insulated him from the number of turned heads.

They settled into their seats as the film opened with the dulcet tones of William Conrad, narrating Chisum's heroic cattle drives into New Mexico, against a backdrop of a series of Russ Vickers' oil paintings of dusty drovers. The last painting gently faded to a scene of Wayne sitting on his horse, near the top of a hill, admiring his ranch.

Eugie was quietly absorbed in the movie, letting out the odd chuckle, mostly at plot points that were not obviously funny. A seemingly deep and meaningful scene of Chisum having a fatherly chat with his niece Sallie induced a shake of her head and a 'Humph.'

The closing credits rolled, and John Wayne rode back up his hill to the sound of Dominic Frontiere's rousing ballad "Chisum, John Chisum..." The lights in the theatre brightened and Eugie's thoughts returned to the 20th Century. She turned and smiled at Danny, who helped her up and walked her back to his car. She was a fit old gal, in no particular need of assistance, but she did enjoy the attention, "Thank you, that was interesting."

It struck Danny that 'interesting' was an odd critique for an action movie, more something you would save for a documentary, but had no vision of Eugie's deeper thinking.

As they pulled up outside the homestead, Eugie turned to Danny and spoke for the first time since they left the theatre, "This will surprise you, but... he was my grandpa."

Danny's expression confirmed his puzzlement. Eugie was never a lady prone to fanciful thoughts or cryptic humor, so he wasn't quite sure how to respond to this bizarre and unlikely revelation.

"John Chisum was a real person... though he didn't look much like John Wayne, and he was more likely to pull out a fiddle than a gun," she added.

Danny had heard of the Chisholm cattle trail across the Red River into Oklahoma, as had any Texan farmer, and had been curious about the apparent misspelling of the movie's title, but his education regarding John Chisum was about to be broadened.

He took Eugie's arm and led her up the steps to her veranda. The evening heat was pleasantly subdued by the breeze from the reservoir; all was quiet apart from the ever-present background serenade of field crickets and frogs.

"Daniel, could you please get some lemonade from the refrigerator in the kitchen, and glasses from the cupboard next to it, then sit with me a while." Eugie requested as she settled into her swing chair with a satisfied sigh.

It had been two decades since Danny had last stepped a foot inside the 'Jones' Place', as it was still known as by his father's generation, in reference to Eugie's dearly departed parents Bob and Meady Jones. It took him a moment to get his bearings and remember where the kitchen was. En-route he was distracted by an elaborately-framed painting of a very distinguished looking, mustachioed fair-skinned gentleman, which was hung in pride of place in the family room, in stark contrast to the room's modest

7

decor. He paused, transfixed for a moment by the piercing eyes of the noble looking gentleman, before continuing on his quest.

He emerged with a pitcher of Eugie's renowned refreshment, and joined her on the swing chair, poured her a glass and handed it to her. He poured his own and took a sip, the lemonade's tart, cool sweetness taking him back through a tunnel in time, to cherished childhood memories of summer barbeques with the Jones family.

Eugie turned, and looked into his eyes with a confident assertiveness reminiscent of the painting he had just perused, "Are you ready for a story that is long overdue to be told?"

Danny, highly intrigued, nodded, "Yep... sure!"

She put down her glass, took a deep breath, leaned forward and placed her hand on her thigh.

She spoke in a tone that reminded Danny of a well-versed history teacher confidently reciting dates and occurrences from before they were born. "John Chisum gave his name to my grandmother Jensie, my mama, Almeady, and my aunt Harriet in 1858, when he bought the rights to them from a California-bound migrant from Arkansas, but the road that brought Chisum and them here to Texas started long before that."

CHAPTER 2

SETTLING IN TEXAS

I n the fall of 1837, John's father, Claiborne Chisum, led a wagon train west from John's birthplace in Hardeman County, Tennessee. Claiborne was a tough, burly, deeply religious man, of Scottish descent, with a full beard and a gravelly voice. A natural leader of men, who did not suffer fools lightly, the perfect combination of character traits for a pioneering wagon master.

The entourage included; thirteen-year-old John, who drove a six-horse team, pulling a Conestoga wagon, John's pregnant mother Lucinda, his elder sister Nancy, three younger brothers; Pitser, James and Jefferson, and their slaves and livestock. Just down the trail away they were joined by John's cousins, their extended families and even more slaves.

Their 400 mile journey took two months to complete. They left Tennessee via a Mississippi crossing near Memphis, and then drove all the way across the new state of Arkansas, then forty miles further west into Indian Territory to get to Ragsdale's Ferry on the Red River.

Texas' Red River County was clear to see, just a matter of 200 yards away across the muddy river, but it would take three days to get all their wagons and livestock over to the Texas side. A few days after that they reached their destination, a new settlement named Pinhook.

It had been a hard journey, which Claiborne was certain contributed to the death of his beloved Lucinda, during childbirth, shortly after they arrived at the settlement, aged just 36. A loss that would leave Claiborne wracked with guilt, and be an important step in shaping the independent, self-reliant man that John Simpson Chisum would eventually become.

Unlike most migrants, Claiborne was already a wealthy man, and within months had purchased over 2,000 acres, of what was at the time the leading edge of the Wild Frontier, and built the first permanent homestead in their community.

Arriving in the republic a year after the battles of The Alamo and San Jacinto, they had missed the ravages of the Texas Revolution, but what they did share with Davy Crocket and the brave Tennesseans, in whose footsteps they had followed, was a passion to turn Texas into something more than that Wild Frontier. Claiborne was a very opinionated man, who had an almost obsessive determination to bring civilization, as he saw it, to the republic and make it worthy of annexation, to become a state of the union.

The biggest threat to the homesteaders and ranchers were the natives. The Indians had never bought into the concept of the land being owned by either the Americans, or the Mexicans who had preceded them. So, unsurprisingly they took umbrage to the steadily increasing flow of incomers into their homelands.

Claiborne felt it was his civic duty to give as much support to the dispatch of the natives as he could muster. To this end, Camp Chisum was established on his land, and in 1838 he signed up as a Captain of a squad of spies under General John Dyer. Their brigade embarked on regular raiding parties as far west as the Trinity River, and played a big part in clearing the natives from a large expanse of prairie.

Some of the land that Claiborne had helped clear would be settled a couple of years later by a trader, by the name of John Neely Bryan. Ironically, Bryan had migrated there from Arkansas after surveying the Trinity Floodplain shortly before Dyer's raids, and had returned with the entrepreneurial ambition of setting up a trading post near the river, to trade with the Indians.

When he arrived, the natives were all gone, but seeing the benefit of having the only natural ford across the Trinity in the county, and the potential for a settlement to develop, he decided to stay. He made his claim, marked out half a square mile into city blocks, and built a cable ferry for the months when the waters ran deep, then simply waited for civilization to arrive. His vision was soon fulfilled, as new settlers moved to his little pioneer town, which he named Dallas.

With no mother around, and his elder sister married and moved on, Claiborne's regular Indian hunting absences left John in charge of his younger brothers, and protecting the ranch for days, sometimes weeks, on end. Despite the responsibility of spending so much time with the herd, or perhaps more accurately, because of his reluctance to take on such a responsibility, he developed a deep dislike for the cattle business. He would not live up to the prophetic family nickname of 'Cow John' until well over a decade later.

For most of his teens and early twenties he was a footloose under-achiever, more concerned with using his good looks to ensnare any of the few available young ladies in town, rather than forging any kind of career for himself; much to the disdain of his father.

In 1840 Claiborne controversially married his own cousin, the widow Cynthia Latimer, who was only nine years older than John, the second time he had married into extended family. Claiborne rapidly got down to the job of producing more children, having another four before the decade was over.

John had never been good at expressing his feelings to his father, and quietly struggled to come to terms with this new relationship, assuming that Claiborne had suddenly got over his grief at the loss of Lucinda in favor of his new love, like replacing an old pair of boots with new ones. Subsequently he emotionally distanced himself from his pa and his new step-mother for a while.

At about this time Red River County was sub-divided, and their homestead was in the new Lamar County portion. The county was named for Mirabeau Buonaparte Lamar, the second president of the Republic of Texas, a man who had distinguished himself at the Battle of San Jacinto, so a good name in Claiborne's patriotic eyes.

In 1844, the Lamar County seat moved to a new town right on their doorstep, named Paris. A French settler, Thomas Poteet, had been tasked with coming up with a name that would reflect the new-found town's importance, to him it was an obvious choice. And the following year Texas fulfilled Claiborne's ambition of becoming a State of the Union.

Despite the hustle and bustle of change, Claiborne always kept a frustrated eye on his listless son, trying to get him involved in his various entrepreneurial projects, whenever possible. Every so often John did impress him, and looked like he was going to make something of himself, but he never seemed to be able to commit to anything for more than a few months.

He was the clerk in a grocery store for a while, but when that did not work out, and only thanks to Claiborne's influence, he got a job overseeing the construction of a road, connecting Tarrant to what would become Sulphur Springs, but he soon quit, causing a huge row with his father.

John felt it was extremely unfair that his younger brothers were not put under the same pressure as he was, and were allowed to follow their whims, which they regularly did to excess. There were reasonable excuses for the middle brother, Jeff, to be cut some slack, due to him being a sickly soul, suffering from epilepsy. Jeff was always going to find life difficult, but James and Pitser had as much duty as John did to uphold the family name.

What Claiborne did not realize was that John had big ambitions bubbling on the back burner. As much as he admired his father and was proud to see him become a respected pillar of their growing community, John did not want to live in his ever-growing shadow, picking up scraps from his table. John's ambition was wealth, great wealth, but he wanted to achieve this independently. At this point he had no specific idea how he was going to do this, but he knew that he was not going to find it in a general mercantile store or overseeing a road gang.

This all said, John was no snob, and not above physical labor. When his father won a contract to build the Cumberland Presbyterian Church, he was happy to support him in the menial role of Hod Carrier, hauling bricks to the masons on the building site. This was followed by construction of the Lamar County Courthouse, a prestigious project that led on to other building contracts, which would occupy his time for a few weeks or months on end, without challenging his limited attention span. Laboring also kept him fit and lean, fitting in well with the image he liked to portray, of being a man who could charm the ladies.

By his mid-twenties John had a scheme maturing in his head, with regards to how he could make his fortune which, despite his desire to take a different path from that of his father, would very much emulate Claiborne's road to respectability. He planned to go into the cattle business, but go into it on a far bigger scale than his father ever had. To achieve this ambition he needed land, and lots of it, which would mean heading further west into the ever-migrating Wild Frontier.

This new plan concentrated John's mind on the fact that he needed a stake, and that he would have to accept settling into a steady job for a while, that paid a bit more than he was earning working for Claiborne. It was time for what he expected to be a long father and son chat.

He eventually plucked up the courage to broach the subject, walked into his father's office and looked across at Claiborne sitting behind his big leather-bound desk, pouring over paperwork, smoking a clay pipe. He sat down waiting for his father's attention, a waft of distinctive smelling smoke blew his way, giving him the opportunity to fain an attention-seeking cough. Claiborne looked up, "What is it Son?"

John hesitated, then mumbled nervously, "Pa... I think it's time I made a life for myself on my own."

Claiborne put down his pipe and papers and replied without hesitation, "Son, I think it's about time that you did just that."

John was surprised at the instant, almost too positive response, but he carried on, explaining his ambitions to go west and start his own cattle business.

Claiborne stood up from his chair, walked around the desk and gave John a congratulatory pat on the shoulder, "Well my boy, I always knew that you had it in you, but do you really think you can stick at it?"

John looked up at his father, "I'm going to have to, to make this business work I'm going to need a lot of men, they'll be depending on me to make a go of it, when I start this, I have to see it through."

"John, you are the man to do it, your brothers are good men, don't get me wrong, but you've always had something about you that was special. You're smart, but you never crow about it, and you're fair, men will be loyal to you my boy."

John was overwhelmed and inspired by his father's confidence in him, he felt like he had just grown two inches taller.

CHAPTER 3

ODD FELLOWS

With the ongoing influx of homesteaders to the county seat, the sleepy 50-acre Parisian settlement had grown to over 300 residents and had become quite the boom town. When the position of Lamar County Clerk came up for grabs in 1850 John applied but was beaten by a fellow named John Craddock. Undaunted he soldiered on, keeping his nose to the grindstone, working with his father until the position came up again two years later, and John got the job.

The new job worked out well for John in several ways, he was earning a good wage, and saving most of it. More significantly, he was well positioned to get the jump on any business opportunities that might arise. Beyond that, his daily routine, and the respect that went with his new importance, would set in motion a chain of events, which would lead to him adopting a far more enlightened view of the world, from which he would never falter.

After being proposed by Claiborne, John received an invitation to join the Independent Order of Odd Fellows. His first reaction was that a stuffy group of old men was not for him, but after some thought he accepted, seeing it as an opportunity to boost his social esteem, rubbing shoulders with the great and the good, the big fish in the little pond, of Lamar County. He did not expect the experience to be life-changing, but the IOOF turned out to be far more than a social gathering. It opened his eyes to a philosophy on life that had evaded him in their harsh frontier world.

The IOOF mantra states, 'An Odd Fellow bases his thoughts and actions on healthy philosophical principles. He believes that life is a commitment to improve and elevate the character of humanity through service and example. He is humble in a way that he never boasts about himself.

'He knows and accepts his strengths and weaknesses and keeps away from badmouthing people and making unreasonable allegations. He understands that certain things in life are unavoidable. He is aware of the vanity of earthly things, the frailty and inevitable decay of human life and the fact that wealth has no power to stop the sureness of eventual death. He then asks the question, how am I going to spend my life?'

This philosophy smacked in the face of the conservative self-sufficient existence that John thought he had come to believe in. It would not sway him from his addiction to wealth, but it would make him consider the way he conducted his life. It also planted the first seed of doubt regarding other elements of his family's lifestyle, a doubt that was further cultivated by a chance encounter whilst lunching one day.

John had become a creature of routine in his new role. Each day at 12:30 pm, on the dot, he would leave his desk and lunch at the general merchandise store, run by his friend and former employer Monroe Grant. Grant and Chisum shared an enthusiasm for chess and would generally have a game on the go.

A teenage houseboy by the name of Bass Reeves came into the store one day, picking up goods for his owner, and took a keen interest in their game. From then on Bass would find any excuse to be in Grant's Mercantile at about that time to watch them play. He had a quick wit and a glint in his eye, John took a liking to the lad.

One day, Montgomery was far too busy sorting a delivery to have time for chess, or to deal with Bass, who had just ambled in. John, keen for a game, decided to dispense with social protocols and offered to teach Bass how to play, ignoring a very puzzled look and a less than polite comment from Grant, regarding Bass' aptitude.

Bass turned out to be a quick learner, and as the weeks ensued, he was playing a good strategic game, beating Chisum in about one in three. Aside from the game, John had begun to earn Bass' trust and confidence, their conversations across the board becoming deeper and more revealing.

"How did you get to be named 'Bass'?" Chisum inquired one day.

Bass hesitated then responded quietly, "It's from my African name Mr. Chisum," quiet being unusual for this normally cocky young man, he whispered, "please, keep that a secret sir."

This was a huge leap of faith for the boy, he was a multiple generation slave; any hint of upholding anything to do with Africa would be beaten out of him by many owners.

"But you're not African boy, you're a Texan now," John stated as Bass made his excuses and left.

The conversation nagged at Chisum, but he respected the confidence. A few days later, as their game continued, curiosity got the better of him, "What is your African name boy?"

Bass already realized that he might have opened a door he shouldn't have, but had no way of closing it, he responded cautiously. 'My mama gave me my Akan name, "Baasaewi", it means Big Fish in American, my mama's smart sir, she tells everyone Bass, so I'm still a fish.'

"But why a fish?" John was puzzled.

Bass really put his head on the fishmonger's block when he responded, "Because a fish is free Mister Chisum, a fish is free."

John looked Bass straight in the eye, "Do you think you will ever be a free man Baasaewi?"

Bass was uncomfortable talking in the store for fear of being overheard, so respectfully asked John to take a walk with him.

They sat in the shade of an old Bur Oak tree, which unbeknown to them was the very spot where a group of Tennesseans had sheltered seventeen years previously, en-route to San Antonio to defend the very way of life they were about to discuss. John had noticed that in their chess conversations Bass' colorful Negro drawl often abated when they got on to deeper subjects, but never had he heard him talk as eloquently as he was about to.

"Sir, please don't ever call me anything other than 'Bass' in earshot of others, be they black or white. I don't know if I will ever be a free man, but I know the day will come when all men and women will be free, maybe even equal."

Chisum responded as if reading from the slave owners' handbook, "But there have been slaves since Jesus were a boy and twice-fold before, is it really such a sin for one man to be the master of another?

"You're fed, you have shelter and you never have to worry about money. Damn it boy, sometimes I'm jealous of our slaves, in the drive from Tennessee, they got fed before I did."

"And I guess your horses did too, sir?"

Chisum shrugged in agreement, "Mr. Chisum, you're a good man; your father is a good man. I know your slaves, they speak well of you, in a different world they might call you a 'friend'. You look after them and keep them safe, but safe isn't free and you are not their friend."

John took a deep breath, "Bass, please trust me, I want to know more, anything you say will be taken to my grave." Pointing in the general direction of his mother's plot where he was destined to lay to rest.

Bass went on to explain the nobility of his Ghanaian roots, the language that the slaves spoke and taught out of earshot of the whites, and the culture that had been passed down to him in songs and stories.

The dignified rebelliousness of his parting statement that day would ring in John's ears for the rest of his life, "With all my respect Mr. Chisum, sir, I'll never be a Texan or an American, I'm African."

This was a lot for a southern gentleman, even one as open-minded as John Chisum to absorb. He had often heard the blacks singing folk songs in English on the trail to Texas, he had found their melodies and harmonious voices a great comfort as he fell asleep at night, but he had never considered that they had a culture and a language that they carried with them. It had not even crossed his mind that the slaves had an opinion about him, any more than he would have dwelled upon what his horse might be thinking of him.

Bass was right; beast and slave had been treated pretty much alike. The comparison reminded him of an unsettling conversation he had overheard as a youth in Tennessee. A neighboring plantation owner, proudly crowing about how he had 'broken' a rebellious slave to within an inch of his life, and Claiborne's later cursing of the boastful bully. Unusual for his father, if Claiborne was going to insult a man, he was never normally shy of saying it to his face.

John couldn't remember there ever being a crossed word between his family and their slaves, thinking back to his youth he had faint memories of playing games with their children, most of whom had come to Texas with them, and were by then hard-working adults. He could not work out at what point he had forgotten all this. As he reminisced, a wave of nostalgia and homesickness for Tennessee washed over him, that he had not felt since the early days after they arrived in the republic. For the first time since his mother died, he felt tears welling up.

As he returned to work, he passed the IOOF lodge, and mused upon the possibility that perhaps he had been an 'Odd Fellow' for longer than he knew. The reality that, despite the patriarchy's charitable and philanthropic mantra, no black man, free or otherwise, had ever become a member of the lodge, sailed right over his head.

CHAPTER 4

BREAKING POINT

John Chisum's future direction would be challenged and channeled by the distraction that either guides or afflicts most men at some point in their life – a woman – he was about to lose his heart for the first time.

Susan Holman was formally introduced to John by her brother, Cyrus, the County's former sheriff, who had befriended Chisum at the IOOF lodge. She was a very attractive and spirited, green-eyed redhead, who despite being three years younger than John could hold her own with any man in a debate. She came from a well-to-do Maryland family, a sixth generation American, who could trace her ancestry right the way back to the very first, witch-hanging, puritan pilgrims of Chesapeake Bay, who fled across the Atlantic from the ravages of the English Civil War in the seventeenth century.

Her mother's family, the Tongs, even had a village named after them back in Yorkshire. John had admired her from afar for quite some time, but with the eligible ladies of Paris still outnumbered by the single men, five to one, a girl could afford to be picky. She had shown no interest in him in his days as a lowly grocery clerk or laborer, but his newfound social prominence appeared to have turned her head in his direction.

As a man long-used to being very much in control of his feelings, this was a very odd time for John. It wasn't as if he hadn't been with a woman before, but he had never been with a 'lady' and Susan most definitely considered herself to be one classy lady. More significantly, John had never explored the mind-distorting experience of being head-over-heels in love before. Though his physical attraction to Susan was strong, his love had been mostly fired up by simply listening to her talk. He had never met such an intellectual woman, so knowledgeable about worldly affairs and politics, albeit that the latter was of no real interest to him, in fact it had crossed his mind that Susan probably deserved the right to vote on such matters, far more than he did.

John, although he did his best to hide it, was very conscious of the fact that he was poorly educated. He could read and write, and had a natural flair for math, but get him on world affairs, or history and he was a fish out of water. He was often quite out of his depth in Susan's company, as he was in smoking room debates with some of the IOOF's more intellectual gentlemen. But in Susan's case that challenge made her far more desirable.

There was a wave of Victorian civilized morality rolling into Texas from the east, the only way John was going to fulfill his manly desires with Miss Holman was to put a ring on her finger. Marriage had not been high on his agenda, it certainly did not fit in with his vision of becoming a free-spirited cattle herder, but his desire for this woman had become blindingly obsessive.

What John was not aware of, was that among most of the highfaluting Marylanders in town the Chisum clan were referred to as 'a bunch of 'crackers', a derogatory term from back east for the less refined frontiers folk. Claiborne's consecutive marriages, to two of his own cousins, had not impressed the Holmans, and John's younger brothers' rumbustious reputations had done nothing to help his cause.

Susan was attracted to John, but wasn't in love with him, though she did like the security that he could offer, at least until a better opportunity came along. However, marriage would have to be on her terms. John had talked about his ambitions, but to deaf ears. Susan had no intention of being dragged any further away from 'civilization' than she already had been. She maintained that she had only come that far west to look after her brother, but John sensed that there was a deeper story explaining her route to Texas but was too nervous of rocking the boat of their presumed relationship to explore it. Their 'romance' had remained at a stalemate for weeks, but John was too smitten to let her go.

Everything came to a head on 2nd March 1853, the seventeenth anniversary of the creation of the Republic. Texas Independence Day remained the most celebrated day in the Lone Star State, outshining the 4th July festivities by a country mile.

They were about to leave for Paris' annual party, when Susan noticed John's fiddle parked by her door, "You are not taking that common instrument with you!"

"How can you call a violin 'common'?" John defended.

"When you can play Paganini in Philadelphia, I'll call it a violin, while you play that New Orleans trash it is a common fiddle, you are not playing it today."

The festivities that year would include a shooting contest; the prize was a very desirable silver-plated Model 1851 Sharps boxlock rifle, plus ammunition. Susan had never seen John fire a gun, but knowing his father's reputation as an Indian fighter, was very keen for him to compete, to impress her family and neighbors with his manly prowess. At two dollars, the entry fee was expensive, but that was not a problem, the stumbling block was that John had never bothered to learn to shoot properly; he had no interest in firearms.

Independence Day always brought in visitors from out of town, but the shooting contest had attracted folk from way outside the county, including a few unsavory looking Mexicans who Sheriff Thomas was keeping a close eye on.

One particularly tall, heavily-muscled, stranger named William 'Bigfoot' Wallace was getting a lot of attention from the small band of single women in attendances, who were sharing a risqué joke regarding the source of his nickname. Wallace was a Texas Ranger from Austin, with a legendry law enforcement reputation. Much to John's annoyance, Susan had aligned herself with a bunch of flirtatious local spinsters, with much fluttering of her eyelashes in Wallace's direction. Wallace was flattered by the interest from the prettiest girls in town but had another purpose for being in the neighborhood on his mind.

This was the first time that John had ever seen his father star struck. As well as being a hero of the war with Mexico, Wallace had a direct link to the hero of Claiborne's childhood stories from the old country. He was a descendent of his namesake, the notorious William Wallace from Scotland, who was executed by the English in the fourteenth century.

The Parisians knew how to throw a good party, but the moment John was dreading rapidly approached. He paid his $2 entry, stepped up to the plate with the Colt Paterson revolver he had borrowed from his Father, and fired four rounds into the practice target, then his final shot into the competition one next to it. The disappointed look he got from Claiborne, as he handed the Colt back to him, said it all, he was darned useless.

A dozen or so more hopefuls, including John's brothers, gave it their best shot, then Claiborne took his turn and almost bullseyed the target, letting out a smug, "Hurrah."

To add to John's embarrassment, Claiborne slapped two shiny new gold liberty dollar coins into the hand of the contest's sponsor, Susan's brother-in-law, George Wright, "Give my boy, John, another chance, it was his first time - he doesn't even own a gun," and handed the Colt, which he had expertly reloaded back to his son.

Wright conceded and in a friendly, but rather patronizing tone stated, "Come on then 'boy', second time lucky," this got a big laugh from Claiborne and the crowd, Susan covered her eyes in shame.

At 28-years-old, John was getting tired of repeatedly being called 'boy', but as usual he shrugged it off. After all it was the first time that he had heard his father laugh since the loss of his beloved sister, Aunt Polly, it was good to hear him getting back to his old self.

John had noticed Bass Reeves showing a keen interest in the proceedings, knowing how much it would mean to him to have a go, and to avoid looking an even bigger fool in Susan's eyes, he gestured in Bass' direction stating, "Let this boy shoot for me."

Bass was excited at the proposition, but loudly admitted, "I ain't ever shot a gun before either, Mr. Chisum, sir."

John beckoned him over and handed him his pa's five-shooter. The audience expected some entertainment at Bass' expense, so no one objected. Claiborne looked a tad disgruntled at his two dollars being wasted, but he had enough pride in his reputation for generosity to keep quiet.

As Bass turned towards the platform John whispered in his ear, "You can't be any worse than me."

John was right, to almost everyone else's disappointment Bass' practice shots got better each time, and his final shot was almost as good as Claiborne's.

Wallace was impressed, "That really your first time, boy?"

"Yes sir, Mr. Wallace, sir."

In a deep droll voice, he joshed, "Well son, if you ever get tired of being a slave, you ought to consider becoming a Texas Ranger."

Susan dragged John aside, "You just made a complete idiot of yourself and a fool of me."

"Hell Susan, I never said I could shoot."

"I don't give a damn that you can't shoot; it's that you would hide behind the coat tails of a no-good houseboy, what the hell were you thinking?" she exclaimed, barely controlling her anger. She did not give him time to answer before firing her own parting shot, "and the boy beat you!" confirming that she did 'give a damn' regarding his gunslinging prowess. She pulled up her skirts and stormed off in a rage. John sat down on Monroe Grant's sidewalk bench, to collect his thoughts.

Whilst they had been arguing, Wallace had taken his turn and put all the other competitors to shame. You could not separate one hole from another on the practice target, and bang on the bullseye with his final shot, to win the Sharps.

John's mind was distracted, trying to make sense of the argument. He took a while to notice a giant of a man blocking out the sunlight. It was Wallace in deep conversation with Sheriff Thomas. The Sheriff bid farewell, and Wallace turned to John, cradling his prize, with a big grin on his face.

John acknowledged Wallace's victory, trying to sound suitably congratulatory, "You won – well done Mr. Wallace."

In truth, he was very disappointed that his father had lost; being the best shot and winning the Sharps would have meant the world to him. But a gloating Texas Ranger was the least of his worries, so he gave him a 'well, get on with it, say your piece,' kind of grin.

"Chisum, I saw what you done for that boy, you're a good man."

This compliment completely threw John, and he felt guilty for pre-judging the Ranger. He responded sincerely and respectfully,

"Thank you, sir, I knew it would mean a lot to him, but apparently a lot less to my young lady."

"It was a nice thing to do and a big thing to do; everyone needs to feel important once in a while, that boy will always remember today. But you sir, need to learn to shoot, come and find me at the Lamar Hotel tomorrow morning."

John returned to the party, to discover Susan dancing with some suited and booted city dandy, she threw him a disdainful look, smiled at her dance partner, and turned her back on Chisum.

A few dances later she sat one out, to get her breath back, so John took advantage of an empty seat next to her, to try to fix things. "Susan?" she ignored him, pointedly looking in the opposite direction, but he persevered, "Susan, please, we need to talk."

She turned to him with fire in her eyes.

He made his pitch, "You win, I'll do whatever you want, I'll stay in Paris, or go east with you, just promise that you will marry me."

She laughed, "John, you are a pathetic excuse for a man, why would any girl want to marry you?"

She stood up and returned to her new dance partner without a glance back. That would be pretty much their last conversation, he had finally seen the true character of the object of his affections, his rose-tinted spectacles had cleared – this gold digger was not the girl for him.

CHAPTER 5

WILLIAM WALLACE

John's mood was low the following morning, but he remembered William Wallace's invite. They rode out to a quiet spot at the edge of Claiborne's ranch, where Wallace gave a very scientific induction into the world of firearms, which couldn't have been in more stark contrast to the excited antics he had witnessed his brothers getting up to, the first time they got their hands on a gun.

They just cleaned and talked about guns for the first hour or so, before he even loaded a shot. Wallace taught him about safety, storing and loading ammunition, which weapon did what job, and the subtle art of squeezing a trigger. John was extremely impressed by his professionalism, no throwing coins in the air or shooting at bottles. The remark that Chisum would always remember from his induction was, "A gun is a tool that you should be happy to never have to use. But if you do have to, make sure you can use it proficiently, and without doubt, because doubt kills more men than having a poor aim. That's mostly why I'm alive and others ain't."

John pitched a very direct question that was bubbling in his head, "How many men have you killed?"

A question that Wallace had been asked dozens of times before, so he gave his stock answer, "I don't keep a tally, it isn't a competition."

"So, if it is too many to remember, how do you deal with the guilt of killing a man?"

Wallace stared out into the distance before responding, few had asked the question in a moral context before, so decided that John deserved a fuller answer, "Son, it's not about there being too many, it's about killing a man, or anything come to that, the fact that you have is nothing to crow about."

He paused then continued, "In my case it is about doing the job I signed up for... kill or be killed, I've never killed anyone who didn't have it coming. You feel for their families but at the end of the day they chose the life they wanted to lead. The bigger guilt, the one you carry forever, is surviving, when those around you don't."

There was an awkward pause, which John interrupted with the obvious question, "Why feel guilty for surviving?"

Wallace was reticent, paused and mumbled, "You ask too many questions, it's history now."

"William, I'd really like to know," John pushed.

Wallace pondered and then decided, 'What the hell', "Okay... It was back in '43, a load of us got captured by the Mexicans and a load of us escaped. 176 of us got caught again," confirming that there were no issues with Wallace's ability to count.

"How do you know the number so precisely?" John queried.

There was a long pause and Wallace's eyes shrank away looking remorseful.

"Because I had to count 176 beans into a jar, 17 of them black. Those delightful Mexicans decided that a tenth of us were going to be shot for escaping, and we had to choose who, so picking beans out of a jar was fairest. But I was smart, I noticed that the black beans were bigger than the white ones, so knew what to feel for when it was my turn to put my hand in, and so I lived."

"William, anyone would have done the same if they'd thought of it, and the odds were that you would probably have picked a white bean anyway."

"Maybe, but I could have also chosen a black bean and saved a life. That is the guilt I will carry to my grave."

They shot some more then headed back to town. Wallace talked more about the war with Mexico, it was something he didn't often discuss but he felt strangely comfortable talking to John. He went on to explain how he had spent his recent years in command of a company of Rangers, fighting Indians and border bandits.

"So, what brings you this far north?" John queried.

"Bounty."

"Are you tracking an outlaw?"

"Nope, runaway slave."

This shocked John, and he began to readdress the thought that this man might be a kindred spirit.

"I don't understand, you admired my kindness to Bass Reeves, but you are chasing a slave. And I guess if he doesn't choose to be caught, you'll shoot him, and if you do catch him, he'll be beaten."

"That's my job."

"With all due respect sir, it's a dirty job."

Wallace took a deep breath, "That it may be John, what you need to understand is I am a good tracker," he stated with no sense of either modesty or pretention, "a good tracker gets into the mind of his prey, like an eagle knows a rabbit. There are few men more admirable than a runaway looking for his freedom and none as hard to catch alive."

"So, you enjoy the challenge?"

"Nope, I enjoy the pay."

"Do you never feel guilty that you're taking money for another man's misery?"

"Nope, if I didn't some other fellow would, and to date I have always brung 'em back alive... then when they run again, I catch 'em again," he smiled, "John, to be honest I'll be a happier man when I don't have to chase 'em anymore, and I won't be for much longer."

John missed the point of the remark, "You're a bit young to be retiring?"

"Retirement would be nice wouldn't it?" he joked to his horse.

Turning to John he continued, "The state has granted me a nice little spread in the hill country, but it'll be a while before I hang my guns up. Nope, I won't be retiring, but the abolitionist's voice is getting louder, the slaves will be free soon enough, so I won't need to take 'em home."

"You really believe that?" John was surprised.

"Yep, if not I'll guarantee you there will be a war!"

John's aversion to politics rapidly turned the conversation around to cattle, he talked about his ambition of becoming a rancher and the Ranger's response was very encouraging. Wallace went on to describe the great expanses of land to the west between the Red River and the Brazos that would be perfect to fulfill such ambitions, so long as John had the courage to get there first with enough manpower to fend off the Indians.

"That's a mighty fine dream John, but that's all it will ever be unless you have the sand to do something about it. You can't run a ranch from a desk in a courthouse."

His assertion revealed that Wallace knew more about John than you would expect from a passing stranger. What John had overlooked was that a good Ranger makes it his business to know about people.

Back in town they were about to part company, when Bass Reeves ambled by trying to get John's attention, intending to thank him for letting him shoot the day before. John contemplated his recent conversation with Wallace, "Bass... a word of advice, if you do ever get 'tired of being a slave', don't go south or you might have the misfortune of meeting this gentleman."

Bass was puzzled by the statement, but knowing of William Wallace's reputation, didn't argue the point, or forget it. Wallace let out a hearty laugh and rode off with a parting farewell, loud enough for some passing locals to hear, "John Chisum, you and I will meet again, I have no doubt; you take care my friend."

Wallace's advice was ringing in John's ears. He knew that if he was to fulfill his ambitions, it was time to be getting away from his desk and move on from Paris. What he didn't know was how quickly that plan would be expedited.

CHAPTER 6

LEAVING PARIS

Fate would take a hand the very next day, when a sharply dressed visitor was brought to John's Office by his father. Claiborne had been delivering to the Paris Inn, where he had found the man, looking quite the lost soul. The stranger was asking where he could invest in cattle, Claiborne took him under his wing, and they shared lunch and a bottle of whisky, at the visitor's expense.

"I have here a gentleman from New Orleans, keen to get into the cattle business." Claiborne announced, "His name is Stephen Fowler, I'll leave you to talk," he then staggered out of the door, offering a discreet wink to his son.

John recognized him as the 'dandy' who had danced with Susan on Independence Day but would do his best to not let that interfere with his professional impartiality. But the irony that he was from New Orleans did induce a quiet chuckle, John wondered if he could play a good tune on a fiddle. "Good afternoon Mr. Fowler, how can I help?"

Fowler's reply revealed a deep southern drawl, "Your paw said that you are the man to give a man good advice, on where to buy land and cattle."

Chisum had both a nature to, and as County Clerk, an obligation, to give honest advice, but was not keen to encourage fresh competition to the detriment of his own ambitions, and particularly not from this city slicker. However, he felt confident that the whole truth would scare the incomer off. He responded with the upper hand of local knowledge, "Well, land is near as damn it free."

Fowler was shocked and clearly taken aback, "Free?"

"Free, if you go far enough west and can protect it from the Indians." John qualified as he gestured to the map of Texas on his office wall and pointed to a spot about ninety miles west of Paris, where 'Gainesville' had been written, by hand, in pencil, "I've a cousin who has just settled here."

He then drew a circle with his finger to the southwest that was neatly bisected by a county line, also hand drawn, "You can file on pretty well as much land as you can protect from the Indians, outside the settlements in Cooke County and down into Denton."

"Well, how bad is the Ind'un problem?"' Fowler inquired hesitantly.

"Not as bad as in my father's day when he rode with General Dyer, or in the '40s when Captain Tarrant would raid out that way with 70 odd men. They pretty much saw off the Caddo tribes, but the Kiowa and Comanche are still troublesome, particularly at night, they'll kill you in your bed."

"I thought them heathens didn't attack at night."

"That's an old wives' tale. You never heard of Comanche Moon? They love a full moon to raid by." John spoke with great confidence and authority on the subject, for a man who had never met a wild native. He went on to regale the visitor with tales of his father's daring deeds in the late '30s and of recent Indian raids he had heard about from the outlying settlements, with a mild to fair degree of embellishment.

It was abundantly clear to Fowler that 'getting into the cattle business,' was not 'the easy road to quick riches that the dumb Texans hadn't taken advantage of,' as it had been described to him by travelers back in Louisiana. Though he had wondered why the folk who were giving such generous advice were traveling east, rather than west.

His journey to Paris had already set him thinking that the frontier life wasn't for him, which had been confirmed by Chisum's animated storytelling. However, he was a shrewd businessman and still saw the potential of investing in the wild frontier. No one will ever know if it was Fowler's good judgment of character, Chisum's charm, the half-bottle of whisky or the convivial surroundings of the courthouse office that inspired so much trust and confidence, but by the end of that day they had struck a deal. Fowler would invest ten thousand dollars in a partnership with Chisum, which would be registered as the Half-Circle-P brand. Fowler would return to the home comforts of New Orleans as a sleeping partner, and wait for the money to roll in.

Wallace was right, 'You can't run a ranch from a desk in a courthouse,' but you can sure as hell start one from there. John's final task of the afternoon was to tear up the nomination form for reinstatement as County Clerk, which he had been procrastinating from signing for over a week.

There was much celebration in the Chisum household that night, until Claiborne decided to take John aside for one of his fatherly lectures, to remind him who was boss of the family, in his own inimitable style.

"John, I'm proud of you, but there's something that needs to be said. You're a good businessman, hell, you're a good man, folk respect you and will follow you, but you aren't up to running this all on your own. You need to keep yourself away from the coalface and learn to delegate. I want you to take James with you. You need a range boss to deal with the day-to-day stuff who talks the same language as the men. It will be the making of him."

Claiborne's criticism knocked John's celebratory mood a tad, but he knew his father was right. James had always been the one to deal with the ranch hands and slaves, everyone respected his little brother in a similar fashion to his father and he had a down-to-earth manner with people that got the job done without a fight.

As John considered his father's words a peculiar irony struck him. Although Claiborne was putting him in his place, he had finally shown him the respect he had always yearned for, to have the freedom to make his own way in the world with his father's blessing. Whereas, despite the great compliment he had just paid James, he still treated the 25-year-old as a boy, who should go where he is told to.

John soon proved his delegation skills, within a few days he had offloaded all his responsibilities at the courthouse to the district court clerk, Jacob Long. By August, John and James were heading west to Gainesville in Cooke County.

The plan was to stay with their cousin Frances Towery and her husband Tom, the town's saddler, until land could be secured, and a ranch house built. The journey took three days on horseback, with an overnight stop with family at Bonham, in Fannin County and then the more bustling frontier town of Sherman. As that was the farthest west that either of them had ever ventured, James decided that it was time for a celebration.

Sherman was a wild town compared to Paris, with a very transient population. There were migrants heading west to California with wives, children and slaves, and in total contrast, gun-toting cattle drovers following the old Shawnee Trail north to Preston and on into the Indian Territory. Sherman was the last big watering hole en-route for these two very dissimilar groups of travelers.

John had never been a fan of the saloon lifestyle; he found it vulgar and intimidating, although it was educational listening to the drovers' stories about the lonesome trails. James however was in his element, loving the spit and sawdust atmosphere of drunks and pretty dancing girls.

One particular girl had caught James' eye. Her name was Josephine, which fitted in well with her glamorous showgirl image, particularly with the fake French accent she put on for the customers. Josephine also took a shine to John and James the moment they walked in the bar. They didn't have the travel-weary look of the migrants and smelled a lot sweeter than the drovers. Finding that the boys were from a neighboring county back in Tennessee opened the conversation and subdued the French accent, James got the lion's share of her attention for being the youngest and in her opinion the better looking. Having the same name as her late father did not do his case any harm either.

While James canoodled, John ended up spending the evening chatting to a colorful and apparently, from the number of drinks he had been bought, popular gentleman, who was working as a guide for a cattle drive from San Antonio to the Missouri river.

"So, how is the meat market in Missouri?" John enquired.

He shrugged his shoulders, "Meat market is okay, it's getting the beeves there, that's the problem."

"What, Indians?"

"Nope, Indians are fine, anyways with me around they are. I'm half Cherokee. I'm on this drive to make sure there ain't no hostility with them. It's the damned Alfalfa Desperados that are causing all the trouble."

He saw the confused look on John's face and explained, "Farmers... don't take offense, but Missouri is getting too crowded. It's full of white folk with ploughs, that's what's putting a spoke in the wheel and they don't want your Texan Longhorns around trampling their farms or bringing sickness to their cows."

"Don't get me wrong, I'm a realistic man, I'm a trader by trade so I know this country needs settlers, but what it needs first is a railroad that keeps ahead of 'em to drive cattle to. We could make new trails further west and keep everyone apart, then these fellows wouldn't lose so many beeves sailing them down the Missouri," he stated, with a gesture to a table of his dusty associates, playing cards.

"But aren't they always going to catch up?" John queried, confident of the accelerating wave of settlement into the west.

"Maybe, but not in my day... and if they do, I'm going to go live with the Indians, if there are any left."

The two men had enjoyed each other's company, but their talk had gone way past the time a man on a cattle drive should be finding his bed. As the trader excused himself, John realized that they had overlooked an important protocol of gentlemanly conversation.

"I never did catch your name, sir."

"It's Chisholm, Jesse Chisholm, I didn't get yours neither."

"I've heard of you, I'm a Chisum too, John Chisum, you haven't by chance got any family back in Hardeman County, Tennessee?"

"Nope, not that I know of, I sprung up way east, near the Carolinas, we're probably kin somewhere though, maybe back in Scotland, that's where my father's family came over from."

They shook hands and parted company, not knowing how much confusion the coincidence of their names would cause lay-folks when trying to untwine the history of these two men long after they were both dead and buried.

John knew of his drinking companion's reputation and smiled at the thought of his namesake referring to himself simply as a trader. The man was a legend, known as the 'Peacemaker of the Plains', a renowned tracker and translator. He was famed for gaining the release of several captured children, some of whom he had adopted.

Most significantly he was reputed to have negotiated more treaties with and on behalf of the natives than any man alive. Even the tribes had called upon his services to resolve disputes between each other.

John went to his bed with much food for thought, his conversation with Chisholm had created as many questions as it had answered, but he was looking forward to seeing his cousin the next day and was excited at what prospects the coming weeks might have in store for him.

CHAPTER 7

GAINESVILLE

When they arrived in Gainesville it was fair to say that they did not find Cousin Frances at her best; in fact, her household was in turmoil. She had lost her father the previous September and her mother, John's Aunt Polly, over the winter. To add to her burden, Frances was also the only person able to tend to Melton, her sickly teenage nephew, who was isolated in an outbuilding suffering from Yellow Fever, a disease she was immune to due to having survived it herself as a child.

To top it all off, her brother James, in what he referred to as a 'bout of melancholia', which Frances described as 'a bout of lust' after the loss of his wife, Nancy, had got one of his slaves pregnant, who had just given birth to a boy they named Sonny. James then had the temerity to return to Paris to die, leaving her with yet another unproductive mouth to feed.

Frances, despite being only 19-years-old, was normally a very resilient, level-headed frontierswoman, but even for her this was a lot to cope with.

John's own attention was also soon distracted by one of Frances' slaves, a beaming light of beauty, in the form of the Towery's Mulatto house girl, Jensie, who welcomed him with a big smile and bright eyes. John had known Jensie since they first migrated to Texas in '37, she was owned by Aunt Polly and would have been about three-years-old when they first arrived. He remembered that she was the cutest, funniest child who used to play around camp with Frances and John's little brother, Pitser, who were about the same age.

Jensie's beauty and paler skin had been her savior, but to some extent her undoing. She had been much favored by her owners, never being sent to work in the fields. Growing up as a house girl she always had pretty clothes to wear, to be the attractive domestic decoration that her owners saw as befitting their social standing. She had even been tutored to read, so that she could recite from the bible on Sundays. The downside to this was that she did get a lot of unwanted attention from men, as evidenced by her 18-month-old son, Philip, the father of whom remained a mystery.

Frances' late brother had been the chief suspect, but he denied having bedded Jensie, a denial that she confirmed to be true. But, no matter how hard she was pushed, she would remain tight-lipped to her grave regarding the identity of whoever had 'taken advantage' of her.

Whilst John may have grown up oblivious to the blossoming of this mixed-race beauty, Jensie had always been aware of him and his reputation amongst the slaves for his kindness and generosity of spirit. She had quietly admired him from afar whenever he visited Aunt Polly in Bonham and had been excited from the moment she heard he was coming to stay, even more so when she overheard that he was no longer involved with the redhead woman.

To escape the chaos of the Towery household John took a room at a neighboring boarding house, leaving James with the family. Sitting at his bureau on the first evening he heard a faint tapping on the door, it was Jensie; she had volunteered to deliver his supper.

John pulled the cloth from Jensie's basket, and a veritable feast lay before him. He called to her as she was heading to wait outside the room, "Have you eaten? This is way too much for me."

"I eat later Mr. Chisum, after my chores are finished."

"Please, join me, I'd enjoy some company," John invited.

"I couldn't, Mrs. Towery would be real cross, I'd be in trouble, please sir."

"Okay, I'll talk to Frances, and then tomorrow, you bring supper for two."

The next day, a bright and excited Jensie bounced up the stairs, politely knocked on the door, and skipped into John's room with her basket. But instead of joining John at the table sat in the corner where she felt she belonged.

"Jensie come and sit with me, I don't bite."

John sensed her discomfort so opened a conversation. He talked about the old times in Paris. He was not sure why, but he felt the need to convince Jensie that he was different, he reminisced about his chess playing days with Bass Reeves, without giving any secrets away.

"I know about Bass being your friend, we all did. Word got here about the shooting contest." Jensie smiled, "that was so special for Bass; you made him a hero."

John was still getting used to what he would come to know as the 'jungle telegraph', a stark reminder that eyes and ears followed him everywhere.

One evening, John was deep in concentration trying to make sense of some local maps he had acquired and did not notice Jensie enter the room. He startled as he realized there was someone looking over his shoulder.

"You made me jump."

"I'm sorry you looked so busy, I didn't want to disturb you."

She looked down at the map, and pointed to Gainesville, "That's us, where you going to build your ranch?"

"You can read?"

"Just enough to go to the store or recite from the bible."

Getting back to Jensie's question, John ran his hand over the map, "I'm not sure yet, where there is space, grass and water... and high ground to watch out for trouble."

"Aren't you scared Mr. Chisum?"

John loved Jensie's polite directness, and felt no need to pretend, "I am Jensie, but I'm more afraid of failure."

John talked more about his ambitions, his father's parting comments, how he saw his future and that he and James would be heading off in a couple of days hunting for land.

Jensie had attentive ears, and John felt comfortable in her presence enjoying her unbridled enthusiasm for his plans. After she left, he reflected on the evening's conversation, even he was surprised at himself for being so open with a slave.

The following evening Jensie turned up punctually, but with a very subdued demeanor, they ate with little conversation. John's mind was on the expedition ahead and Jensie's was elsewhere.

She went to leave, then plucked up courage from deep inside, and turned to face John with her head bowed, "Mr. Chisum, would you like me to keep you warm tonight?"

John was taken aback and hesitated, then responded defensively, "I have never taken advantage of a slave, nor of any woman without her willingness."

Jensie looked up at him, her beautiful big brown doe-eyes bored into his, "John Chisum, I am willing, freely willing."

"Jensie, how old are you?"

"I'm 19, coming up to 20."

"My God, I've got horses older than you are!"

Jensie paused, then dug deeper with faith in her belief and trust in this man, "Do your horses love you?"

"You think you love me?"

Jensie had passed a point of no return; she looked down at her feet, "I have loved you for an age and then some." She started to cry.

John instinctively stepped forward and gently pulled her to him. She buried her head deep into his chest. He was intoxicated by the sweet smell of her perfect skin.

He stepped back, holding her by her trembling fingertips and gave her a smile, which she nervously returned. She held his hand tighter, pulling him back closer again, while fighting her flight instinct. He kissed her gently but clumsily on the forehead. She looked up to kiss him properly, he responded, less clumsily this time, and then Jensie led him to his bed.

He sat on the edge, of his bed and his moral code, his head in turmoil. His one sure thought was that he did not want Jensie to be scared and run away with sordid tales, which wouldn't do either of them any good. He looked at her face in the flickering oil light, he could see the love and desire in her eyes. He had no doubt that he wanted her as far more than a bed warmer.

Jensie nervously unbuttoned her blouse and let it fall to the floor, John's eyes widened at the sight of her voluptuousness. She giggled, eyeing him mischievously.

"What's funny?" John asked.

"You white men, you so love the bosoms." She dropped her skirt, pointed at her curvaceous posterior and stepped towards him, "Now this... this is my beauty."

In the morning John and James were up before dawn in nervous anticipation of their forthcoming adventure. If John had happened to look over his shoulder as they headed south out of town, he would have noticed a tearful dusky beauty standing on the Towery's veranda, praying for his safe return as he disappeared over the horizon.

John's mind was torn between the events of the night before and the job in hand with its challenges ahead, as significant as those challenges were, he could not get Jensie's sweet smell out of his head.

James interrupted his train of thought by asking, "What you grinning about?"

"Aw nothing; just pleased to be on a horse, on a beautiful day, with my little brother doing what we came here for."

"Hey, not so much of the little!" James switched tracks, "Do you think Pa really is proud of us coming out here?"

"He says he is... I hope he is, he wouldn't say it if he didn't think it, you know Pa."

They rode on, both in quiet contemplation. John was overwhelmed by the majestic, untouched, beauty of the Southern Great Plains. He could imagine herds of ancient mastodons (hairy elephants) grazing the long grass and being hunted to extinction by families of nomadic Paleo-Indians, twelve thousand years before. As told to him by the Cooke County Clerk, William Twitty, a keen amateur historian and archeologist, a story which he would captivate visitors with whenever he wanted to show off his local knowledge. It had turned out that he did have an interest in history after all; Susan would have been so impressed.

As John had described to Jensie, there were three essential criteria to finding the ideal place to stake his claim; clean water nearby, good pasture, and an elevated position where you could see trouble coming in time to do something about it. They spent the first few days zigzagging south and west, finding nothing truly suitable. With the Cooke County seat being in Gainesville, and having already struck up an acquaintanceship with William Twitty, John had hoped to find land or at least build his ranch house, within the county's boundary, but it was looking ever more likely that that ambition was not going to be fulfilled. After the third day they made camp next to a river they had been following for most of the afternoon, somewhere near the border with Denton County. That penciled line on the map in his courthouse office, which already seemed a lifetime away.

It was a beautiful clear night. While James cooked the fish supper that he had caught, John counted at least three shooting stars. He always considered them a lucky omen. A big sky can make a man feel very small, but John's thoughts drifted to the bigger picture of his life.

"Do you think much about family?" He asked his brother.

"What, back in Paris?"

"No, I mean about making a family?"

James pondered for a moment, "Well, I wouldn't mind making some babies with that girl in Sherman... or at least trying to!" he exclaimed with a wink.

"Oh yes, Josephine, the not-French girl, she sure is pretty, do you see her as the marrying kind?" John teased.

"Aren't all women the 'marrying kind' if you've got what they want?" James responded cynically.

"Maybe, I thought Susan was the one, I sure figured that one out wrong. I guess I didn't have what she wanted." John admitted.

"How about you and the not-white girl?" James asked cautiously.

John was taken aback, but kept his cool, "What do you mean?"

"Jensie, Cousin Frances has noticed her sniffing around you, and is not best-pleased, to say the least."

John dismissed the notion, "She's a sweet girl that's all there is to it," he instantly felt ashamed at his dismissal of someone he was developing serious feelings for, but decided that it was best that he kept his mouth shut, until he fully understood what he was getting into. It was likely to be a chilly night, and it would have been nice to have her there keeping him warm, and more, he thought to himself.

"Yep, she's sure sweet on you, brother." James pursued.

John changed tracks, "Anyways, I'm not sure this is the place to bring up a family, not in our business when we are going to hardly ever be home," thinking of the testing times, when his father had been away in the past.

He waved his hand toward their bedrolls, "Let's get some sleep, I've an inkling tomorrow is going to be a good day."

They broke camp at dawn and followed the meandering river south-east. After an hour's ride John accepted that they were no longer in Cooke County, and had crossed into Denton, which would likely mean a bigger challenge to registering a claim. They trotted to the top of a ridge, with the river descending below them, to find the magnificent splendor of knee-high grass all the way to the horizon. They could see clearly for a mile in every direction, John could barely contain his excitement, it was perfect.

"This is the place... this will be our home James."

They gathered a pile of rocks to mark the spot, a minor but symbolic construction, inducing a manly hug between the brothers.

CHAPTER 8

THE CATTLE BUSINESS

Danny had listened intently, fascinated by Eugie's story, subduing a head full of questions while she told it. He had steadily redefined his vision of the larger than life gunslinger, he had seen on the movie screen, to the mild-mannered businessman she had described. But some math had been clicking around in his head.

"How do you know so much? This would have been decades before you were born? I don't even know who my grandparents were."

"We have always passed on our family stories by word of mouth, to preserve our identity. My grandmother told me everything she could remember, or had been told about that time, and before, on my 14th birthday, when she decided it was time for me to be a woman. I got the whole family history, and her recipe for vanilla and lemon cake... and lemonade of course," she said hinting for Danny to refill her glass, "and this helps," she added, pulling a raggedy edged notebook from her handbag, and then returning it before he could get a proper look.

Eugie diverted the conversation, "Is that true, that you know nothing about your grandparents?"

"Only a little, on Ma's side, she was French, my father met her when he was part of the occupying army after World War One, she was only 18 and had lost all her family in the war, her parents were Jacques, like the scuba diving fella on Calypso, and her mother was Claudine who mama was named after, dad married her in Paris, of all places. Then ten years later, when she was expecting me, brought her home to America. On his side all I have got out of him is that 'there is some Mexican from way back', but he does not know where or who, and I never got to meet any of his family."

"That is truly a shame," Eugie consoled.

Danny was keen to get back to the subject in hand, "So, did you ever meet John Chisum?"

Eugie's reply was quite cryptic, "I never actually met him, but I was almost at his funeral."

"You said he bought Jensie from a migrant in 1858, so how come he already knew her from being owned by family, a decade and some before, I'm confused?"

"Danny it's late, and yes, it was a bit more complicated than that, I need my bed, we'll talk more, soon enough."

Eugie could see that he had taken the bait, so as she turned towards the house, the canny old girl pitched her challenge.

"I never did get to see that ranch; I know it's somewhere north of where Bolivar is now, I've been inkling to visit for an age. And he was buried back in Paris, would be nice to see if we could go find his grave some time. If I paid for your gas, would you mind taking me on a road trip, a chance to try out the camera, McKinley bought me for Christmas, and get some snaps for the family album?"

"Sure, I'd love to, I'm free next weekend." Danny replied eagerly.

"That's great, pick me up on Saturday, and then I'll tell you more."

"Do you know the addresses?"

"Roughly, but perhaps you could do me a favor and take a trip to the library? Maybe do some research on the Chisum family for me?" she responded deviously.

Come Saturday, the two of them were in the Dodge heading north en-route to Bolivar. They turned off on to 'Chisum Road', looking for the trail to the ranch; Eugie spotted a 'Jingle Bob Trail' street sign, "It'll be up here somewhere," she pointed out to Danny. The Jinglebob was the distinctive ear cut that Chisum marked his cattle with, to prevent rustling.

Undaunted by a gated dirt road, they drove on past a reservoir, and up to a modest modern farmhouse on top of the hill. Eugie noticed a four-foot-high stone marker in the corner of the garden wall, with Chisum's name on it, "This is it."

Danny knocked on the front door to ask if it would be okay to look around, the elderly owner graciously agreed, but the tired expression on his face was quite revealing.

"Sorry, I guess we're not the first visitors since the movie came out," Danny apologized.

"That's fine, at least you knocked, most just wander around as if they own the place, perhaps I should run a tour? You'll want to start at the state monument," pointing at the stone they had just spotted.

They sat on the grass in front of the memorial and read the inscription. Eugie huffed and shook her head, "Well, the only things that aren't wrong on that are his name and the years he was born and died."

Pointing at the inscription she explained, "He died in Arkansas not Paris, and it was '54 not '56 that John and James built their 'Great White House' up here," she turned to try to picture the scene that had been described to her 70 years before, "also, his birthday was August 15 not 16, and he died December 22 not September 22.

My birthday by the way... next month," she added as a less than subtle hint.

"John's dream was to own a large white house with a big veranda. But before he could even think about building the house, he and James needed to head off to Denton County's seat at Alton, to file their claim with the County Clerk," she stated, pointing south east.

They found the clerk, a convivial portly Irishman named A.P. Lloyd, at his log cabin general store, which doubled as his office, somewhat less salubrious surroundings than John's former workplace.

Lloyd was excited to see them. John talked about his grand plans, and it was clear to Lloyd that, should he succeed in pursuing them, this could be the next push of the Wild Frontier, bringing civilization to Denton County in its wake. The county's population numbered just a few hundred at this point and was barely sustaining itself as a community, so desperately needed new settlers.

John marked up their claim, on yet another hand updated map, at a point they named Clear Creek, which Lloyd notarized. John mused that leaving Cooke County had been far less painful than he had expected.

"I guess this means that you are in the market for buying cattle now then?" Lloyd queried.

"Yep, that is next on my agenda, after I've found a safe bank." John confirmed.

"I hear old man Matthews, in Colorado County, wants to get out of the cattle business, he's 60, tired, and I hear say he's had enough of beeves, and wants to stick to cotton."

"Any idea how much he's looking for?" John inquired.

"The going rate down south is about six dollars a head; I reckon he's got about 1,000 up for grabs."

John's eyes lit up, "How far south, how do I find this Matthews fella?"

"Well, the direct route is about 250 miles, but do you have good horses with stamina?"

"We sure do." John replied with pride.

"Then I suggest you pitch in with the 2nd Dragoons company that are camped down by Hickory Creek," he pointed over his shoulder with his thumb, "they are waiting for some railroad surveyors, then they're heading south to San Antonio and then west on the Gila Trail, or thereabouts to California. They cover forty miles a day, if you can keep up with them, they'll keep you safe to San Antone. From there you head east towards Houston on the low road, for a little over hundred miles, to Columbus, ask the way to Eagle Lake. Then just follow the hoof prints."

"And a bank?" John reiterated.

"Well, you'll find no real banks around here, your best bet is Groos the German, he's setting up a new store in San Antonio, he's an honest fellow, as straight as you could ever hope to meet, he'll look after your money."

Lloyd shut his shop up and led them around to the Dragoons' campsite, two neat rows of tents, next to the river. The sentry recognized Lloyd and let them pass freely into camp. He led them to the largest tent, pulled open the flap and ushered them in, to where two officers were having a heated debate over a letter. One turned his head, eyed up the two smartly dressed strangers and frowned.

"Damn, they've not sent you from Washington to tell us as well have they?"

"Nope," Lloyd interrupted, "these are cattlemen looking to head south with you, I'll leave you all to talk" and bid them farewell.

This was the first time John had been called a 'cattleman' in his own right, and he liked the sound of it. He introduced himself and James, while the grumpy officer waved the letter at them, "Sorry, damned bureaucrats are forming a new regiment; want to call them 'cavalry', they'll be changing our name next, then telling Mr. Colt to rename his guns."

He reached out his hand to John, "I'm Lieutenant Tree, Arthur Tree, I'm in command of this detachment, and this is Lieutenant Alfred Pleasonton. Alfred is a regimental adjutant heading to San Antonio on Army business. So, you'd like to ride along with us?"

"If that's possible we would be very grateful." John replied.

"It may be son, but your horses will need to be tough to keep up with us, we ride a hard pace."

"Our horses are homebred sir, of the best you'll find, they are outside the clerk's office if someone wants to look them over."

Tree called for the guard posted outside the tent, "Philips, go check their rides up at Lloyd's store."

"Sit down gentlemen; tell me what your intentions are."

John went on to explain his great plan.

"Very ambitious, Mr. Chisum," Lieutenant Tree acknowledged, "what protection have you got from the Indians up there?"

"Well sir... I was kind of hoping that was where you come into the picture, the Army will need meat; I'll keep my prices keen in exchange for firepower," John bartered.

"I only have twenty men in Company B, who are already stretched; I can't make any promises, as for meat, that is more Alfred's department."

Lieutenant Pleasonton was about to pick up the conversation, when the soldier returned and nodded approvingly, their horses had passed muster.

Alfred continued, "I will definitely be interested in buying your meat, but as Arthur says, we can make no guarantees about your safety, you'll need to be self-sufficient, you need men with guns. There are enough veterans from the Mexican war settling round here looking for work, keep them well fed and on a fair wage, you'll get who you need."

Arthur Tree interrupted, "We'll be heading south at dawn, if you're here you can ride with us."

The Chisums checked into the Alton Hotel for the night, giving them their last chance to sleep in a proper bed before they reached San Antonio.

The surveyors arrived that evening and joined them and Lloyd for dinner. John was fascinated by their exploits, mapping potential routes for a railroad network, to join up the country. He remembered his conversation with his namesake, Jesse Chisholm, and smiled. Progress was coming faster than the 'trader' had expected.

Lloyd donated an old copy of his clerk's map, for John to mark up routes of potential interest, for the future expansion of his business plans, and an hour of very productive scribbling ensued. Lloyd also offered to get word back to Gainesville that they would be gone for a while.

CHAPTER 9

THE ROAD TO SAN ANTONE

At first light they headed south. When they stopped to water their horses, a few hours later, at what would become known as Denton Creek, little could John know that he was on land that would be owned by a future daughter of his, and then by his grandchildren. One of whom would be regaling a friend with stories of his adventures over a century later, just a hundred yards from where they stood.

Their first night's camp was at Fort Worth, which was in the process of being decommissioned, as the frontier and its protectorate moved west. By the second night they arrived at the Brazos River crossing at the new town of Kimball. While the Dragoons set up camp for the night John tagged along with Lieutenant Tree, to track down the town's founder, Judge Kimball.

He did not take long to find; the army were always a welcome sight in town; the charismatic New Yorker had seen them ride in and dashed to meet them. Kimball gave Tree an update on the Indian situation. In short, some of the outlying farms had lost a few cattle, but no serious problems since his last visit.

John took the opportunity to introduce himself and explained that he hoped to be coming back soon with a herd of cattle.

Kimball responded enthusiastically, "Well, that is why I built the town, best crossing of the Brazos for a hundred miles. If you've got the gumption of your pa, you'll do well."

"You know my father?"

"We've met; I've got family back in Lamar County who didn't fancy coming this far west. You'll likely be the first proper herd to cross, send a rider ahead and we'll throw a party for you. You can supply the beef," he added jovially.

A few days later, after making good progress, John sensed tension in the ranks and trotted ahead to talk to Lieutenant Tree, "Is there a problem?"

"Scout has spotted signs of Indians ahead, small band, they could be Comanche, always trouble."

The company gathered tighter and slowed their pace to save their horses' energy for a potential gallop. Sure enough, they soon came across a band of natives, but a sorrier looking bunch you could not imagine.

One of the fitter looking Indians rode his horse towards them, the scout and Tree reciprocated. A short conversation ensued and the two returned. The scout trotted back to one of the company's pack horses and came back with a large parcel under his arm which he delivered to the Indian.

Lieutenant Tree returned to Chisum, "Tonkawa... friendly Indians; sided with your Texas Rangers against the Comanche at Plumb Creek. Poor souls are starving, given them enough to keep them going 'til they can get to the reservation at Fort Belknap."

"What reservation?" John enquired.

"Just been built, A few tribes will be there, will be customers for your beeves. Talk to Alfred, the army will be feeding them."

"If they're starving then why haven't they eaten their horses?" John queried.

"That would be a last resort, you're dead without a horse around here when everyone else has got one; they'd eat each other first."

John laughed hesitantly.

"I'm serious!" Tree retorted, "the Tonkawa are cannibals... but friendly cannibals."

John had heard wild tails of such, but he'd always thought they were stories to frighten the weak-minded, but Tree did not seem to be the kind of fellow to spin a yarn.

Late morning, a couple of days after not being eaten, an impressive three-story building, with a scaffolded dome above it appeared in the distance. The largest man-made construction John had ever seen in person. The elaborate building looked totally out of place in such wild country, like a pyramid rising up from the Giza Plateau in Egypt. As they got closer a bustling town came into view surrounding it. Tree pointed towards it, and confirmed what John had already suspected, "Austin."

Throughout Texas' days as a republic, with its administrative roles shared by several towns and cities, there had been much politicized debate about where a capital should be. After statehood Austin secured the title; and a while later construction started on the ostentatious Capitol building that lay before them, to replace what was not much more than a cabin. By the time the Chisums and the Dragoons passed through, the city's population had swollen to over 1,000 souls.

Eight days after leaving Alton they finally arrived in San Antonio, a truly bustling city, three times the size of Austin. New friendships had been forged and much learned en-route. A friendly 'fare thee well' was tinged with sadness, not least of all because the Chisums were losing their protection.

It did not take long to find Frederick Groos at his smart new Commerce Street store. He had just been joined in the business by his two younger brothers, Carl and Gustav. Frederick explained that he was breaking his brothers in, while they learned their trade and the language.

John soon realized that this fellow was far more than a storekeeper, and part-time banker. He ran a highly organized freighting business, with 140 high-wheel carts pulled by 280 oxen, forging a route to Fort Duncan and to Rick Pawless' Eagle Pass trading post, by the Rio Grande River. To say that John was impressed by the gentleman's enterprise would be an understatement.

As the conversation got around to business, Frederick Groos ushered him into a back office.

"Mr. Groos."

"Call me Frederick."

"Frederick, I have it on good authority that you're an honest man."

"Whose authority might that be?" Frederick queried.

"A.P. Lloyd."

"The Clerk in Alton?"

John nodded in acknowledgment.

"Yes sir, he said you are a man I could trust."

'Sir' was not a title that John used lightly, and seldom to someone younger than himself, but Groos was turning out to be quite a fellow, who certainly deserved the accolade.

Frederick responded, "In which case he clearly feels the same about you, Lloyd is a good judge of character, he would never send a waster my way."

They talked about John's plans, and an equitable agreement was reached. John would invest a large chunk of his capital in Groos' business, which he could draw upon as required, with certain limitations, Groos in turn would give the Chisums 'unbeatable prices' on supplies, which he would freight out from his warehouse in Austin.

"That will be perfect." John acknowledged "I'll drop an order in first thing tomorrow; it will be two full wagon loads."

John had an inspired thought, "As you will be unlikely to have a backload, if I can have an 'unbeatable price' I'll buy the wagons and four oxen off you. You can leave them all with Lloyd at Hickory Creek in Alton and let him know I'll settle up livery when I get back, your men can hitch their horses to the back of the wagons to get home."

Frederick came up with the 'unbeatable price' John wanted, and they shook hands to bond the deal. What John did not know, was that he had just planted the seeds of a friendship with the Groos brothers, which would last his lifetime.

John left the store feeling very pleased with himself; satisfied that he had secured a good deal. It was one of the first times James had witnessed his brother negotiate a contract, he was suitably impressed, "Pa sure would have been pleased to see you in action today."

John smiled; his day was complete.

They headed down the road to the comforts of the boarding house run by Frederick's good friend, William Menger, and his wife Mary. While John went to his room to write an extensive shopping list, James decided to meet some of the locals and have a taste of Menger's renowned home-brewed beer.

CHAPTER 10

ESCAPE FROM SAN ANTONE

At first light, whilst San Antonio was mostly still asleep, the brothers posted their order at Groos & Co, and then headed east out of town into the blinding rising sun. But as soon as they crossed the San Antonio River, two rough looking Mexicans appeared through the haze, guns drawn. John recognized one of them, from the shooting contest back in Paris.

James moved his hand towards his gun, "Don't be crazy, you'll never make it," John warned.

The Mexican, who John had recognized, overheard and replied, "Wise words Señor Chisum. Both of you keep your hands where we can see them and head up there."

He motioned with his gun towards a quiet side road, then after a couple of hundred yards, out of sight of Commerce Street, he instructed, "Here will do, stop and turn around."

The Chisums obliged.

"Señor Chisum, you still not carry a gun?"

"Nope," John affirmed.

"Well, no matter, you don't know how to use one anyway, but to be sure, open your jacket... very slowly."

John obliged, to confirm that he was not carrying.

"You should learn to shoot Señor; this is a dangerous country for an Americano carrying so much money," he observed, sounding sinisterly friendly.

He turned and pointed his gun at James, "Okay, baby Chisum, I want your right hand in the air, then undo your belt with the other, and drop your gun on the ground."

As the Mexicans' attention was drawn to his brother, John drew a Colt Pocket Dragoon from a concealed holster that Tom Towery had built into his saddle, and swung around his horse's neck. By the time he hit the ground he'd shot one bandit in his shooting arm and the other in his horse.

'GO!' he screamed to James, who kicked his mare and galloped through a gap in a ruined adobe wall, with John's horse having the good sense to gallop after them.

The horse John injured had dropped to the ground, with the two shocked Mexicans ducking for cover behind it. John encouraged them to keep their heads down with his three remaining shots, as he ran to where James was hiding.

James passed him the makings to reload. The quickest John had ever managed to do that at home was about three minutes, but that was without his hands shaking. James, wracked with nerves, got into what he saw as a strategic position, ready for a gunfight that they would most likely be outgunned in.

A rifle shot rang out, shortly followed by a second, then silence, apart from a horse grunting in agony. A deep American voice called out, "Chisums, hold your fire... you can come out now."

After John had finished reloading, they cautiously made their way into the open, guns cocked, to be met by a tall man carrying a familiar looking silver-plated Sharps rifle.

William Wallace smiled, "John Chisum, you've been practicing."

Before responding, John walked over to the Mexicans to finish the job, one clean shot through the head put the poor horse out of its agony. The Mexicans were already deader than doornails, dispatched by Wallace in a similar fashion. John felt sick at the sight of their brains spread in the dirt, but his nausea was far outweighed by his gratitude to be alive.

"Mr. Wallace... we are in your debt, on at least two counts."

He turned to his little brother, "Who were you talking to, when you were drunk last night, and did the conversation happen to include the fact that we were off to buy cattle?"

James looked sheepish, and then raised his palm to slap his own forehead. He did not need to say anything, but the expletive he mumbled spoke volumes.

"James, you need to learn to keep that mouth shut, until your brain catches up with it."

Wallace interrupted the sibling chastisement, "He didn't talk about much else; even I got bored with hearing it."

"You were there?" James queried, "I didn't see you."

Wallace took off his hat to reveal a shaven head, and pulled an eye patch from his top pocket, quoting, "In regione caecorum rex est luscus," showing off his grasp of Latin.

"Uh?" James replied.

"In the land of the blind, the one-eyed man is King," Wallace translated.

"Anyways, John, I'm glad you took my advice about a gun, though I'd recommend finding one with a bit more stopping power than that toy. As for these two lowlifes... it would probably do your reputation a power of good for you to take the claim on them. That is of course if you give me the $200 bounty, that's on what's left of their heads," he qualified.

"Thank you William, no offence, but it's not the reputation I want," and before his brother could get a word in, "you neither James."

Wallace gave a respectful nod, "Fair enough, I'm sure I can find a home for the Criollo gelding that you missed as well."

"You know what the bounty is on them, so I'm guessing you know who they were?" John deduced.

"Yep, the Gonzales brothers, they robbed a payroll in Austin a week ago, I've been tracking them, was going to ambush them and take them in alive, but then you happened along, and they ambushed you instead."

"You used us as bait? Why didn't you arrest them at Menger's, last night?" James protested.

"Not intentionally, you two just turned up at the wrong place, at the wrong time, and added some spice to the occasion. I cussed when I saw you. And you don't arrest a couple of desperados in a bar, it's likely to turn into a kidnap or firefight, and then nice folk get hurt.

"It's a shame," Wallace stated in a sympathetic tone, "these two were honest fellows after the war, went to California in '49 with gold rush fever, to make their fortune, and were doing okay, until the Hounds ambushed them and took everything."

"Hounds?" James queried, with a vision of a wolf pack in mind.

"The Hounds were a clan, with a high opinion of their white superiority, they hated Mexicans, and pretty much anyone who didn't speak English as their native tongue. They called themselves 'The San Francisco Society of Regulators', but 'Hounds' was what the 'Frisco Police Department named them. In truth, half the police were in cahoots with them anyway, and I'm ashamed to say that some of them had served with me in the war. These Gonzales boys grew sequoia-sized chips on their shoulders and have been robbing 'Americanos' ever since."

The Chisum brothers learned a lot that day about how intelligence, resourcefulness, and the ability to adapt to a changing situation, were essential skills for a good lawman. It wasn't all about posses and quick-drawing in the street.

John pointed at their formerly more talkative protagonist, "That one was in Paris, the day you won the rifle."

"Yep, they both were, I didn't have papers then to recognize 'em, their lucky day, I guess. Or perhaps not, seeing as how things have panned out for 'em."

Wallace wandered over to the bodies, and bent down to take their guns and bandoliers, which he offered to John, "These will get you started, and some, Colt Walkers."

"Isn't that looting?" John asked, trying to determine where Wallace's moral watershed lay, regarding the assets of the dead.

"Hell no, it's repatriation! These beauties were designed by my old friend Samuel Walker; they were probably taken from our men during the war. Sam would have been pleased to see them back in the hands of an honest American, if he'd survived."

Wallace paused, pondered and looked towards the Chisum brothers, remembering old battles and lost friends.

"We can at least take one accolade away with us from today," he observed.

"What's that?" James enquired.

Wallace pointed beyond them, "Well, we are the first Americans ever to win a gunfight here, and without the Mexicans getting off a shot."

The Chisums turned towards the chapel behind them, with its new bell-shaped facade. In the heat of the moment they had not recognized the most infamous building in Texas, the iconic Mission San Antonio de Valero, more commonly known as, 'The Alamo'.

Wallace cut back to the moment, "So, you're heading for Colorado County, that's four days ride through some rough country, if these two know you are carrying money, others might too. My job here is finished, so I'm happy to sign on as your scout for a dollar-fifty a day, plus expenses."

John saw the sense in Wallace's concern and offer, so happily agreed.

Wallace kicked the boot of one of the dead Mexicans, "Let me sort out these fellows with the Sheriff, then we'll make tracks."

What Wallace had failed to mention, was that a few years before Samuel Hamilton Walker's death, at the Battle of Huamantla, he was also one of the 159 who picked a white bean, that fateful day in Mexico, but without the benefit of Wallace's insight.

Footnote: Samuel Walker was one of the most celebrated heroes of the war with Mexico. His remains would be returned to Texas a few years after the Chisums' Alamo gunfight, to be re-interned in the Odd Fellows cemetery, just a mile east of where they stood. To rest beside the ashes of some of the brave souls, who defended the shrine that they were standing in the shadow of.

CHAPTER 11

BUYING BEEVES

Two hours later, with extra supplies secured from Frederick's store, they were heading east again, with the Mexican's sturdy Criollo in tow, earning its keep as a pack horse. As they left town Wallace made sure everyone could see that he was accompanying the brothers, a warning to anyone foolhardy enough to follow.

It soon became clear that Wallace's style of scouting was very different to that of the Dragoons. Whereas they would mostly keep to the main trails creating a wake of dust, relying on force and numbers for security, Wallace would keep off the trodden path whenever possible, often riding along shallow river beds. It was a style John would adopt himself, when traveling in a small party.

Apart from a wagon train heading west, and Gamaliel Good's stagecoach heading east, they didn't see more than the distant smoke of a campfire until they got to Colorado County.

Columbus gave them the opportunity of a roof over their heads for the night, and a bath, before trying to find the Matthews fella. If they had followed Good's stagecoach, they would have been there a day earlier, but John was not troubled, he had enjoyed Wallace's company, and his education. As for Wallace, he was on a day rate, plus expenses, so was happy with the stopover. James, as ever, was enjoying the company of the Latino ladies in the bar, all be it a tad wiser in the art of discretion in conversation.

In the morning they followed the directions the hotel manager had given for finding Eagle Lake, "Just follow the geese." They saw no eagles, but as predicted their morning was punctuated by huge flocks of migratory wildfowl, which had been pond-hopping to the lake for winter. A magnificent sight, and a telltale that cooler weather was on the horizon, perfect for driving cattle.

As they arrived at the lake, A.P. Lloyd was proved correct; there were clear signs of cattle tracks. There were also other tracks, which the Chisums did not recognize.

James pointed them out to Wallace, "Are those bear?"

Wallace laughed, "Well... if they are, that bear has got short legs and flat feet. Nope, they'd be 'gator, here for a goose supper."

They followed the cattle tracks south and within the hour were pleased to see a few healthy-looking longhorns on the horizon. As they rode over the ridge, they were met by the magnificent sight of the biggest herd of bovines John had ever seen.

"So that's what 1,000 cows looks like!" he exclaimed.

The herd parted, and five men cantered towards them, led by two white riders on horseback, followed by three black men on mules, who John presumed to be slaves.

The smaller of the white men, a scruffy, stubbly looking young fellow, trotted forward and in an aggressive tone shouted, "What you want?"

"I'm looking for Mr. Matthews." John replied.

"I'm Matthews, what you want?"

"John Matthews? I was expecting someone older."

"My uncle," then again in the same monotone, "what you want?"

"I'd like to do some cattle business with your uncle." John responded politely.

Matthews Jr. turned to one of the slaves, "Elijah, take them to the cabin."

They followed the slave south through the Matthews' cotton fields, James whispered to his brother, "I hope Uncle John is easier to deal with."

As they approached the Matthews' cabin quite a sight befell their eyes, at least two dozen alligator hides stretched drying on the veranda.

Matthews appeared from the cabin, gun drawn, backed up by one of the biggest men Chisum had ever seen, "What you want?" he yelled at them.

'Nope, the uncle was going to be just as difficult,' John decided.

"I hear you want to sell your cattle, I might want to buy them." John proposed.

Matthews lowered his gun and his tone changed, "All right then, come in and talk, I might want to sell them to you... Elijah, see to their horses."

They dismounted, handed the reins of their mounts to the slave, and stepped into the shade of the cabin. Matthews ushered them to a large table, where he planted a jug of sour mash. Wallace declined and found a chair in the corner to observe proceedings. John introduced himself and James and joined Matthews at the table.

"So, how many beeves do you want?" Matthews grunted.

"How many have you got?"

"At the last count, a thousand and fifty, and calves, and a hundred mustangs. I'm ready to sell you all the cattle, and half the horses."

"I'll take all of them off your hands if the price is right."

"You got here at the right time. We just rounded them up to move to the winter pasture, so that'll make your life easier. Price is seven dollars a head for the beeves and twelve a horse – take it or leave it."

John was familiar with the 'take it or leave it' gambit, a standard for testing the metal of who you are negotiating with.

"That is a fair price... if I was buying 10 cows, but for the whole herd I'll pay two dollars a head, eight dollars each for the horses."

"You are kidding me?" Matthews slapped his hand down on the table, "I've got three hands and four slaves running that herd, I can lay off the hands, but I need to feed the slaves, all they know is cow poking, I might as well shoot 'em at that price."

John was unclear whether Mathews was referring to shooting the cows, the hands or the slaves. He replied, "To be honest that's not my problem, but I might be able to help you fix it. Are the four slaves fit and single?"

"All fit, three of them single, Abe is hitched to my house girl, Lucy," he stated, pointing to a nervous looking girl standing in the shadows at the stove.

John drew a deep breath, "Can we have some privacy?"

Lucy was ushered out.

John continued, "Okay, here is the deal, I'll buy your herd at four dollars, I'll hire on your hands and I'll give you another two thousand for the slaves if you include Lucy."

Matthews laughed, "Lucy is worth a thousand or more on her own. You can have the boys but not her."

"I will not be responsible for splitting up a couple!"

Matthews paused and double checked the math in his head. He repeated John's opener, "Okay, here is the deal... the herd plus calves, fifty horses, Elijah, Joshua and Stephen. Abe can stay here and pick cotton, for six thousand dollars, cash on collection."

"Include their guns, saddles, and whatever strings of horses and mules the men run, and if that big fella outside is one of them, whatever elephants he rides, and you have a deal Mr. Matthews."

Matthews paused for dramatic effect – "You have a herd Mr. Chisum."

"Oh, this is just the start of my herd Mr. Matthews!"

"Out of curiosity, where are you taking them to?" Matthews inquired.

"Kimball then north," John responded.

"A lot of Indian country to go through," Matthews noted, then with a surprising streak of humanity, stated, "Look after my boys."

Wallace took the opportunity to jump into the conversation, "That will be my department," then turning humbly to John, "if you want to keep me on?"

John remembered Wallace's subtle show of strength when leaving San Antonio and picked up his cue, "May I introduce my scout, William Wallace."

Matthews looked surprised, "Bigfoot Wallace, the Ranger?"

"Yes sir, he would be me."

"You are in safe hands then Mr. Chisum."

Show of strength complete John tied up the final loose end of business, "I'll be back to collect first light tomorrow," he shook Matthews' hand and departed with James and Wallace in tow.

As Wallace turned to leave, he added, "Can you make sure the men have two days supplies to get them to Columbus?"

Wallace found a wooded spot a few miles away, out of sight of the Matthews' place, to camp for the night. James lit a small fire, in the Texas Ranger fashion he had learned from Wallace, and they settled down for the evening.

Wallace opened the conversation, "You surprised me today John; and I am seldom surprised these days."

"How's that?"

"I never thought I'd see you buy slaves."

"Just because I bought them doesn't mean I feel I own them, anyways I did not buy them; they came free with the beeves just like the calves did."

But the fact that Matthews would happily split up a man from his woman, sooner than a calf from its mother had seriously troubled John.

"You have a strange concept of free," Wallace replied, and then changed the subject, "You also need to heed the advice that you gave your brother. There was no need to let on we were going to Kimball, we will be conspicuous enough for sure, but the less people who know where we are headed, the better."

John acknowledged his poor judgment with a nod, "True."

"Anyway, pass me that map of yours," Wallace requested.

John slipped A.P. Lloyd's marked up map out of his saddle bag and handed it over.

Wallace laid it out on the ground and went on to describe the route home, "We won't be going back to Columbus like I told Matthews. North of Eagle Lake we'll turn north-east and head to San Felipe on the west bank of the Brazos. I know the town well, the Rangers used to be based there. You can get supplies there and I'd suggest hiring on a cook with a wagon, then we'll follow the river north. We should get to the Kimball crossing in two to three weeks. After that I'll bid you farewell. I have Ranger business to attend to in Fort Smith."

"Seems simple enough, and fair enough, you've been a great asset to us, and no doubt we'll miss you when you're gone," John acknowledged.

Wallace smiled and winked, "Sure, simple!" then headed off to his bed.

John climbed into his own bedroll but stayed awake for another hour running the events of the day, and the adventure ahead through his mind.

CHAPTER 12

BRINGING HOME THE BEEVES

They broke camp at dawn, to return to the Matthews' cabin, where they were greeted by his nephew, who was in a far more jovial mood, than when they had met the previous day.

"Mornin' Mr. Wallace, Mr. Chisums, my uncle will be right out, sirs."

John mused that perhaps the lad didn't like cows and was impressed that he had learned a few new words overnight. In truth John had simply underestimated how big a celebrity his scout was in those parts.

Matthews appeared and introduced John to his new employees; Art Williams, Charles Argent and big Jim 'Jimbo' Brown. They too seemed in fine fettle, John could not decide whether the source of their good mood was the fact that they still had a job, or because they no longer had to work for the Matthews, either way he was pleased to see it.

John, William and Matthews went inside, where six thousand dollars and ownership papers exchanged hands as witnessed by Wallace. A Texas Ranger's signature was a good notary to have on any document.

Matthews made a parting observation, which made John feel guilty for his earlier disdain towards the family, "Mr. Chisum, I admire your grit, it's quite a thing you're taking on, I wish my brother's boy out there was so bold. Don't get me wrong he's an honest lad, but I'm sad to say he's mostly a waste of space. He'll get my entire plantation one day and most likely ruin it, but your family should be proud of you, and I wish you well in your endeavors."

They shook hands and John headed out the door.

Outside, the three slaves had just appeared on their mules, having cut out John's fifty mustangs, he greeted them, and they responded politely. Their expressions were blank, he could not read their mood, but was wise enough to appreciate that the uncertainty of their future would be forefront in their minds, something which he planned to address at the earliest opportunity.

He also noticed several more slaves standing outside a cabin. Their emotions were much clearer to see, two of the older women were sobbing.

John cursed to himself, "The skin trade is a dirty business."

He beckoned his new crew to him, and introduced James and Wallace, despite the latter not really needing an introduction.

"Okay, William will scout the trail; you know your herd, who's going to be foreman?" Argent stepped forward and no one disputed his claim.

"Okay, place your crew Argent."

"I'll ride point with Bigfoot; Jimbo, Josh and Steve can eat dust on drag. How about you Chisums, are you riding with us?"

"We surely are, James and I can rope and cut, use us where you need us."

"Alrighty, James would you mind outriding the right wing and flank with Elijah, you'll be wrangling the horses as well. Mr. Chisum sir, you can take the left with Bungy," pointing to the fellow who had been introduced as Art Williams, "To be honest sir, we could do with a few more men, if you could hire them on at some point, it's a big herd."

"Fair point, duly noted," John acknowledged, "okay, are you ready, Mr. Wallace?"

"I was born ready, Mr. Chisum."

With the drag pushing from the rear and the Chisums, with their new colleagues, squeezing the wings in, the herd slowly bunched up until Argent was ready to point the bell cow north, and the drive could officially begin. John was tempted to let out a 'yee-haw' but was too scared of spooking the cows, or of making a fool of himself.

That evening they made camp on the border of Colorado and Austin counties, they had covered twelve miles, all be it that they were heading north-east, when home was a little to the west of north of them. After supper Wallace ushered John to one side and whispered, "Probably a good time to get to know your men."

John nodded and joined them at the campfire; he had thought of an opportune opener, "Bungy, where on Earth did you come across a name like that?"

"It's a nickname that my family is proud to carry Mr. Chisum." Bungy replied proudly, "my father, Richard Williams, is Welsh, he was an Ordinary Seaman on HMS Victory and fought under Nelson at Trafalgar, all the seafaring Williams are called Bungy, it's a Naval tradition."

Argent snorted, and then explained for his new boss' benefit, with the barely detectable remnants of a French accent, "My family was on the other side of that particular conflict, Bungy and me exchange views on it a lot."

John smiled "So, you were in the navy Bungy?"

"Yes sir, I signed up on the USS St. Mary's, at Galveston in '45, when I was 21, under Commodore Robert F. Stockton, and spent the Mexican war as a fighting-top sharpshooter."

"You're the same age as me. That must have been an important job," was the best response John could think of, having no personal experience of war, and having never seen the ocean.

"It was at times sir, and thank you, but to be fair it was mostly spent hoping not to get scurvy, cleaning my gun, and being afraid of dying."

"Bungy can shoot the whiskers off a coyote at a thousand paces. That's why I've got him riding with you Mr. Chisum, to look after our payroll," Argent injected to lighten the moment.

John laughed.

Bungy did not want to take too much acclaim on his shoulders, so pointed out, "Charlie and Jimbo were also in the Mexican war, and they're both useful with a gun. We're not famous like Mr. Wallace but we've all got history in that particular conflict.

"Most of which we'd like to forget," Argent interjected.

"Amen to that brother," Wallace replied, "Bungy, I did notice the Hall rifle you are carrying, not that many enlisted got to take 'em home."

"Yep, I was allowed to keep it for 'services rendered'. I'd love to see how it compares to your fancy Sharps some time, Sir."

"That would surely be interesting," Wallace acknowledged, "but save the 'Sir' for the boss there, you can call me Wallace, or you can call me William, you can even call me Bigfoot, but only Rangers who I outrank call me 'Sir'."

John had noticed that Jimbo was very quiet, so attempted to draw him into the conversation, "Just how tall are you Jimbo?"

The response was delayed and monosyllabic... "six... six."

Seeing John had gone up a dead-end, James took over and turned to Elijah, his new companion on the trail, "Can you boys shoot?"

The question was mostly rhetorical, as they were all carrying revolvers.

Elijah replied cautiously, "Well sir, we can all make a lot of noise, but gunpowder costs money, we don't get much practice."

Argent interrupted, "These boys have all got their skills, Elijah is a natural with horses, almost as good as his cousin, but Matthews would never have sold him to you, Steve and Josh are great nighthawks, I swear that all noirs can see in the dark."

Elijah's head bowed, John could not work out if it was due to thoughts of missing his cousin, being second best to him, or simply being dismissed as a 'noir'.

Steve took Argent's hint and got up to saddle his mule for his shift, watching the herd.

John saw an opportunity, and grabbed it, "Have those mules pulled draught?"

"Yessir," Elijah responded.

"How many of the horses are broke in?" John asked.

"Out of my half of Matthews hundred, I'd got through breaking fifteen."

"How many of those fifteen are with us?"

Elijah replied with a bit of swagger in his voice, and a big grin on his face, "Twenty of them, Mr. Chisum," he winked, and then added, "ma cousin, Jacob, will forgive me."

John smiled, "Well, I'm in Cousin Jacob's debt. Pick yourselves the best three each in the morning. We can use the mules elsewhere; you can break in the others as we go."

"Yes'um sir," Elijah replied gleefully, accompanied by big toothy smiles from Steve and Josh.

Wallace turned to John and quietly advised, "They'll be harder to catch if they run."

"I don't think they'll run," John reassured in a similar tone, "certainly not with you around!"

They woke to a beautiful autumnal morning, the sun glinting off the copper leaves of the neighboring thicket of beech trees. The mood in camp was good; John's chat with the men had allayed a few concerns.

John looked over to Wallace, who he had come to unwaveringly regard as his mentor and thanked the heavens for their chance meeting back in Paris, and for being reunited in San Antonio. They were clearly destined to become great friends.

With the cattle on the move again, Wallace returned to join Argent on point. He had developed a routine of riding a few miles ahead to scout for problems, and then later in the day, to look for potential campsites. Argent was always keen to see him reappear after his sorties, and had already developed great faith in Wallace's scouting abilities; his reputation had not been unwarranted. In between his rides out they would chat about the Mexican war, and generally concluded how awful it was, Wallace being particularly evasive on certain incidents that his reputation had him associated with.

Argent took the hint and decided to move on to another subject, "I've heard a lot about you as a Ranger, but never connected you with cattle."

"Ha, I can't stand the things, a thousand pound or more of trouble, with two brain cells, wrapped up in a leather bag, looking for the best way to kill itself."

"So, why are you on this drive?"

"Simple, I had nothing better to do, and I like Chisum."

"We were worried when we heard Matthews wanted to sell up, there isn't much work around Colorado County outside cotton picking, and I hate that as much as you hate cows," Argent admitted, "he does seem like a decent man, I think he'll be a good boss."

"You could not do much better I reckon," Wallace confirmed, then changed the subject, "Charlie, I do have one cattle question for you; something that I have always wondered about, but promise me that you will keep that I asked it to yourself."

"Okay," Argent replied, with great curiosity, expecting a deep and meaningful test of his knowledge of the industry.

"Why do they follow a cow, just because it wears a bell?"

Argent laughed heartily, "They don't, we let them follow the steer that we notice they like to follow, and we put a bell round its neck so that we can find the beast in the morning. Ha-ha, I could trade this story for whisky in the saloon, but my word is my bond, I'll not tell."

Wallace did feel a tad embarrassed by his lack of bovine knowledge, but shrugged it off, "Hell, every day is a school day!" then kicked his horse and cantered off on his next reconnaissance.

Meanwhile, on the right flank a deeper conversation was ensuing, between Elijah and James.

"When we left there were two women crying, who were they?"

"That would've been Steve and Josh's mama, they're brothers, and probably their aunt, they were sad to see them go."

"Are Steve and Josh okay?"

"They're sad, they cried some last night, but it was gonna happen one day, just happened a bit sudden, and going so far away, they knows they'll most likely never see their mama again."

James knew this revelation would upset John, so decided to keep it under his hat.

When not retrieving strays, John had spent his downtime quietly observing his men; he was pleased with what he saw. Apart from information being fed back from Wallace to Argent and subsequent directions sent back down the line, they just quietly got on with the job. There was no particular hierarchy, white man and slave worked together like clockwork. However, he was conscious that his men could not keep up this pace for weeks - this clock needed a few more cogs.

That night they camped just west of San Felipe, near the Brazos River, they would be turning north in the morning, heading in the general direction of home for the first time.

The evening's campfire conversation was on more practical issues than the night before. John stoked the fire under Jimbo's stewpot, then stood up to address his men, "I'm going into town in the morning to get more men and supplies, oh and some more plates," he joked, as he observed Jimbo testing dinner out of the pot with a spoon, and burning his mouth.

"Charlie, how many men do you need?"

Argent was quick to respond as he'd been fretting on the subject, "Two would be good, four would be better."

"Okay, do you want to come with me and help choose 'em?"

"I'd better stay on point, William and me are working well together, once we get the drag moving take Jimbo, he may not say much, but he listens lots, knows the town and is a good judge of men."

"Would it leave you too short-handed if I take Elijah as well? I want to do some horse trading."

"That should be fine tomorrow; we will be funneled between trees and the Brazos, so not too much work on the wings." A short while later John caught Charlie Argent on his own; so, took the opportunity to interrogate him, "What is it with Jimbo Brown, is he ornery, or has he got some kind of problem?"

"No, you could not meet a nicer fellow, if you are on the right side of him. He's always been quiet, but I only met him after the war, Bungy knows him better. I've seen many come home troubled, could be that, could be just that he's spent too much time around the Matthews, or perhaps because he's English, they are strange folk," he joked.

John had got so few words out of the fellow; he had not even noticed his nationality.

As everyone not nighthawking headed to their bedrolls, Wallace grabbed John's attention for a quiet word, "San Felipe is a rough old town; you keep your wits about you tomorrow! Don't leave it too late to find us, nights are drawing in and no moon tomorrow, even with Elijah's nighthawk eyes a herd is hard to find in the dark, even one this big."

"I'll be okay Pa, I've been taught by the best remember." John winked.

"Hey, don't get too cocky, Son."

CHAPTER 13

SAN FELIPE

As they headed to town leading the three mules, John soon confirmed what Argent meant about Jimbo being quiet. He could barely get a string of more than three words out of him. While on his other flank he had Elijah, who had learned early in life not to talk unless he was spoken to.

Apparently, John asking, "How much do you know about mules?" definitely fell into the category of being spoken to, and by the time they got to town John had not only expanded his knowledge of that particular hybrid. He'd also gained an extensive understanding of jennies, jacks and hinnies, which you could breed with what horse and which you couldn't. Elijah's enthusiasm for equines was boundless.

On reaching the outskirts of San Felipe John pulled his horse to a halt, "Right, first order of business, we need men, where do I find them, Jimbo?"

"The tavern, midday," Jimbo quietly replied and pointed.

"Okay then," John acknowledged, "second order of business, where's the fairest horse trader?"

Jimbo pointed to a barn further down the street, "Fuhrmann."

"Jimbo, can you go order supplies," he handed him a list and a purse of money that equated to over two month's pay. Jimbo nodded, not bothering to question how they were going to carry the large quantity of goods back to the herd, Chisum was the boss. He handed over the reins of the mule he was leading to Elijah and steered his horse away, stabbing his finger towards a general mercantile store where he would be heading.

"While you are at it, see if you can find someone who can cook as well as you can?" John added.

Jimbo shook his head and quietly muttered, "Unlikely."

John and Elijah trotted over to the stables that Jimbo had recommended; the sign over the door confirmed it to be the premises of 'Mr. Hans Fuhrmann'. They hitched up their horses and mules to the long rail outside, and wandered in to Fuhrmann's barn. A large, bearded fellow with arms like tree trunks was working on a wheel with a spokeshave.

He spoke with a deep, strong, Germanic accent, which made Groos back in San Antonio sound all-American in comparison, "How can I help you?"

John introduced himself and offered his hand to the German. Fuhrmann shook it with a vice like grip, and nodded an acknowledgement to Elijah.

As was his way, John cut straight to business, "I'm looking for a small wagon, a mule and harnesses."

John had taken on board Wallace's advice about a cook and a wagon but did not want someone who could quit if the mood took them. If he was in control of the wagon, he was in control of the cook.

"It will have to be a very small wagon if you only want one mule." Fuhrmann joked.

John smiled, "I have three outside, I need a fourth."

Hans put his woodworking to one side, and wandered out to look over John's stock.

"Good mules Mr. Chisum," he turned to Elijah, "I recognize you; you're from the Matthews plantation, do you tend to these?"

"I do, Sir," Elijah replied cautiously.

Hans gave him a respectful nod.

"Elijah, you know your mules, have a look out back in the corral; you'll find something there, if that's okay with you Mr. Chisum?" Hans queried.

"That's fine,"

"You want a wagon, I've got a twelve-foot Murphy in the barn that I bought off a migrant, I have tidied it up some."

"What happened to the migrant?" John asked, knowing that a migrant without a wagon was as lost as a bullet without a gun.

"Still about some place, they read the stories of Stephen Austin's San Felipe and thought it would be El Dorado, they run out of money, or rückgrat. This town never really picked up again after the Mexican war."

John could only guess what rückgrat translated to, but got the gist.

"So, what brought you here?" John asked; his natural curiosity piqued.

"Me, I simply ran out of money," the German smiled.

"But I'm doing fine now," he added, not wishing to compromise his negotiating position.

"Show me the Murphy," John requested.

They returned to the barn where Hans tugged on a tarpaulin to reveal a freshly painted blue wagon. He had done a fair job of 'tidying', but it certainly carried a few battle scars, if only the holes and split timbers could talk, he pondered. It was similar to the ox carts he had purchased from Groos, but that did not matter; he knew that if it no longer had any purpose, he could always sell it on in Denton County, probably at a profit.

He reminisced fondly about the huge Conestoga 'Prairie Schooners' that his family had used on their own migration to Texas, but you could buy five Murphys for the price of one of them, and these little wagons were far more practical for a cattle drive.

For negotiating effect John poked a finger through what appeared to be a bullet hole, sighed and stated, "This will do if the price is right."

Elijah came wandering back from the corral leading a mule; the big grin on his face spoke volumes, "And I'll take that mule," John added.

"Okay, you want harnessing as well; this came rigged for four, $150 for the lot?"

Elijah put his hand up to interrupt negotiations, wandered over to John and whispered in his ear.

John turned to Hans, "It's a deal, if you can include harnesses for an extra four horses for the hill country. Elijah wants to look after his mules."

"You are a hard bargainer Mr. Chisum, but I like a man who looks after his stock, ja, it's a deal."

After talking some more John left the mules with Hans so that he could adjust the harnesses and set them up for four-in-hand daily driving, with the eight-in-hand option when terrain got more difficult.

John rode over to the tavern with Elijah, happy with their morning's endeavors.

He had visited a lot of drinking houses in his day, but had seen few as rough as the San Felipe Hotel. It crossed his mind that he would most likely wipe his boots on the way out.

They approached the bar, and John ordered two beers.

A voice further up the bar interrupted proceedings, "Hold on there, we don't serve niggers around here."

John paused, saddened that a good day was suddenly turning sour, and attempted to take the intellectual high ground, "Would you be the proprietor of this establishment?"

"What's that to you, city slicker?" the aggressor responded.

John was amused at the 'city slicker' reference, but after looking around, he judged that he was certainly the smartest fellow in the bar.

The bartender leaned over to John, "You'd best go, Rufus is still drunk already, and trouble."

The advice was sound, and John never did truly understand why he ignored it, in favor of his next statement, but in the fullness of time would be glad that he did.

"My employee and I are thirsty, and would like a drink, two beers please," he repeated.

"My employee and I," the drunk mimicked, "are you saying he's a free man, let's see his papers."

John looked along the bar, "Elijah's papers are none of your damn business."

The angered drunk stomped over to John, drawing his gun.

John held up his hand, "Hold on I'm unarmed," which he confirmed by opening his jacket.

"What the hell does that matter?" Rufus exclaimed.

"It doesn't," John confirmed, jabbing the drunk in the throat with his right fist, followed by a knee to his testicles and the hardest punch he had ever delivered, square between the eyes." Rufus hit the floor unconscious. John decided on the spot never to use that punch again, it hurt and contemplated that his hand might be as broken as Rufus' nose.

Before he had time to check, two of Rufus' drinking buddies pulled and cocked their guns, echoed by a third from behind John. Elijah's eyes were fearful, he was sure he was about to die.

Rufus' companions hesitated as a calm English voice behind Chisum commanded, "You two, put your guns on the bar or I finish the job Mr. Chisum started."

They did just as they were told.

John turned with a sense of relief, to see 270 pounds of Jimbo Brown behind him, and an equal sense of disbelief that he'd just strung an entire, grammatically correct, sentence together. John looked at Elijah; they both shrugged their shoulders in amazement.

Jimbo continued with his newfound eloquence, "Drag your friend out of here, you can pick up your guns after we leave town."

As the three drunkards departed John turned back to the bartender, "Make that three beers."

"Make that four!" A short, greasy, skinny fellow standing behind Jimbo injected.

"Cookie," Jimbo explained, reverting to his more familiar turn of phrase.

"Make that six, and they're on us!" A man playing cards at a nearby table yelled out.

"Old friend... other fellow too." Jimbo endorsed.

They joined the two card players at their table and it turned out that these were the men that Jimbo had hoped to find, he introduced them, pointing with his finger.

"Mac... Ken."

The latter responded, "Kentucky, but Ken is just fine." The former offered his hand to Chisum, "Calum Macleod".

John had to ask, "So a Scot?"

"Third generation American, but Scottish to the bone", Mac replied proudly.

Within minutes, expedited by Jimbo's further endorsement of, "They'll do," the two were hired on.

John asked, "Is there anyone else in town worth their salt?"

"You just beat up, and threw out, the only others around here who know how to rope a steer," Mac replied.

"They would not have made good 'employees', not worth an ounce of salt," Ken added with a smile.

While Mac and Ken collected their worldly possessions, the rest of the crew returned to the general store, to pick up their order, plus some less 'city slicker' looking attire, for John and his brother. They caught up with the herd a while before sunset, as recommended.

The mood around the campfire that evening was very upbeat, old friends catching up with each other, good food and coffee in abundance, and the story of the boss' bar fight getting more dramatic, as each told their version of it.

John was pouring a coffee at the wagon, feeling more than a little pleased with himself, when Wallace wandered over to him, "Sounds like you had quite a day."

"I certainly did," he replied with a slightly smug look.

"For a man who 'doesn't want to build up a reputation' you took quite a chance just to buy the boy a beer," he stated, pointing up to the faint silhouette of Elijah, nighthawking on the ridge above.

"Maybe, it just seemed to be the right thing to do at the time," John replied defensively.

"Perhaps it was, but be careful, you won't always have a Jimbo covering your back or an angel on your shoulder."

John thought for a moment, "Then perhaps I need to make sure that I do, always have a Jimbo or Bungy covering my back."

CHAPTER 14

INDIAN COUNTRY

Mac and Ken fitted in from the off, taking a lot of pressure off the rest of the men. John apologized to Argent for not bringing back more hands, and was pleased with his foreman's objective response.

"Two good men are way better than four bad ones, or greenhorns Sir, we'll be just fine."

They made good progress over the coming days, until one afternoon when Wallace came back to the point looking uncharacteristically perturbed. Argent held up the herd while Wallace trotted back to talk to Chisum.

"We've got a band of Penateka Comanche ahead. Do you mind losing a few of your leanest beeves?" Wallace asked.

"Whatever you need to do," John replied sincerely, with a fearful tremble in his voice. He knew he would have to deal with 'proper Indians' one day, and had always feared this moment.

"Okay, I need everyone to swap to fresh horses, you and Bungy cut out five cows from the drag, that have been slowing you down, and bring them up to the point." Wallace directed.

"That'll take a while; can't you just take some from up front?" John queried.

"John, I'm in no hurry, I'd frown upon giving away your best stock. Bungy, make sure that Hall of yours is ready for some action."

"Why fresh horses?" John puzzled.

"That's plan-B, run like hell." Wallace replied with a wink.

An hour later the Comanche appeared ahead. When they were about 500 yards away Wallis and Bungy led the scrawny cows out towards the Indians, with their big guns on show, half way there Wallace shouted out, "Tukamukaru tosahwi."

The Comanche looked to their leader for orders; one asked the question that was on all their minds, "Why does he want us to 'wait in ambush'?"

The leader frowned and replied, "I'm not sure, white men are crazy, let's just see what happens." He raised a long lance in acknowledgement.

Wallis and Bungy trotted back to the point and dismounted.

"Are you sure about this?" Bungy queried.

"I sure am sure; me, you, me, you then me, left to right, head shot." Wallis explained and took aim.

"Whoa there!" Bungy interrupted, "these ain't deer, longhorns have got skulls like a stove door, it'll just bounce off at this range and give 'em a headache. Aim lower at the chest, heart the size of a pumpkin, hard to miss."

Wallace accepted the advice humbly, "Okay, I'll take the one facing us the others will turn when they hear the shot, you pick your steer."

'Bang – Bang – Bang – Bang – Bang', followed by another 'Bang' and a faint echo as Bungy finished off one of Wallace's that was still standing. Wallace turned to him with an impressed nod. Bungy had matched his six-second reloading time with a rifle that was 25 years older.

The Comanche, rode forward, two to each steer, roped their hind legs and dragged them to the edge of the neighboring forest out of the way of the herd. The fellow with the long lance raised it again, and Wallace responded by raising his rifle, he then motioned to the drag to get the herd rolling.

John trotted up to Wallace, "Very dramatic and some fine shooting, but why did you not just give them the cows?"

"Psychology Mr. Chisum, pure psychology. By shooting them we are keeping the Comanche busy, they can only drag a cow so far before ruining the hide, they'll be most of the day here butchering. Shooting from afar, taught them how far and how well we... or at least, how well Bungy can shoot, another show of strength."

Chisum realized that this was yet another day in school, but decided to take the opportunity to further his education even more, "How were you so certain it would work?"

"I wasn't... I was considering plan-B, until I recognized the fellow with the long spear, the one I told to 'stay put and wait'. His name is Tosahwi, means 'Little Knife', he's a smart fellow, and knows what's best for him. I've come across him before, a short while back. Most Comanche don't look for a fight for no reason, and only then when they are sure they will win it, they are not savages. They'd have hoped we would get scared and run, and then they would have had the horses too. A bolder raiding party might have gone after your slaves... sorry, your 'employees', for ransom, so I gave them a distraction to reconsider that option."

"They would have kidnapped slaves but not us?" John asked, surprised at the thought.

"Sure, who pays ransom for a cow puncher? You just hire another one."

"So, that'll be the last we'll see of them?" John asked in hope.

"I'll answer that next Wednesday." Wallace replied. Wednesday being the day they planned to cross the Brazos at Kimball, and be out of Penateka territory.

As it would happen the question was answered a lot quicker, in the morning the Penateka appeared again behind the drag.

"Another five?" John resigned himself to gradually losing his herd.

"Nope, just two and I'll tell them, 'That is all they're getting'."

"Screwies?" Jimbo queried.

"Only the worst for the Indians," Bungy replied.

Wallace turned to Bungy with a puzzled look on his face and repeated, "Screwies?"

"Jimbo loves to educate, it's English for a runt cow."

Two were cut out and left behind, then Bungy stood next to Wallace armed and ready.

"Give us a countdown Jimbo." Wallace requested.

"Three, two, one, fire!" Jimbo boomed.

Only one shot rang out but both cows hit the dirt.

"Mine hit the ground first," Bungy boasted.

"Sure it did, it was shorter." Wallace replied.

Wallace called out to the Comanche in their native tongue. Who then tried to work out why the man with a thousand cows, would be shouting, 'We have famine'.

Wednesday couldn't come around soon enough, and to the delight of everyone it came around a day early. At noon on Tuesday Wallace trotted back to the herd with the news they had all been waiting for. They would make it to the crossing at Kimball before the end of the day and the townsfolk were real excited that they were coming. John took it upon himself to spread the news, giving each man an advance on their pay, including his three slaves, much to their surprise.

Later that evening, John, James and Wallace were happily sitting on Judge Kimball's porch, bathed and shaved, except Wallace skipped the shave, smoking nice cigars and drinking Kimball's homemade beer. It wasn't quite up to Menger's standard, but after eighteen days on the trail, no one was too bothered.

"Days don't get much better than this." John commented.

"I'd have to agree," Wallace added, patting his pocket that contained an unexpected bonus.

"Yep!" John continued, "Fifty head sold, for three times what I paid for them, two new hands hired, a bath and a change of clothes. William, when you head north tomorrow would you mind taking James with you, pick up the supplies from Lloyd, pay for storing them and livery. Then get everything onto the site at Clear Creek for when we get there, so we can start building a bunkhouse for the men."

"No problem, Mr. Chisum, Sir!"

John returned a smile; he was truly having one of the best days of his life.

CHAPTER 15

HOMEWARD BOUND

As the hands started moving the cattle across the Brazos, John wished his Brother and Wallace a safe journey. He was not sure who he would miss the most, but he certainly knew who made him feel the safest.

On the fifth day north of Kimball, after a cold night, they woke to a majestically beautiful November morning. The cattle were enjoying the last of the Fall sun on their backs, and the men were in good spirits, hoping to get to Fort Worth, the last big milestone in the final leg of their drive, by sundown.

It was Jimbo who first noticed something was wrong, there was no birdsong. He headed over to Chisum to borrow his telescope and looked north, dark blue clouds were gathering on the horizon, "Blue Norther!" he exclaimed.

John had experienced a Blue Norther before, but from the comfort of a homestead. It was going to get very cold, very wet and very windy, very rapidly.

"Okay, bunch up the herd, they'll have to fend for themselves tonight, we're heading to Fort Worth," John commanded.

It pained Elijah to leave his horses, but Chisum was right, there was little they could do for them.

They covered the eight miles at a Dragoon's pace, and some, with the north wind directly in their faces and dodging tumbleweeds en-route. By the time they reached Fort Worth the wind had picked up to over thirty miles an hour, bringing torrential rain with it. The fort was by then abandoned, apart from a small patrol of guards, who pointed them to a barn for their wagon, mules and horses, and unlocked a barrack for them to shelter in for the night.

In contrast to the weather outside, the men had a comfortable evening and the unexpected opportunity of a lukewarm bath, but all thoughts were with the herd as the window shutters rattled, and the roof sounded like it was about to head south. John noticed Elijah praying, and offered some comforting words, "Your horses will be okay, Son."

By dawn, as they emerged from the cabin, the wind had dropped to a stiff breeze, the water troughs had frozen, and the ground was littered with a layer of hailstones. They left Cookie and the chuck wagon at the fort and headed south at a more reasoned pace, severely worried at what they might find.

As they came over a ridge the herd was spread before them tightly packed, sharing warmth, but the horses were missing. Knowing how horses think, Elijah quelled panic. He headed for a spinney of evergreens, where they were sheltering under the pine trees, tails into the breeze.

One was lame, always a hazard on the trail, a hoof shaped bruise on its hock revealed that it had been kicked, but not lame enough to become dinner. Elijah would nurse it to their new home.

After a second, less dramatic night back at Fort Worth, they were on the road to Denton County, and to what was to become home.

Arriving at Clear Creek a few days later, John was pleasantly surprised to see construction had begun. James had hired on two local fellows, of Lloyd's recommendation, who had built a corral for their horses, mules and the four oxen. And started work on a bunkhouse for the men.

One of them passed John a letter from James. It explained what he had done, and that he hoped John approved, and stated that he was heading back east on a personal matter.

John decided that it was time that he also headed somewhere on a personal matter, he put Argent in charge and rode on up to Gainesville.

He got quite the hero's welcome at the Towery homestead. James had regaled the family with stories of Mexicans, Indians, bar fights and gunfights, they were very impressed by his association with Bigfoot, but mostly relieved that he was safe, as the town had also experienced the brunt of the Blue Norther the weekend before.

He heard some delicate footsteps on the veranda, followed by a squeal of delight, as a certain young lady realized that he was home. She dashed into the room with a beaming smile, only to receive a scornful look from Frances. She subdued her excitement but could not subdue her beating heart.

As things quietened down John caught Frances on her own and laid $500 in front of her, "I want a half share in Jensie."

"Your whore, I thought of selling her while you were away, to teach you a lesson. You men are all the same; you can't keep your peckers in your pants. You can't find a woman, so you want to buy one."

"Jensie, is no whore, if something develops between us it will be natural, and none of anyone else's business."

Frances looked at the King's ransom before her; she could certainly do with the money, "Well, I guess you will sleep with her anyway, and it's better than sleeping with your cousin," a reference to his father's serial borderline incest, rather than to any romantic candle she might have burning for John. Though in truth she did care for him, in more ways than a cousin with a husband should, making the vision of him snuggled up to a slave girl even more abhorrent to her.

John moved his gear back into the boarding house, and the routine of Jensie bringing over his supper was resumed. She was so excited to have him home, but equally nervous of what the future was likely to have in store for her.

He smiled as she came in, and stood up to take the supper basket off her, "Please, please sit down," he requested in a slightly nervous formal tone.

Jensie sat on the edge of the bed with no clue how this was going to turn, her eyes looked tearful, so John got straight to the point, "Do you want to be my woman?"

Jensie thought on the question to see if there were any alternative interpretations, other than the one stated, there were none, "I already am John Chisum; the question is 'am I your only woman?' forever your only woman?"

"Yes, you are... every night on the trail I thought of you and seeing your face again, it kept me going. I love you."

"You know that I love you too, but can this be, do you want to marry me? Can that be?"

"I don't think we could ever get properly hitched, but married in my heart. And... as of this afternoon I half own you."

Her reply was the first thing that came into her quick-witted mind, "Which half?"

John went on to explain his earlier conversation with Frances, and that she would be able to spend every night that he was home with him, if she wanted to.

Jensie thought on this life-changing revelation, "How can you own someone, and love them."

"Well, if I did marry, I would own my wife under law."

"But you have bought me... half of me, that ain't no marriage."

"I bought a share in you, to make sure Frances can never sell you, she can't do anything without my agreement. It is to keep you safe."

John put his hand around her beautiful long neck and pulled her towards him, he kissed her sweetly then deeply. Supper was cold by the time they got around to eating it.

CHAPTER 16

BUILDING A RANCH

Christmas had always been a special time in the Chisum household, the one time in the year that virtually everyone got a day off work, or at least most of it. John was sad to be away from family, and had considered going back to Paris but was far too busy. At least that is what he told everyone. For him Christmas was where the heart was, and that was in Gainesville with Jensie. He expected to feel a bit isolated that year but when he got word that James was returning, mid-December, he was genuinely excited.

James did not turn up alone though; he had a familiar looking, very attractive young lady with him, Josephine, the girl from the saloon in Sherman. The bigger bombshell was that they planned to get married before Christmas.

The brothers headed south the next day, to inspect the construction work at Clear Creek. John had heeded his father's advice and delegated to his crew, keeping 'away from the coalface'. It had turned out that Mac was a skilled carpenter and builder, so Charlie Argent had happily agreed to him being put in charge of the project. As Charlie colorfully put it, "I know cows and horses, I even know sheep, but I don't know shit about shingles."

As they rode, John tested James' ambitions, "I guess we are going to need a bigger house, for you and your bride."

"Well, I won't be much use to you if we live in town, but this will help." James handed over $100.

"You won at poker for once?"

"No, not played a game since last time, I've got a wife to look after now, need to be responsible... it's a wedding present from Pa. I spent a few days with him before coming back."

John did a quick calculation, of how little time that left, for his little brother to have seduced and engaged his fiancé.

"You are a fast worker, does he approve?"

"Oh, hell yes... adores her, and expects grandchildren within the year."

"Are you sure this is the place to bring up a family?" John queried, resurrecting a campfire conversation, from what seemed a year before, but was, in reality just a few months, barely a mile from where they were riding.

"No less so than Paris was in its day, and Jo wants children, so there ain't too much choice in the matter."

As the brothers came over the last hill their crew's efforts were plain to see. Things were moving on at a great pace. Smoke was billowing out of the bunkhouse chimney, and a frame had been crafted for the house.

John visited once or twice a week; and always found something positive to say about what had been accomplished. The infrequency of his inspections instilled in his men that he trusted them, and meant that he got to see real progress, they were truly exciting times.

Mac put down his hammer to welcome them, it was clear that he was enjoying this break from poking cows. The cows were also enjoying a break from being poked, grazing on the long grass, and putting some tallow back on after the drive.

Mac showed them around, proud of his endeavors. One of the most impressive feats of engineering was a hole in the ground that you could almost fit the bunkhouse in, which was to become the icehouse and meat store, "Better than digging graves," Mac pointed out, alluding to the dugout's alternate potential, as a hideout in inclement weather, or other emergencies.

"Looking good Mac, but the house needs to be twice as long."

Mac turned to the plans lying on his woodworking bench, "But?"

"Nope, you have done just fine, but a change of plans, it needs to be twice the size with two front doors."

John went on to explain his brother's good fortune, which was met by much delight from the fellows in earshot. Every new family was a blessed celebration in their harsh environment. With the expectation of lots of babies coming along, for the next generation to perpetuate the 'Manifest destiny', of God-fearing folk's determined domination of their expanding country.

A twitch of the curtains at the modern Clear Creek ranch house reminded Danny that they might be outstaying their welcome on the owner's lawn, "Let's move on to Gainesville", Eugie suggested.

Danny helped her up, "One thing first though," Eugie paused, turned around, and walked over to the ranch house door, much to Danny's bewilderment.

She returned with the elderly rancher in tow, passed him her new Instamatic camera, and prompted Danny to stand next to the historical marker with her, despite its erroneous information.

"Say 'Cheese'," the rancher requested and clicked the shutter release.

"One more for luck," Eugie encouraged.

The 'odd couple', as the rancher would call them, when regaling his wife with stories of the day, waved goodbye and headed back down Sons Road towards the highway. Eugie noticed a graveyard off to the right in the distance, and had a better than good idea as to who might be buried there, but decided that their story had to wait for another day.

As they turned on to I-35 Danny resurrected the conversation, "So, Josephine and James moved in next door to John and Jensie? A whole lot of 'Js' in that household," he joked.

"Not quite, Jensie was still half owned by the Towerys, and still very much in service, she may have been nearly 20 but her face looked about 14 and she had a few years left in her as a house girl."

James and Josephine got married on the Wednesday before Christmas, John was best man of course, and in the absence of Josephine's dear-departed father, the job of walking her down the aisle fell upon Jimbo, who had volunteered due to him being the 'eldest hand'. The job did not involve too many words, so James and Jo felt safe to go along with his reasoning.

The wedding was also an excuse for everyone to have an extra day off work, and come to town, two Christmases at once. John never missed an opportunity for a party, and getting his fiddle out, especially since there was no longer anyone around, who would dare to admonish him for his choice of instrument.

The double-sized ranch house was completed in the spring, finished off in two coats of Blue Norther resistant white paint. The conspicuousness of the 'Great White House' on top of the hill was a mixed blessing, it was easy to find by folks who you wanted to, but equally easy to find by those who you didn't.

Throughout the first few months at Clear Creek there were several attempted raids by the Comanche, and John was losing a lot of stock to rustlers. A carrot and stick routine was developed, derived from Wallace's demonstration of a show of strength, on that first cattle drive.

The 'stick' came in the form of having two guards on patrol 24 hours a day. At the first sight of hostiles, "INDIANS", the unsubtle codeword for a native attack, would be shouted out, and either

Bungy or Jimbo, or both if they were around, would rush to bear arms. Jimbo's marksmanship had improved somewhat, due to a combination of Bungy's tutorage, and the new Slanting-Breech Sharps Carbines that John had acquired, as part of his security regime.

If you shoot an Indian you start a war, if you shoot his pony you embarrass him and ruin his season, both of the marksmen proved that they could reliably take down a horse with a single shot, at a quarter of a mile, so the natives seldom came any closer than that.

The 'carrot' was an animal proof crate which was set up on a bench about half a mile from the ranch house that the hands had come to call the 'bird table'. Once a week a salted, butchered 'Screwy' would be placed in it on ice. The Comanche soon got into the routine of collecting it the same day, and the rustling of Chisum's cattle declined dramatically.

The full success of the strategy was proven soon enough. Jimbo and one of the hands were taking the meat out in the old blue Murphy, as they got within a hundred yards of the bird table, half a dozen Comanche appeared the other side of the hill. Jimbo could have turned, but outrunning the Comanche in a wagon was extremely unlikely, would have been a sign of weakness, and could well have resulted in their mules being shot from under them, so they soldiered on.

The cowhand laid the ice and meat out, while Jimbo stood guard. Job complete they backed away to their wagon and a lead Comanche held up a lance in acknowledgement. They turned and returned to the ranch house at a sedate walk, but with their hearts pumping like they had just run a mile.

The white house would get regular visits from the military, out of Fort Belknap, who were always made welcome. Later that summer John was pleased to see a familiar face, Jesse Chisholm, scouting for them. Jesse joined them for dinner at the bunk house and the conversation soon got around to the natives.

Jesse looked up from his supper and pointed in John's direction, "Did you know that you're pretty famous among the Comanche?"

"Am I?" John queried, with ego temporarily boosted.

"No, the big fella," Jesse pointed higher at Jimbo who was standing behind John, listening to the conversation.

"And the other one who can shoot," Jimbo pointed to Bungy who stood up and wandered over to hear more.

"They have given you names. 'Little Man Big Gun' and 'Big Man Louder Gun'. I guess you use a few more grains there big fella."

Jimbo nodded an affirmative. Neither he nor Bungy would ever get to hear what their names sounded like in Comanche, but both were tickled by their newfound celebrity status amongst the tribe, but moreover from hearing it from a renowned hero of the West, like Jesse Chisholm.

CHAPTER 17

MAKING BABIES

Danny parked up outside the Cooke County courthouse, an impressive four-story, limestone clad, Beaux Arts style building with a central domed clock tower above it.

"This was the fourth courthouse," Eugie explained, "it started off as a log cabin, but that got knocked down by an angry steer, about the time the Towerys moved to town. The next one was a bit fancier, but that burnt down, so did the one after that. Then they built this cathedral, when I was in my twenties."

Danny had visited Gainesville numerous times; he had even been in the courthouse to sort out his taxes, but never thought of it as anything more than a dull municipal building. He'd never really looked up, and considered how it would have been a landmark, to those who watched it emerge from the ashes of its predecessors, a magnificent milestone to the growth of the county and State. A wave of patriotism flooded over him, he was proud to be a Texan, and would make sure he looked up more often in the future.

Eugie got her bearings from some of the older brick-built town houses, on the other side of the square, and pointed to a corner of the city block that the courthouse stood on, "That was where the boarding house stood, where Chisum stayed when he was in town and my mama and aunt were born, let's take a walk."

She slipped her arm into Danny's for a stroll around the perimeter of the courthouse's one-acre grounds, "Where did we get to?"

"Big Man Loud Gun," Danny cued almost correctly.

"Oh yes, Indians... John was spending more time away from home than at home, negotiating deals with the military and such like. Selling meat to Fort Belknap, for the reservations they were responsible for, turned out to be quite the goldmine for him. He even got money up front, which he surely needed. His reputation as an honest cattleman spread far and wide, helped somewhat by a certain Texas Ranger, recommending him at every opportunity," she paused at the spot where the boarding house would have been, "but when he came back here his mind wasn't on cattle."

John and Jensie's unions were less frequent than they would have liked, but were always enthusiastic, later in 1854 he would return from a trip to discover that she was 'with child'.

After the initial excitement of learning that he was likely to become a father (a pregnancy going full-term, with a live birth at the end of it, was not something anyone took for granted in the Old West, to the point that it was considered bad luck to assume it, you just prayed and hoped), John found himself in a moral dilemma. Should he go public about his relationship with Jensie, or hide it like the men of high self-esteem, but low character, who he had known get their slaves pregnant, out of either simple self-gratification or to expand their stock of free labor. But it was a dilemma that he could put off for a few months, while he cosseted Jensie in the boarding house, to give nature its best chance.

In the spring a healthy baby girl popped out, who they named Harriet, she became quite the tomboy, and was often called Harry when she was up to mischief, a name she refused to be addressed by when she was a little older.

Sadly, John was still away most of the time, so missed most of the magic moments of fatherhood. Harriet's first word, at eight months old, was of course 'Muma', and she was an early walker at just nine months. The next time that John came home they did their best to teach her 'Daddy', but it just came out as 'doodoo', a word she had already learned to describe a certain bodily function, much to John's embarrassment and feigned laughter.

This should have been a gloriously happy time for Jensie, but John had decided to keep their relationship a private affair. A mask of dispassion was worn whenever they were in each other's company, beyond the walls of the boarding house. The only exception to this was in the exclusive company of the closest of John's family. There was a deal with Frances that if John did not 'embarrass' his extended white family in public, she would accept Jensie and his daughter as part of hers, in private.

Later that year the Chisum family was further blessed, when Josephine also gave birth to a daughter, who she and James named Mary. She was the first child to be born at the Clear Creek ranch, leading to a huge party, in stark contrast to Jensie's very private and modest celebration of motherhood.

Jensie had begrudgingly accepted not being able to say who the father of her child was, but did get jealous whenever she saw James and Jo playing outdoors, with their new daughter. She resigned herself to keeping those feelings to herself and simply counting her blessings, instead of envying others, as her 'good book' told her to. She had a beautiful daughter, fathered by a man who she had no doubt loved them both, in his own peculiar way.

A year later, when Jensie got pregnant again, John was determined to be a better father. After their second daughter, Almeady, was born he spent most of his time in Gainesville. He was useless at changing her napkins, but tried to make Jensie's life as easy as possible, at any and every opportunity. He wasn't shy of running errands for her, and had learned to cook things other than meat.

The different domestic situations John's daughters experienced, in their formative months, had quite an impact on their future relationships with him. As they grew up, he never got to see either of them as often as he would have liked, but he was always much closer to Almeady, who would exchange letters with him at least once a year when she got older.

Claiborne's wish of becoming a grandfather may not have been fulfilled 'within the year', but he was delighted to become one, despite not being overly impressed by the source of John's progeny. Sadly, he did not get to know the inspirational individuals his grandchildren would become, including those not yet born. He died in October 1857, aged sixty, when Almeady was just six months old.

John had become very independent of his father, but he took the news of Claiborne's death hard, regretting that they had not had more time together since he moved west. John had taken him for granted, as being an indestructible constant in his life, the man to aspire to, impress and have the best advice on hand to set him right if he was going wrong, he never considered he would lose him, so relatively young.

What was particularly poignant was that Claiborne had left instructions that he should be buried with John's mother, his first wife, Lucinda, to be 'reunited in death'. Contrary to John's assumption, his burning grief at her loss had never been extinguished. This, unsurprisingly, was difficult for his second wife, Cynthia, to accept, and made the funeral a little awkward. Cynthia would go on to outlive Claiborne by twenty years, and be buried alone.

Claiborne's passing filled John with as much anger as it did grief. There were so many things he never got to tell his pa, mostly about how much he loved him. But life out on the Wild Frontier had to go on; he buried his grief at the family plot in Paris and went home to cuddle his daughters, but he would carry his anger with him for quite a while longer.

John stayed around Gainesville until Meady, as his new daughter had become known, was a walking talking eleven-month-old. Then decided that it was time to get back in the saddle, and devote more time to his other duties at Clear Creek.

Eugie paused, which gave Danny the opportunity to hit her with the stack of questions he had queuing up.

"What do you think the real reason was, for John to hide their relationship, he did not need to kowtow to family pride; he was bigger than that?" he stated, confident that he had got to know the man.

"You know, I've had lots of thoughts on that over the years, and I still don't really know. Perhaps it was simply family honor, or maybe John being a very private person, possibly a bit of both. I do have my own theory though, but no proof of it."

"Go on?"

"Well, they were dangerous times and the Chisums were a rich family, the fear of kidnap is a reasonable possibility."

"Wouldn't that be the same for Josephine or any other rich man's wife or children?"

"No outlaw in his right mind would dare kidnap a white woman. The whole town would be after you, and lynch you before the sheriff got his boots on. Taking a slave was about the same as taking a horse, you could still get hung for it, but no one, outside the owner, would be interested in chasing you."

"Didn't John being away for a year get folks suspicious?"

"He visited the ranch enough that they did not think he was dead, and later his pa being dead gave him the excuse that he was sorting out 'family affairs'. Not far from the truth if you think about it differently."

"One other question... your family has kept this a dark (he instantly regretted using that word) secret for over a century, why share it with a stranger now?"

"Oh, bless you Danny; you're no stranger... why today? To be honest I don't fully know... that movie did make me cross. A hundred years on, maybe it is time for the real story to be told, or maybe you are just special, Daniel Johnson," she patted his hand reassuringly.

"So, how did that California-bound migrant come into the picture?" Danny pursued impatiently.

"Oh yes, tired Mr. Baines, that was one life-changing afternoon, in May 1858."

CHAPTER 18

JOSEPH BAINES

Tom Towery arrived at the white house, accompanied by a very tired looking stranger, on an equally tired looking horse. He introduced the fellow as Joseph Baines, John invited them in, and they sat around his dinner table.

Tom started to explain the stranger's presence, "Mr. Baines is here from Arkansas, he has teamed up with William Bell's wagon train out from Paris bound for..."

Baines impatiently picked up the story, "Mr. Chisum, Sir, I bought a hundred head of cattle in Lamar County to take to California, when I got to Bonham I met up with this wagon train and realized I'd made a big mistake, cattle ain't for me. I was talking to Mr. Towery, and he brung me here."

John laughed, "You gave up, after a few days?"

"When you put it like that, it sounds pretty poor and foolish, I ain't proud of myself mister. Any roads, there is a fella who offered me a share of 'is gold mine, just need to manage it, suits me better."

At this point, John felt to some small degree, morally obliged to point out to Baines that he was stupid, and that he was almost certainly being conned. Baines might well have been buying real shares, in a real gold mine, but the rush had panned out in '55, there'd likely be no gold at the bottom of it. But he sensed that a deal was coming, so put his moral compass back in his pocket, and kept his mouth shut.

Tom took over, "I want to buy the cattle, and I want to make a go of it, like you have John, then Frances and me head to California."

"So, you have come here to borrow money?" John queried.

"Well no, not really," there was a pregnant pause, and then he continued nervously, "the only assets we have left to sell are Jensie and the girls."

John's fuse was lit, but he kept his cool, "Do I need to remind you that you can't sell Jensie, due to me half owning her?"

"Well that's the thing John, you don't. Your name never got on the papers."

John nearly let out an expletive, but Baines conveniently interrupted, "I don't want your slave, certainly don't want her children. I've agreed with Tom that he can have the herd for $1,000 or equivalent. They'd be equivalent, and I'll sell 'em on, I can get to California a lot quicker carting them, than I can with 100 beeves. I can see that you have your own story here, so I'm thinking, why don't I be fair to your arrangement, and just sell his share of the slaves to you, Mr. Chisum."

John bottled up his personal interest, to retain his negotiating position, and opened proceedings in a business-like fashion, "It may not be recorded, but I made a verbal agreement with Mrs. Towery and paid $500 for a half share in Jensie. So, Mr. Baines, the share that you have agreed to buy from Mr. Towery is worth another $500."

"But she has had two children since then, your..." John raised a hand to stop Tom in his tracks.

"Okay, $700 for Jensie and her daughters, and that's as far as my cash box will take me," he lied.

Baines pulled a list out of his pocket, "I hear you sell guns and supplies, and trade 'orses, mine is ready for the boneyard. If you can throw in these an' a better 'orse we may have a deal."

John continued to keep his cards close to his chest, and wandered outside on the premise of having a closer look at Baines' sorry looking gelding, but more for fresh air, and thinking time. He spotted Elijah coming out of the stables and called him over… "What do you think?"

"Worn out, not been treated well, worked too young, I could give him a new start."

"Okay, pick me something out to sell, something that looks the part but is grumpy in the morning."

"Oh, that would be Moody Alice."

John returned inside, "Yep, that horse is dog food."

He worked his way down Baines' list, pricing up the order. Just as he finished adding up, he heard a horse trot up, "Have a look outside Mr. Baines."

Baines was impressed to see a very solid looking mare, being calmly ridden bareback, with just a head collar. He returned to the negotiating table, "That'll do fine."

"Okay, $60 for my horse, $10 back for 'dog food' and $150 for the rest of your shopping list, $700 in cash, $900 in total, and my final offer.

Baines nodded his approval, as he was not paying for the shopping list, price did not matter; Tom Towery was seldom as smart as he liked to think he was, and had not kept up with that.

"Okay Thomas, what money you got on you?" Tom returned a confused look, then pulled $6.42 out of his pockets.

"Nope, that 'hidden' money belt you always carry."

The penny dropped, and he begrudgingly laid a further $80 on the table.

John slid the 42 cents back across the table, he never rejoiced in breaking a man, pocketed the $86 and headed to his study.

He returned a few minutes later with a note for Tom to sign confirming he had received a balance of $814 for full ownership of Jensie and two daughters. He passed $700 to Baines, along with his list signed as 'Paid in Full', "Your order will be waiting for you in my barn and icehouse, pick it up when you head west."

So, a three-way deal had been struck, which would indelibly and disrespectfully misrepresent John's relationship with Jensie, in Cooke County's slave records, for time immemorial, to be debated by historians and genealogists for centuries to come.

Baines headed outside, to saddle up his lovely new 'orse.

Chisum turned on Towery, "You bastard, I should kick your ass."

"I'm sorry, I was in a corner, Frances and me, we are running out of options."

"What about Philip?" Chisum enquired.

"Well, I own him, I've been investing in him for nigh on seven years, and he is coming of an age to be useful. He's mine."

Towery headed for the door, opened it, and turned to Chisum offering him a handshake; a hand was returned but not in the manner expected. It turned out that John could throw a harder punch than that one back in San Felipe, leaving Towery sprawling on the veranda.

"Explain the black eye to Frances, if you don't, I will."

Baines observed Tom's unorthodox departure, and resolved to never mess with John Chisum.

In the morning, John headed up to Gainesville to settle things, and found Frances at home.

She got in first, "I had nothing to do with it."

"I did not expect so, but what about Philip, what's going to happen to him?"

"John, I adore him like a son of my own, he is the sweetest child; no harm will come to him here."

"Your husband seems to be equally possessive of him," John replied, planting a seed of concern.

"John, you need to talk to Jensie and work this out, she is yours now, and you need to take her away. I won't be feeding her anymore. Just know I will never get in the way of her seeing her son... for as long as we're in Texas."

After some business in town, John retired to the boarding house. Jensie arrived 'home' early. John had seen her confidence grow over the years but had seldom heard her so direct.

"So, John Chisum, you own both halves of me now."

"Yes and no."

"What does that mean?"

John passed an official looking paper across the table, "You are free."

She evaded the enormity of the moment, "Free to do what?"

"Whatever you want to do."

"Be your wife?"

"You are, in all that matters."

John diverted to the subject on his mind, "Philip, the Towerys still own him."

"Are you going to buy him?" Jensie demanded.

"I probably could, but would that be the best thing for him?"

Despite having given much prior thought to the subject, Jensie paused before replying, concerned how John would react to her adamancy... "No, it wouldn't, the Towery home is his home."

"Not with his mama?"

"No, here is his home, Mrs. T has said I can visit whenever, you are not his father, his place is here. Our girls and me are coming with you."

The next day, paperwork was notarized by the County Clerk, Jensie, Harriet and Meady had become 'Chisums', and were heading south to the white house. Jensie Chisum was delighted with her new name, but not with how she came about it.

Later that month the Chisum household would celebrate yet another happy event, the birth of a feisty little lady, who Jo and James would name Sallie.

Danny picked up on the name, "Sallie, roses and wheat in her hair," a song from the John Wayne movie.

Eugie lost her thread for a moment, "Oh that bit really did make me cross, that fatherly chat with Wayne."

"Because Chisum wasn't her father?" Danny queried.

"No, because James would have been there with them, it was James who took Sallie to New Mexico. They killed him off in the movie and replaced him with Ben Johnson's 'Pepper'. I know it's Hollywood, but why would they do that? Anyways we have a whole war, and some, to get through before then. There is more to tell about Gainesville, there is a little park off Main Street by a creek, can you take us there?" she requested, pointing east.

CHAPTER 19

WAR COMETH

By early 1861, as William Wallace had predicted almost a decade before, war was on the horizon, and slavery was at the bottom of it. By February, six southern states had seceded from the union, but Governor Sam Houston was keen for Texas to remain loyal to the new President-elect, Abraham Lincoln. Houston was offered substantial armed support by Lincoln, to reinforce his point of view, but he turned it down. Houston was not going to point guns at fellow Texans.

Instead, the secession decision went to a democratic state-wide referendum; the result was 75% in favor of leaving the Union, and the subsequent allegiance with the Confederacy when war was declared on April 12.

In a statement a week later Houston predicted that it was a war that the South was unlikely to win. Wise, forward-thinking men like John Chisum agreed with him. It is worthy of note, that whilst Denton County voted narrowly in favor of secession, Cooke County voted against it.

At the Clear Creek ranch, nothing changed abruptly on April 12, with the general view being that the war was going on 'back east'. Everyone knew their job, got on with it and with each other; be they slave, freeman or white man. Chisum was a fair-minded boss, and his hands were loyal. The ranch was a hard-working rural idyll with little time for politics or bureaucrats, but from the day that Texas seceded from the Union there had been steadily growing concerns amongst his hands, as to their future.

An inverted juxtaposition had developed; whilst slaves were free of any commitment to the war, the same could not be said of the white ranch hands. As well as social pressure to 'do their bit', rumors of aggravated conscription into the Confederacy were rife. Whilst a few were keen to enlist, some of the younger hands were resentful that they could be plucked away from their chosen way of life, whilst their black counterparts had relative security in their tenure.

John's preference for neutrality on the war debacle was brought to a head when he received a visit from a Colonel Norris, from the Adjutant General's department. Norris needed to feed an army, and was prepared to pay top dollar for 750 head of cattle, $40 per head to be precise. There were two catches, they would need to be driven to Vicksburg, Mississippi, and part of the deal was an agreement that in the absence of a local military presence, John's men would take on responsibility for protecting the settlers within 100 miles of his ranch, an area the size of South Carolina.

As daunting as the task was, John was in no position to turn down $30,000, and the 'policing' duties would give some insurance that his men could avoid conscription, if they chose to.

"How do you plan to pay for the cattle, Colonel?" John enquired, guessing what the answer would be.

"In Greybacks," Norris replied, spreading twenty freshly printed Confederate $100 bills on the table. You can take this as a deposit.

John had already decided that Confederate banknotes, which were not backed by gold or assets, were likely be worthless if, or more likely, when the South lost the war, but he could pass some on to reduce his escalating bills. $2,000 would cover his payroll for a couple of months and trickle down into the local economy.

"Okay, I'll take your deposit and we will draw up a contract, but the balance will be paid in gold, on delivery," John insisted.

"That is highly irregular, Mr. Chisum."

"So is not feeding your army, Colonel Norris."

The deal was struck, and John pulled some pre-printed contracts from a drawer that just needed dates, destinations, quantities and values filling in.

As Norris got up to leave, John halted him with a parting request, "One more thing to sweeten the deal?"

Norris held up the contracts, to indicate that the deal was done.

"Nothing onerous," John assured, "would you happen to have a recent newspaper, it is hard to keep up on what's going on out here in the backwoods."

Norris smiled; in his brief encounter with Chisum he had ascertained that he was certainly no backwoodsman, "I'll send one in."

Word soon got around the ranch that some senior military gentleman had come a calling, and the hands feared for the worst. John wished he had his father, or Wallace around for guidance, but no, it was time for him to step up to the plate on his own.

Inspiration came from the Colonel's newspaper, where Sam Houston's warning words were in print. Houston could help concentrate the minds of his men.

Riders were sent out to send as many white hands back to the ranch as could be found. Chisum had never differentiated between black and white when he gave his Christmas speech, or any other special announcement. The fact that he would do so then got alarm bells ringing amongst the men. Some were convinced it was a call to arms, as a private army, as had happened on numerous plantations across the south.

Two days later the men were gathered in front of the ranch house. Chisum emerged in his Sunday best suit, looking like he was heading for Washington. You could have heard a pin drop in the Texan dust, as he climbed up on his favorite blue wagon.

"Men... it is always good to see you here and safe... I've heard there has been talk that I am forming an army... well, there is some truth in that."

There were muted whispers among the men, John raised his tone.

"BUT not an army that is going to war... A war that Sam Houston does not think we can win."

John pulled the newspaper from his pocket, put on his reading glasses, and shared Houston's words.

"Let me tell you what is coming. After the sacrifice of countless millions of treasure and hundreds of thousands of lives, you may win Southern independence if God be not against you, but I doubt it. I tell you that, while I believe with you in the doctrine of States' rights, the North is determined to preserve this Union. They are not a fiery, impulsive people as you are, for they live in colder climates. But when they begin to move in a given direction, they move with the steady momentum and perseverance of a mighty avalanche; and what I fear is, they will overwhelm the South."

John paused to let Houston's dire warning sink in.

"I've struck a deal. We are going to police this territory while the army is away. We are to protect the settlers as best we can. I know some of you are worried about conscription, but with your duties here I will do my best to protect you from that. I also know that some of you want to enlist, I will think no more or less of any man who wants to go or stay. Both will meet huge challenges over the coming months or years.

"I've signed a contract with the Confederates to drive a herd up through Arkansas on to Mississippi and then down to Vicksburg to feed their army. I'll need twelve men; those who want to enlist can have the first call on this drive, and be free to go and sign up at the end of it."

There was a short hubbub among the men, then their ranks parted to let Argent and Bungy step forward.

"You will be dearly missed," John quietly stated with sincerity, but he was not overly surprised that these two comrades-in-arms felt obliged to fight.

Three of the newer hands also stepped forward to volunteer. John expected it to be a tough drive, but he would lead it himself, partly to show solidarity with his men, but moreover to remind their customer how they agreed to pay. James would be left in charge of the ranch.

A few days later, John would have a more discreet meeting with his black hands in the hay barn. He explained all that he knew.

"We have tough times ahead, but it is likely the South will lose this war and you will get the freedom you deserve," he pronounced from the heart.

"I'm happy to draw papers today to set free any man who wants to take their chances out there. But I need to warn you, as freemen you may well face conscription, if this war gets dirtier."

Elijah, who had become the natural spokesperson for the slaves, stepped forward.

"We knows what is coming Mr. Chisum, we are not going to fight for those who want to keep us in chains," a phrase he used purely as a metaphor, no man had ever been put in chains on Chisum's ranch, except for a couple of horse thieves who Bungy had caught rustling.

Elijah continued, "You treat us fair and like free men; who else pays a black man, and what else would we do, we're not going anywhere until this war is over, and probably then some."

His words received a nod of approval from his fellows.

"It's back to work then," John exclaimed subduing a sigh of relief, while making a promise to himself and to God.

Danny interrupted with another burning question, "Just how many of Chisum's cowboys were black?"

"Hard to say, it varied, I reckon a half of his permanent 'employees' less when he hired on white travelers for roundups and cattle drives, similar all over Texas after the war."

"I never knew," Danny replied with genuine surprise.

Eugie reached out and squeezed his arm in a motherly fashion, "Hollywood again son... Hollywood. One day someone will make a proper movie of those times."

The drive east started within days, a week later as they approached Paris, John dropped out from the drive to check up on his other brothers, who he had been remiss in keeping in touch with since their father died.

He found Jefferson at home. Jeff had signed up in Colonel Maxey's Lamar Rifles as a 4th corporal, a bold commitment for a man suffering from epilepsy, but his condition soon got the better of him, resulting in him receiving a medical discharge, and being sent home. He took a pragmatic view on the matter, "At least being ill might have saved my life."

Pitser, the youngest sibling had also joined the infantry and headed east, no word had been heard from him for months, so he could have been anywhere.

After a visit to his parents' grave, to contemplate what Claiborne would have made of all the malarkey, John headed back to his herd.

Their trail through Arkansas turned out to be no harsher than their regular cattle drives. The war was still way east of them, apart from occasionally coming across units of infantry, in their smart new gray uniforms, marching to the railheads at Memphis, Vicksburg and Monroe. Some were singing 'Dixie', the

Confederates' adopted anthem, to raise their spirits on the long walk to war.

John recalled Houston's words and wondered what was ahead for these mostly young men, how many would survive, and for those who did, what state their mind and their bodies would be in when they returned? His thoughts drifted to Jimbo and how he had sounded almost excited when he had been asked to sit out this drive, and guard the ranch.

As John had half-expected, when he arrived in Vicksburg there was some memory loss over the terms of their contract. Pointing out to the receiving officer, who had railcars to fill with beeves to ship east, that there were alternative customers, jogged his memory. Gold soon arrived, and the herd was released into his custody. A gambit that would have probably got Chisum lynched and his herd confiscated later in the war.

One piece of business remained, paying off his men. The five who had decided to go to war had become six on the trail. John handed each man a drawstring pay purse with a reassuring chink. He shook the hand of each in turn, and wished them well in their uncertain future.

He mounted his horse and dispensed a parting offer, "Try to save that pay until this mess is over, and use it to come and find me, if I'm still alive there will be a job for you. If you come across my brother Pitser, tell him he is in my prayers, as you all will be." He saluted his men and turned for home.

When the men got around to checking their pay, they were pleased to discover a generous extra bonus in gold coins.

Footnote: With the benefit of hindsight, if Houston had taken up Lincoln's offer of armed support, it is highly likely that the war would have ended far sooner, or possibly never even started, with countless thousands of lives saved. Houston died before he could discover if his prediction was fulfilled. However, he did live long enough to read how uncivil the war would get. There were nearly 60,000 casualties in just three days at the Battle of Gettysburg, just a few weeks before his passing.

CHAPTER 20

JIMBO BROWN

At Clear Creek war still felt a long way away, but to protect his family and men, John adopted a policy whereby no one ever left the ranch, unless they had a reliable gunman at their side.

Whenever any of the Chisum family needed escorting into Gainesville, there was no shortage of volunteers to accompany them. There would always be a nice dinner, and a hotel room for the night included in the trip, thanks to the Butterfield Overland Mail stagecoach requiring 'civilized' accommodation for their passengers. Whilst some of the penciled-in pioneer settlements had failed, and been rubbed out on the County Clerks' maps, Gainesville was by then printed on them for perpetuity.

The uptake to mind the family was enthusiastic. John had to make a roster of his best men, to fairly determine who was next in line for the privilege of escort duties. But it troubled him that there was one hand, who never put his hand up. So, one day, when the next recipient on the roster wasn't available, he seized the opportunity, and told Jimbo to saddle up and head into town with him, in the hope of getting to know his eldest employee a little better.

On the way to town every angle he used to try to open Jimbo up failed dismally. He'd had deeper conversations with his horse. On their arrival John headed to the office of Samuel Gooding, the latest incumbent of the County Clerk chair, to go about his business. A short while later business was interrupted by a kerfuffle outside. The clerk's assistant rushed in, "Mr. Chisum, you need to come outside, your man has gone crazy."

John dashed out, and tried to make sense of what he saw. There were four young men bloodied and beaten, and Jimbo was being arrested.

"What happened," John demanded.

Jimbo shook his head, and was carted off to jail, John followed.

Deputy Sheriff James Davenport could only tell what he had been told. Jimbo had taken on a group of boys and beaten the hell out of them. Davenport knew what an uncommunicative soul Jimbo was, so agreed to let John into his cell to try to get to the bottom of it all.

John found Jimbo huddled up in a corner, like a scared child. He waited patiently, but after half an hour caved in to the need to break the stalemate. Playing on Jimbo's innate sense of responsibility, he stated, "You know I have things that I should be doing, but I'm staying here until you talk to me, and tell me what happened, however long it takes."

Jimbo looked up but did not respond.

John decided to go off on a tangent, to try to open up the can of worms before him.

"Why don't you like coming to town?"

The ploy worked, Jimbo sat up, paused and replied. "Don't like crowds... don't like the way strangers are scared of me... or look at me like I'm stupid, when I talk."

"Is that what them boys did today?"

"No... I'm sorry Mr. Chisum... they didn't, but I can't abide bullies."

"Who was being bullied?"

"They were beating up on a little fella, calling him a 'Yankee', I had to stop it and teach them a lesson. I can't abide bullies," he repeated.

John had two options. He could end it there, and charm the Sheriff into letting Jimbo go, or take advantage of the situation to find out more. He went for the latter.

"I hate bullies too, my friend."

Jimbo was like a blocked drain, John was sure that he just needed to dig away at the right spot to let all that was bottled up flow out, and was determined to find that spot.

"Have you been bullied?"

A while later, "...Not here ...but I was ...back in England, way back, but that's no one's business."

John had found the spot.

"You are right, it is no one's business, but I'd like to make it my business, tell me your story before I met you, then I'll take you home. I'll sit here all night; and all tomorrow if that's what it takes."

"If I tell, you promise to never tell a living soul, no one knows, but I'll tell if you promise."

"I promise, I'll never speak of it," John assured.

John had no idea how deep the drain was that he was about to unblock, but unblocking it would teach him to never make assumptions about a person again.

Jimbo was born in 1816, at Knightsbridge Barracks in London, and christened 'Edward James Thomas Brown', the son of a senior officer in the Royal Horse Guards, who had fought with distinction at the Battle of Waterloo. Edward's father died shortly after his fifth birthday, his mother could not cope, so handed him over to the Royal Military Asylum, a boarding school in Chelsea.

An 'asylum' gives an image of a Dickensian madhouse. In reality it was an enlightened charitable institution, which had been established to care for the orphans of the Napoleonic wars. It was a unique boarding school for its day, taking in both boys and girls. Boys were ranked as Cadets, given military training, and taught trades like shoe mending and carpentry, in case the army was not for them. Girls learned art, cookery and other wifely skills. Edward excelled at the military aspects of his schooling, but outside that felt far more at home in the company of the girls, sharing their domestic pursuits, which explained how he had learned to cook so well.

The Chelsea asylum was not without its problems though. Edward's lanky frame and sensitive demeanor made him a prime target for bullies. The bullying went unchecked because, 'it would make a man of him,' his life there outside classes, was a living hell.

The natural direction from the asylum was to join the army, a direction he took at the earliest opportunity. With his exceptional cadet record and his family history, he was offered a commission in his father's regiment.

He completed basic training with honors; and after a couple of years of exemplary service, had grown into himself, and risen up the ranks. His quiet, discreet demeanor made him a perfect candidate for bodyguard duties, for the lesser Royals.

A year, later after the previous incumbent had requested a transfer, he was assigned to protect the King's niece, the daughter of his late younger brother, Prince Edward. A troublesome little seventeen-year-old, titled Princess Alexandrina, known as Drina to her few friends.

Alexandrina was a complicated individual, who despite being only five feet tall, had taken great delight in intimidating Edward's predecessors. But Edward was different, she liked him, he wasn't much older than her, and less stuffy than those who had come before.

Girls always seem to have a thing about men who share their father's name, and when she discovered his love of art and poetry a firm friendship developed. They also shared a common bond of both losing their fathers at an early age. Prince Edward had passed when Drina was just nine months old.

Teddy Brown, as she called him, didn't say much, but when he did it made sense, she enjoyed and trusted his council above most others.

Her world changed dramatically in 1837, at about the time the Chisums were crossing the Red River into Texas. Her uncle died leaving no surviving legitimate heirs, or siblings to inherit his throne, so the crown went to Princess Alexandrina, who dropped her Russian forename, to become Queen Victoria, at just eighteen years of age.

In the lead-up to the coronation Edward became a constant supporting companion to Drina, he infused her with the confidence and courage she needed, to take on the huge responsibility of becoming Queen.

An unmarried monarch was virtually unprecedented, and after the lack of offspring, which created the heir debacle when her uncle died, Victoria was under pressure to find an acceptable suitor, and get on with the job of King making as soon as possible.

Her 'choice' for securing a strong European bloodline was somewhat incestual, her first cousin, Prince Albert of Saxe-Coburg and Gotha. Protocol dictated that the monarch had to make the proposal, so in October 1839 Victoria informed Albert that he was marrying her.

Prince Albert resented the friendship between Edward Brown and Victoria, a resentment which festered into a deep jealousy over the first couple of years of their marriage. Despite Victoria's endless protestations, Albert arranged for him to be reassigned away from Royal duties.

They were both devastated, but there was no way she could intervene further, without revealing the true depth of their friendship. After Drina, Edward couldn't care less about romance with any other woman. No one could live up to his Queen, in his affections.

There was a new diplomat in town, by the name of Dr. Ashbel Smith, who Sam Houston had sent over from Texas as an ambassador for the republic, with the grand title of 'Minister Plenipotentiary from the Republic of Texas to the United Kingdom of Great Britain and Ireland and France'. His brief was to establish trade arrangements between the republic and Europe, and consolidate Texas' overseas political relationships.

It was a big title, but with a small office, rooms above a grocery store in St. James Street, and a similar apartment in Paris, France. However, protocol dictated that he be supplied with a bodyguard, and Edward got the job.

Smith turned out to be a fascinating, and extremely well-educated fellow. Also a good story teller, his tales of the Texan Wild Frontier had Edward spellbound, a whole different world to the gray streets of London.

Ashbel arranged for Edward to be his permanent bodyguard. They would spend most of their time in London, and a few months each winter enjoying the warmer French climate. Edward soon picked up the language, but he would never let on to Charlie Argent. He also got to travel to Rome when Ashbel was granted an audience with Pope Gregory XVI, a memorable and humbling day for both of them.

When Texas gained statehood Dr. Smith was rapidly recalled by Houston, and Edward was assigned to escort him home on a ship to

Galveston. On their arrival the good doctor was handed over to a detachment of dragoons, to escort him to Austin.

Smith gave Edward a leather hold all, containing £160 English pounds, to take back to London, with instructions to pay the rent owed on the St. James Street office, which he had neglected to settle in his rush to get home.

During his night ashore Edward reflected on his life in England, how he hated ships and seasickness, and what opportunities he might pursue in the new world if he exchanged the £160 for dollars with anyone in Galveston heading for England.

So, he became a thief, dropped his first name to become Mr. James Brown, and went absent without leave – a Court Martial offence. But in reality, no one would have ever known, his ship sunk on the return journey, with all souls lost.

Jimbo's story was interrupted by the sunrise shafting through the jail's window and James Davenport unlocking the cell to let them out.

John had one burning, but rather coarse question, which he could not resist asking, "Drina and you, did you? ... you know what I mean, did you?"

Jimbo shook his head. John would never know if that meant that he hadn't, or if he was too discrete to tell. He immediately regretted asking such an indelicate question and the subject of Drina was never brought up again. But from that day, whenever someone in John and Jimbo's company got a bit highfalutin, boasting about where they had been, or who they had met, the two would simply exchange a private knowing smile.

Danny saw a flaw in Eugie's story, "If Chisum took Jimbo's story to his grave; how do you know about it?"

"Because writing isn't speaking," she answered cryptically.

"Anyway, back to the uncivil war," she pointed at a lonely looking pink granite stone amongst the park's pecan trees, "let's go take a read."

CHAPTER 21

THE TURNING POINT

They wandered over to the pink monument and Danny read out the inscription.

"Facing the threat of invasion from the north and fearing a Unionist uprising in their midst, the people of North Texas lived in constant dread during the Civil War. Word of a "Peace Party" of Union sympathizers, sworn to destroy their government, kill their leaders, and bring in Federal troops caused great alarm in Cooke and neighboring counties. Spies joined the "Peace Party" discovered its members and details of their plans. Under the leadership of Colonels James Bourland, Daniel Montague and others, citizens loyal to the Confederacy determined to destroy the order; and on the morning of October 1, 1862, there were widespread arrests "by authority of the people of Cook County." Fear of rescue by "Peace Party" members brought troops and militia to Gainesville, where the prisoners were assembled, and hastened action by the citizens committee. At a meeting of Cooke County citizens, with Colonel W.C. Young presiding, it was unanimously resolved to establish a Citizens Court and to have the Chairman choose a committee to select a jury. 68 men were brought speedily before the court. 39 of them were found guilty of conspiracy and insurrection, sentenced and immediately hanged. Three other prisoners who were members of military units were allowed trial by Court Martial at their request and were subsequently hanged by its order. Two others broke from their guard and were shot and killed. The Texas Legislature appropriated $4,500 for rations, forage used by State troops here during the unrest."

"Wow... I'm shocked," was all Danny could come up with. He had lived around North Texas virtually all his life, but had never heard of these events.

"They were hung from an elm tree right here, some are buried under our feet in shallow graves, and then some got dug up by critters or washed away by rain down the creek. Yes, shocking it is, the truth is even more shocking. 'Citizens Court' my ass, kangaroo court more like it, whoever paid for that monument was wearing gray blinkers."

John had gone away on business, and as was their routine when he was away, Jensie and the girls spent their evenings in the other half of the white house, with James and Josephine.

Late one evening Jensie heard a horse snort outside, she peered out of the door to investigate and was pleased to see John's mare, Jennie, in the moonlight, but was concerned that his beloved horse was not tied, and was still saddled.

She dashed back to their half of the house. Fear turned to relief when she saw John's silhouette illuminated by a candle, he was reading, but to her alarm was sobbing. She approached him cautiously; she had not seen John cry since the death of his father.

"What's happened?"

John was startled from his deep thoughts, and composed himself, after what seemed an age, he spoke... "It's too ghastly to tell... man is an evil beast."

Jensie knew when to change tracks and queried, "What are you reading?"

John held up their bible.

"Do you want to read some to me?" Jensie suggested.

John paused, and then shouted, "What it says is wrong."

She lit an oil lamp to see him clearer, and gently took the bible from his hand, saving the page, and quietly read.

"For now we see through a glass, darkly; but then face to face: now I know in part; but then shall I know even as also I am known. And now abideth faith, hope, charity, these three; but the greatest of these is charity."

"We've read Corinthians before John, they are my favorite verses, why are they now so wrong?"

"It's not charity that is the greatest, the greatest is not even written," he turned to Jensie and looked deep into her eyes, "the greatest is LOVE, and I fear there is none left in this ruined world."

Jensie leaned forward and gently kissed him on the forehead and whispered, "Trust me, there is my love."

John stood up and angrily paced the floor, tripped on Jensie's Indian rug and cussed. A gun dropped from his belt and rattled across the floor into a dark corner of the room.

"What the hell?" Jensie squealed, "I've not seen you carry a pistol since you built this place, you had your men for protection."

"I bought it in town, I thought I was going to need one today, it would not have saved me for long though. They have turned into a mob, first time I've ever seen Mac Macleod scared, thank God I didn't take Jimbo, he would have got himself killed."

"Who have John, why?" Jensie begged.

"The good citizens of Gainesville, because of the conscription, they want every man younger than me to enlist in the Confederacy, they would expect me to go to war too, if I did not have this," he stated sweeping his arm in the general direction of the ranch.

"Or if they thought that I no longer owned you, or the others."

"You own my heart... you own your men's loyalty," Jensie consoled.

John continued, "Two weeks ago; they put together what they called a 'Citizens Court' trying anyone who was against enlistment, for being Union sympathizers or spies, mostly men who just wanted peace and to be able to protect their homes and families. They started off by hanging Jacob Lock, Doc Chiles, his brother and four others last week, and then they shot two more who escaped."

"My God!" Jensie exclaimed.

"That was just the start of it. Yesterday they lynched fourteen more without trial, even Nathanial Clark. For Jesus' sake, his son is fighting for the damned Confederates."

He paused, took a deep breath. and then quietly revealed, "I watched them hang Rama Dye."

"Your friend... who built the schoolhouse?"

"Yes, a good man, one of the best, older than me, too old to go to war, five children and his new wife, Mary, to look after. They have tried Mary's father, Arphax, as well, he's to hang on Monday from the same elm tree.

"Rama recognized me, and stared at me as they strung him up, I've never seen such a look of betrayal in a man's eyes, but there was nothing I could do... nothing."

John rubbed his eyes to stem the tears; Jensie did the only thing she could, she held him tight.

"All God-fearing men on both sides. All reading from this same damned book. What God would allow this to happen, what God would stand back and watch this happen, like I had to?" he shouted.

"John, it's not your fault, you didn't start this war, and you have done your damnedest to keep out of it."

"Their blood is on my hands Jensie, do you know why I was in Gainesville?"

"You said 'to tie up some old business'."

"Yes, this old business," he replied, handing her an important looking letter.

Jensie read it out loud, "To confirm, John Simpson Chisum is commissioned as Regimental Quartermaster and Commissary... signed General William Hudson, October 17, 1862. What does it mean?"

"It means I don't need to fight; I get to protect my family and don't get hung for it. My needs are no different to any of those men who are dangling from that elm tree, but because I'm seen as 'rich' I can do what I like, I've sold my soul to the Confederacy."

"You always tried to protect your men from conscription, why shouldn't you do the same for yourself?"

"Yes, but not like this, I never thought it could come to this."

"So, what are you going to do?" Jensie asked with a tremble in her voice.

"I'm obliged to be the Confederate's servant, in a war they will not win."

"So, you are fighting with them, and for them?"

"No, I will sell them beeves until this madness is over."

"So, are you saying we just sit the war out here?"

"No, it's time to move on; there is land down west on the Colorado, away from this hell hole, no squatters, few Indians and next to no war."

"When do we leave?" Jensie queried.

"I leave in the spring," he paused... "but I'm not taking you with me, where I'm going is no place for the girls."

"You can't leave me here."

"I can't take you there; I'll find you a safe house back east away towards Paris but, God-willing, far enough away from this damned war."

"So, you are leaving us!"

"No, I will be back every chance I can, I just need to know you and the girls are safe, I'm away more often than not anyway, when the war is over we will work out what is best."

Jensie was heartbroken, but as ever tried not to show it. Whether she placed John's peace of mind above her own, or whether her slave instinct of 'acceptance of one's fate' was still buried just below the surface, even she could not tell. But she knew she had never seen John's faith in God and humanity so tested.

She also knew many of the folks that John had talked about, and would soon discover more, who he had not mentioned, who were hung from that 'Great Elm', or shot. They were mostly enlightened folk, who had shown her and the children kindness, if there were Yankee spies among them, they would have been few.

Jensie went outside to unsaddle, feed and water John's horse. There was a chill in the air, but the stars were bright and beautiful. She followed the line of Ursa Major, the 'Fry Pan' as she called it, to Polaris, the North Pole star, which had always been her guiding light. It was hard to comprehend the evil that was being committed, less than twenty miles from where she stood, that was sharing the glow of her star. She stared at it and quietly asked, "Why?"

Lost in her thoughts she did not see him approaching from behind, but knew the reassuring feel of John's arm around her. She turned and looked up into his eyes, and something inside so strong, could not be kept inside any longer.

"Marry me John, please just marry me."

He hesitated and stepped back, his reticence telegraphed his answer, and tears welled up in Jensie's eyes. Angrily she spurted, "If I was white, you'd marry me."

John shook his head, and quietly replied, "You still don't know me."

"Maybe I don't, but I trust you more than any person on this Earth, even more than our children, why won't you make me proper yours?"

John's tone sharpened, "For exactly that reason, when I told the slaves they were free to go I swore before God that I would never own a person again. Marriage is just owning, I could not love you any more than I do, I'll never love another a slice of what I do you, and I will never marry."

Jensie took that as the final word on the subject, and turned back to her chores, John followed to help. It reminded her how well they always worked together, nothing needed saying, and they were always at one with each other, more so than any married couple she had known. Horse settled, they walked back to the house, John stopped and pulled her towards him in a fond embrace and whispered, "You are not my woman... but wherever I am, I will always be your man," hanging on to that thought she led her man into the house to see how she could further ease his pain.

Eugie paused from her story; Danny looked across to her and noticed tears rolling down her wrinkled cheeks, "Are you okay?" he asked gently, "do you want to take a photo?" he asked foolishly.

"No, not here, I'm fine, let's go to a happier place... to Bonham."

"To Bonham," Danny replied, fired up his big block V8, and gunned it on to Route 82, heading east.

Footnote: The events of those two weeks were one of the darkest episodes of the Confederate cause. Political sensitivity being so strong, the true story of the atrocity that would become known among historians as 'The Great Gainesville Hanging' would not be spoken of outside scholarly circles for another four decades. A more definitive monument would be erected in Gainesville's Pecan Park early in the 21st century.

CHAPTER 22

MOVING ON

An hour later the Dodge was parked outside yet another courthouse, Fannin County's, although this one was nowhere near as impressive as Gainesville's.

"No clock tower," Danny noted, exercising his newfound interest in architecture.

"It used to have a beautiful wooden one, but the tower and roof burned down when you were little. Then a few years ago they clad it in stone to make it look modern, they call it 'Art Deco'," Eugie explained with similar authority on the subject.

"So, this is kind of where it all begun," Eugie sighed, and noted Danny's puzzled look.

"John's Aunt Polly lived here for a while, would have been late 1840s. She owned Jensie then, Frances inherited her when Polly died. Before John became the important County Clerk, he would come over to Bonham on errands for his pa and stay over. He never noticed Jensie, just as well really, she was only about 14 at the time, but she sure noticed him, he owned her heart from then on. You'd call it a 'schoolgirl crush' these days, but it was much deeper than that."

Danny struggled with Eugie's simple acceptance of the ownership of her ancestors, like they were pieces of furniture to be passed on in a 'last will and testament', but did not want to distract her from her story with a moral debate.

"So, can you work out where Jensie lived when she left Clear Creek?" he prompted.

"Old Bonham was a little east of here, but that's all gone now, all this sprung up when the Texas and Pacific railroad came to town ten years later. But after her girls had left home she lived there for a while," she pointed at a Victorian apartment above a café, "so here is as good a place as any to tell the story of it."

"Do you want me to see if we can go have a look around?" Danny offered.

Eugie gave it some thought... "No, don't disturb anyone. I'd like to remember it as it was. Anyways that's much later in the story.

"So, after Christmas 1862, JC moved Jensie and the girls hereabouts, it was a garrison town, headquartering General McCulloch's cavalry regiment, but was well away from the war, so the safe place for the girls that John had promised. Grandma liked to keep busy and loved to sew, it turned out that there would be plenty of soldiers needing sewing."

Come spring, John started moving his share of the cattle and horses about 200 miles southwest to land at the junction of the Concho and Colorado Rivers. (Not to be confused with the 'Mighty Colorado' that flows through the Western states down to Mexico.)

James and Josephine stayed at Clear Creek, along with their then three children. James took over John's local policing role, and was given a military rank. His duties at home would keep him well away from the battlefields, just as they had for John. They had lost a lot of pasture the previous hot summer, but there was still enough grazing left for James' portion of the herd.

Tom Towery was conscripted, so in his absence James ran the Towery's tiny herd with his own. A while later Frances moved down to Clear Creek, to escape the dire town that Gainesville had become after the hangings.

John had raised enough capital, from the army contracts, to buy out Stephen Fowler, his ever-silent business partner in New Orleans, and be totally independent. He built his new ranch on similar lines to Clear Creek; a fortress, but with better water and grazing. The summer would mostly be devoted to moving the remainder of the herd west to fatten up on his fresh new grass.

One afternoon, that November, Mac was on guard duty and spotted a stranger approaching the ranch, on hearing the other security codeword, 'STRANGER', Jimbo appeared with his carbine and spyglass.

He stared through the telescope for a few seconds, and then exclaimed "My God," passed it and his gun to Mac, jumped off the scaffold and ran through the gates towards the incomer. Mac was totally baffled, so, following the procedure for such confusing circumstances, called out for someone to, "Fetch Chisum."

John appeared, "What's up?"

Lost for more useful words, Mac could only come out with, "Jimbo can jump, and he can run."

John climbed the scaffold and took the spyglass, only to repeat, "Oh my God!"

The stranger pulled their horse to a halt, and awkwardly got off from the wrong side. Jimbo stepped forward to offer a fond embrace.

"Is that lady riding side-saddle?" Mac asked.

"Nope, and that ain't no lady." John corrected.

As Jimbo and the clearly lame stranger got closer, Mac joined the chorus, "My God."

As each took in the sight of an old and dear friend, whittled down to a peg leg, John took the lead, "Charles Argent, you are a sight for sore eyes, what the hell happened?"

Charlie avoided the obvious answer, and simply replied, "Gettysburg."

John took a deep sigh, "I told you to find me, but, how did you?"

"Jensie," Charlie replied handing him a letter, "but there is much more to tell, for a beer, and a chance to get the weight off."

"Jesus, of course, you come inside." Jimbo and Mac followed, they were not going to miss out on this conversation.

John put the letter in a drawer; he had more life and death questions to ask, before he should be looking at matters of the heart, "Bungy?"

"I'm sorry; I lost him on the first day of the battle, along with thousands of others."

"Damn, damn, damn!" John replied, thumping his desk, accompanied by shaking heads from all in attendance, "but thank God you found us... you said Jensie sent you?"

"Oh yes, Miss Chisum is my salvation."

"Last I saw her she was sewing uniforms at the Bonham fort?" John queried for clarification.

"A bit more than that now," Charlie qualified, while unbuttoning his shirt.

He revealed a nine-inch scar neatly healing, "She's a nurse now, at the army hospital, next to headquarters, she sewed me back together, and many others," John and the hands winced, thinking of the pain that his wound must have inflicted.

Charlie continued, "Miss Chisum is the most beloved woman in Bonham, black or white."

"That is good to hear, never was there a more caring soul," John acknowledged, hiding the depth of his true feelings.

"It is much more than that, she has opened up her house to those of us who needed a quiet place to stay and recover. Her beautiful children are a wonder; watching them run around and play gave me back a belief in life, a belief that this country has a future. She saved my soul, but in truth John, you saved my life."

He pulled a battered and holed leather drawstring purse from the breast pocket of his tunic and threw it across the table, it no longer chinked. John opened it, and pulled out a solitary gold dollar coin, it was dented, clearly hit by a bullet.

Charlie tapped his breast pocket and John noticed an equally neatly stitched up hole, presumably also Jensie's handicraft, "You said to hang on to them coins to bring me home, I did, and they did."

"Any more news? My brother?"

"We kept our ears out for Chisums but never heard anything about Pitser. But James is doing fine; he is supplying Bonham with beeves, I met him at Jensie's house.

"Oh... and, Sam Houston has died."

"Yes, we heard, end of an era for sure, so what you going to do now?"

"I've been discharged, I'd be glad to get out of this uniform and get back to what I know best, if you have a job for a one-legged man?"

"He can have my job back," Jimbo interrupted.

Jimbo Brown had been foreman since they moved west; a job that had brought him out of his shell quite a bit, though a man like Jimbo did not have to say too many words to get the job done.

"I think we have room for two foremen on this range, you are hired back on, but I'm afraid the pay has not improved."

"I'd work for you for food Mr. Chisum; you will always see me right."

Danny impatiently interrupted the story, "The letter, what was in the letter?"

"Oh yes, the letter," Eugie reached into her bag and pulled out a 107-year-old envelope, and gently extracted its contents.

Danny took it off her with equal reverence, and opened it to reveal the most beautiful handwriting, and read.

"Dearest John,

"I hope this letter finds you in good health, as am I and the girls.

"If you are reading this Charles will have found you, his wounds are healing well, but his mind has a way to go, be kind to him as I know you will. The girls love him, and I have named him their Godfather, I know you won't mind as he remains a good, just troubled man. I hope you can help with the other half of his recuperation.

"James and Jefferson are also well, but no news of Pitser. Josephine and their children stay with me at times. Sallie and Mary are so bonny, they play with our girls like sisters, it is so sweet, it is such a shame your father is not alive to see it, he would be proud.

"I'm a nurse now, they call me Miss Chisum, who would have thought it of a house slave, I wear a smart uniform, though had to make it myself.

"Life is busy, but I miss you so much John, at night I leave a pillow next to me for you and imagine I is looking into your gentle eyes, and you are making me laugh.

"I don't laugh much these days, except with the children. I've seen things that no woman should ever see, and heard horrors that I will never tell. If the politicians had to be locked in a barn with swords and guns there would be no wars, amen.

"Please come see me when you can.

"Your ever loving, not-wife.

"Miss Jensie Chisum."

Danny handed the letter back to Eugie, "Oh, what a love to have, why didn't the damned fool just marry her?"

"We will never truly know what was in his mind," Eugie answered, honestly.

"Did John visit her much?"

"Every year or so when he left Clear Creek; it was a difficult and dangerous journey. Even less when he first moved to New Mexico, but more often once the railroad came along, and he always brought roses, yellow ones when he could get them."

"She must have got real lonely at times."

"At times, but not always," Eugie answered reservedly.

CHAPTER 23

CHARLES ARGENT

Danny sensed there was a story that needed dragging out, "Come on, tell me more."

"Did you know that before the Civil War, there were no lady nurses?" Eugie challenged.

"I didn't," Danny replied with surprise.

"By the time Jensie got to Bonham the hospital would take any help they could get, even from us blacks. She started by mopping floors, changing bedding, and feeding those who could not feed themselves. She would bring a little cheer to the soldiers and write letters for them. Either because they did not know how to, or had lost the limbs to do so."

Jensie made a big impression on the doctors and surgeons, her warm smile and humanity bringing a little light into a very dark place. She earned their trust and was given more responsibility; dispensing medicines, be they few, changing dressings and even assessing the wounded as they arrived, when the doctors had no time to, one of whom would be Charles Argent.

He had a crushed leg and a horrible saber wound across his stomach, loosely held together by field dressings, and stinking of infection. Jensie could prioritize his treatment without bias, he was near death. Charlie recognized her and grabbed her hand, "Don't let me die," he cried, "please stay with me."

She held his hand as he was stretchered in for surgery. The surgeon threw a bucket of water across the table to wash away the blood, after his previous failed attempt to save a life. A sawbones dispensed with Charlie's leg, while the senior surgeon cut away the infection around his saber wound.

He called to Jensie and pointed at the wound, "Hold here, while I stitch him up."

Jensie tried as instructed, but struggled to hold the gash together. She looked at the surgeon, his hands were shaking. He inserted the needle but ripped the ragged skin, "I can't do this!" He exclaimed.

Jensie reached out to show him her steady hands, then held his, "I've stitched everything from a wedding dress to a saddle, you hold, I'll sew, trust me."

They swapped places, and Miss Chisum was never asked to mop a floor again.

Charlie's wounds slowly healed, but his mind was in a bad place. With a desperate shortage of beds in the hospital, and the risk of re-infection rife, Jensie offered a room at her house for him to recuperate in.

For the first two weeks he would rarely get out of bed, other than for sanitary essentials, and occasionally got caught out on those. Jensie began to question whether she had done the right thing, inviting this broken man into her home, but she had chosen to, so would have to deal with it. However, her kindness alone was not working; a different approach was needed.

Day 1: "Charles, you stink, take a bath."

"I suppose I do."

Day 2: "You don't smell any better, and my girls are looking for a dead skunk."

"Maybe there's one in the woodshed."

Day 3: "Have a bath or get out of my house."

No reply.

Day 4: No conversation, Jensie threw a bucket of warm soapy water over him.

Day 5: No conversation, Jensie threw a bucket of cold non-soapy water over him and he got no dinner.

Day 6: Jensie picked up a bucket of water of unknown temperature or consistency ready to throw over him.

"Stop! In God's name stop," he screamed.

"Take a bath!"

Charles took a bath, Jensie scrubbed his back, took and burned his bed linen and night clothes, and brought fresh ones; avoiding telling him that she acquired them from a dead man.

Day 7: Charles heard children laughing and playing through the window, and smiled for the first time.

Day 8: Charles heard the children again, had another bath, put on his cleaned and repaired uniform, and hobbled downstairs on his crutch.

Jensie greeted him in the garden, "Mr. Argent, it is a delight to see you, and you smell so lovely."

"Okay you win... out of interest, what was your next move?"

"Well, I was considering getting my girls to tell you that 'you stink worse than the outhouse' and throw iced water over you... would that have been cruel?"

"Yes... no... I'm sorry... thank you... it's good to be outside."

She took him back to the hospital to be fitted with a wooden leg. In truth there was not much fitting involved; there was a pile of them in the yard in every size, all second hand, mostly hardly used, no whittling required.

Charles felt emasculated among complete men, but found comfort in playing with the children, who never judged him. He was the same man they knew from when they were little, he just had a different leg.

Jensie came home one afternoon a week later, after a particularly tough day, and spied the three of them sitting under her apple tree, he was teaching them to sing 'Frère Jacques'. The girls sung in sweet harmony.

"*Frère Jacques, Frère Jacques,*
Dormez-vous? Dormez-vous?
Sonnez les matines! Sonnez les matines!
Ding, dang, dong. Ding, dang, dong"

She hid and listened, with tears of joy rolling down her cheeks.

She encouraged him to take walks with her, to get used to his new leg, and to not be afraid to be seen. When he tired she held his arm, which was a great comfort to him, in more ways than he let on.

Jensie got to hear that neighbors were gossiping about the new man in her house. Which was a concern and irritation to her; she valued her reputation above everything, apart from her children.

That was when the thought struck her – if she could help Charlie, she could help others. If neighbors were gossiping about one man in the house, she would invite more. Several took up the offer to spend their days at Miss Chisum's. To enjoy the quiet, read her books, to talk if it helped, or simply get away from the smell of death that hung over the hospital.

At first Charlie was quietly jealous of Jensie's attention being shared, but soon found that it gave him a new purpose. He knew exactly what these young men were going through, and could help them through it.

Jensie rejoiced in watching men, who had given up on life, cheating at cards for matchsticks, and joking at each other's expense.

Charlie was a worry to her though, she would hear him cry at night, and sometimes he would wake up screaming from a bad dream.   His body was getting stronger, but she was deeply concerned about his mind.

He was keen to get back in the saddle and could borrow horses from headquarters. Jensie had never ridden before, so Charlie offered to give her lessons. She was unsure whether to accept, as John had always promised to teach her, but things always got in the way, and he never got around to it. She was a quick study, and they were soon riding out for miles together.

The inevitable question cropped up on one of their rides, "Jensie, why is there no man in your life?"

Jensie hesitated, and despite having a well-rehearsed answer, felt her heart beat faster, "My girls are my life. I have no room for a man in it."

"But you are a beautiful woman; so many men would want to look after you and your girls," he hesitated, and continued quietly, "I'd like to look after you... I love you Jensie."

Jensie had sensed Charlie's feelings developing and if she was honest enjoyed knowing he had them, but was dreading this moment, "You can't love me Charlie, I can't love you."

"Why? Because I'm not a whole man?"

"No, not that, never that, don't ever think something like that."

"So, because I'm white?"

"No, never that either, why would you think such things of me... I can't love you because I love another."

Charlie knew he should leave the subject before he made a fool of himself, but could not help himself, "Who?"

"I can't tell you."

"The father of your children?"

"You know?"

"They've obviously got a father."

"Yes, their father?"

"Tom Towery?"

"No, no never, not my girls!"

Charlie paused, "John Chisum?"

Jensie's silence spoke volumes.

"My God, it's Chisum!"

"Swear you will never tell a soul, if you care for me one dot, swear!"

"I won't tell, I promise. Everyone has always wondered who their pa was, Chisum's name came up, but everyone thought no, he could have any woman he wanted, we even wondered if he didn't care for women."

"Oh, thank you very much Mr. Argent, so I'm not good enough for him, because I'm black?" she barked angrily.

"No, I didn't mean it like that, never that," he stated, emulating her words.

"Touché," Jensie replied, showing off some French that he had taught her.

"Charlie, I do care about you a lot, my children love you, but to me you are like a brother... a brother I love dearly."

"We ought to head back," he suggested, in an attempt to retain his pride, by taking the lead.

"Do you promise never to tell, promise? Only close family know," Jensie demanded.

"I swear," he crossed his heart with his finger, "if I had to lose you to anyone, there could not be a better man on this Earth, he saved my life, I need to buy myself a horse, and go find him."

A few days later he spent the last of his intact gold coins on a gelding and supplies, and stole a map from the quartermaster's stores.

The girls came to see him off with big hugs.

"Muma says you are our Godfather now," Meady revealed with her sweet little girl voice.

He looked at Jensie, "Really?"

Jensie nodded, stepped forward and handed him a sealed letter, "Would you mind giving this to him?"

Charlie returned the nod, as he turned to leave, she stopped him, to give the warmest of hugs, followed by a very un-sisterly long kiss goodbye, to a man she would never see again.

Danny let out a deep breath, "Did she make the right decision?"

"Who knows? I only hope she decided what was right for her, and made it for the right reasons."

"Do you want to head on to Paris to see Chisum's grave, it is less than an hour down Route 82?" Danny offered.

Eugie pondered on the thought, "No, let's save that for another day and try to keep this story in order. Anyway, it's getting late, McKinley will be fretting, and we haven't eaten since breakfast. Take me home and I'll cook you both some supper, and we can talk some more, I promise I'll get us to New Mexico before the day is out."

CHAPTER 24

HEROES RETURN

As they walked into the homestead, McKinley briefly looked up from his newspaper to welcome them. A childhood memory wafted to Danny's nose from the kitchen, 'Venison and Beans'. Venison might seem a bit up-market to some, but during the Great Depression it was a staple to anyone in Texas, and beyond, who could hunt and butcher, like McKinley and Danny's father could.

Eugie kissed McKinley on the forehead, "Thank you sweetheart that smells delicious."

Dinner was served, and Danny was encouraged to 'tuck in', which he did enthusiastically. He had become sick of the monotony of V-n-B as a child, and had not eaten it for decades, but it was truly 'delicious' cowboy comfort food.

"You sure haven't lost your appetite, Son," McKinley smiled.

Eugie joined them and slipped an intrinsically worthless, but historically fascinating, and highly collectable banknote in front of Danny. He had never seen a Confederate $10 bill before. She picked up the story.

"Come May 1865, news arrived at the ranch that the war was over. There was some party that night. John ceremoniously burned the worthless Greybacks he had left. Just $100, he'd wisely been passing them on, as fast as he got them, but found that one in a drawer some time later, and kept it for posterity."

For the second time that day Danny picked up a piece of paper that had been handled by the man himself, and was strangely awestruck.

Eugie continued, "Folk started coming home from the war, and new settlers and squatters arrived in droves. The slaves were freed, but Chisum's simply read that as meaning they were free to keep their jobs and mostly stayed."

"Not all, I thought everyone was loyal to Mr. C?" Danny queried, always looking for the devil in the detail.

"Not all, emancipation had come at such a price, some felt obliged to explore it, but some didn't enjoy it that much, and came back."

Men would regularly arrive at the ranch looking for work. John was charitable but could only take on so many greenhorns; he needed men who knew their trade. Some who most certainly did would arrive a few weeks later.

Charlie Argent was on watch, when a herd of horses appeared from the north-east, he could make out five men driving them. As they got closer, he let out a deep sigh, and called out, "Get Chisum."

John appeared and was bewildered; he had never seen a one-legged Frenchman doing an Irish jig before.

"They're home," Charlie shouted.

"Who is?" John replied with hope in his heart.

"All of them Mr. Chisum... all of them that matters."

John grabbed the spyglass, looking from left to right, there was his brother Jeff with a stranger, someone on drag who he could not make out for dust, another stranger on point, then he looked to the other flank and felt tears welling up, "Pitser," he shouted.

"Look at the drag again, Mr. Chisum, you make the call," scared that his eyes had been deceiving him.

John looked again as the dust cleared, and the tears flowed, he turned to anyone in earshot and screamed, "BUNGY!"

A chorus of 'yee-haws' rung out from the ranch.

Out on the trail Charles Goodnight turned to Jeff and dryly queried, "Do you always get such a warm welcome?"

Jeff replied with appropriate modesty, "I think that is most likely for the Welshman on the drag."

"Popular hand," Goodnight retorted.

Mac opened a corral for the horses, and was surprised to see Chisum's old brand on them.

The riders dismounted. Charlie hugged Bungy, John hugged Pitser and Jimbo was up for hugging anyone. Christmas had surely come early.

John needed to get to the bottom of the story, "Bungy, we thought you were dead."

"News of my demise was greatly exaggerated, Mr. Chisum," Bungy replied.

Bungy was injured and unconscious after the first Gettysburg battle, the same battle that cost Charlie his leg. When he came to, he had been left for dead, and the battle had moved on. But there was a Union rifleman in a similar state who kept him pinned down for a day.

They eventually got to talking, and Bungy could tell that the fella was in a lot of pain, so they made a pact that they wouldn't kill each other, and would go their separate ways.

Bungy came out of his dugout first, but the rifleman did not surface. He found him in a sorry state with a badly broken leg. So, he splinted it up, patched up the gash, where the bone had been sticking out, with a field dressing, and hobbled with him back to Union lines. On their slow march Bungy found out that his burden was named David Stephens, and that his grandfather was from Tredegar, on the banks of the Sirhowy River in Wales, Just thirty miles from Bungy's ancestral home. War had never seemed more ridiculous to him than it did that day.

Out of sight of the Union camp they shook hands bid each other farewell. David gave Bungy the last of his field rations, limped into camp, and as promised never raised the alarm. A day later Bungy found the Confederates, but his unit had been wiped out, and the few who were still able, reassigned. So, he joined the one he'd found, where it turned out that Pitser was a Quartermaster Sergeant.

"Madness," Danny stated with conviction.

Eugie went over to her cabinet, picked out an old book, opened it at a poem by Rudyard Kipling, titled 'Recessional' and passed it to Danny, "He wrote this for Queen Victoria, read the first verse."

> "God of our fathers, known of old,
> Lord of our far-flung battle line,
> Beneath whose awful hand we hold
> Dominion over palm and pine—
> Lord God of Hosts, be with us yet,
> Lest we forget—lest we forget!"

"Lest we forget... amen." Eugie repeated.

As the likes of Houston and Chisum had predicted, after in excess of 600,000 fatalities and countless more men, like Charlie Argent, suffering life-changing injures. There was no true winner, apart from the slaves who won their freedom, which they would have won anyway without a war, and the men who sold guns.

Footnote: Reconstruction was officially defined as the twelve years after the war ended, but allegiances to the Confederacy remained alive in the hearts of many families in the southern states for far longer. For well over a century the Confederate flag would be flown with pride outside homes, offices and on statues, even made into bumper stickers, like the one on Danny's Dodge. But, by the end of the millennium, there was a growing wave of political correctness, aimed at relegating that era to the vaults of the library, and redefining the Rebel Flag as a shameful symbol of the past.

CHAPTER 25

GOODNIGHT-LOVING TRAIL

While friends and family were reunited, and caught up with each other's death-defying stories, the returning heroes' traveling companions waited patiently, until Pitser realized that introductions were in order, and overdue.

"John, you will remember Oliver Loving, and this is his business partner, Charles Goodnight. They've been with us since Clear Creek."

"Oliver, I didn't recognize you," a slight social gaff, considering that John's sister was married to Loving's cousin, but it had been a while since they'd met, "you cannot know how pleased I am to see you gentlemen, and who you have brought home to me. This is surely a day for the history books." Little did John know just how prophetic his words were.

Looking across at the horses, and guessing their ages, John's mind was racing, "Would those be the ones we lost to the Comanche raiders, three years ago?"

"They would indeed, or what's left of 'em," Loving replied, "they took some of mine this Spring as well, so we teamed up with your brother's men to go to Colorado and fetch 'em back, this is your half of the herd, according to James."

"Well, it sure is kind, and honest of you to bring them here."

"Honest is my nature, Mr. Chisum, and when I want to do business with a man it's always good to start from a position of trust?"

"What sort of business do you have in mind?"

"Cattle business – we've been offered a contract to supply beeves to Fort Sumner, New Mexico to feed the Indians. We don't have enough, and I hear you've been blazing a trail that way, we wondered if you wanted to pitch in with us?"

"A partnership?" John queried cautiously.

"A partnership," Goodnight confirmed, feeling a bit left out of the conversation, as was often the case, due to him being a generation younger than Loving.

"I'm not good on partnerships," Chisum stated, "and you've already got two in yours, but I'm sure we can do a deal... Fort Sumner you say, I hear there is good grazing to be had west of the Pecos."

"They say, 'West of the Pecos there is no law; west of El Paso, there is no God.'" Loving quoted.

"And not too many settlers either, my sort of place," John added, in more practical terms.

The trio would make their first drive early the following year, and Chisum would establish a new ranch at Bosque Grande, in Lincoln County, forty miles south of the fort.

Goodnight and Loving made two more drives to Fort Sumner, and on to Santa Fe. The last of which would sadly lead to Oliver Loving's demise. While on his way to the fort, ahead of the herd, with intentions of negotiating a price, he was seriously wounded in a Comanche ambush. He made it to the fort, but succumbed to gangrene, followed by a painful death.

Goodnight was heartbroken. All he could do was fulfill his friend's last request, and return his body to Weatherford, Texas. A pilgrimage which would become the stuff of legend in Western folklore.

The contract with the fort lasted for a couple of years, until the Navajo were repatriated to their homeland at the Four Corners region around Monument Valley. As depicted as being Texas in Wayne's 'The Searchers' movie. Chisum continued working with Charles Goodnight, to extend their trail north up into Colorado to feed miners, and on to Wyoming.

Back in Texas, John's stock was being rustled on an industrial scale. He had been shrewd in using his unique Jinglebob ear cut, to make his cattle impossible to rebrand, but that did not prevent calves being stolen, or beeves taken to unscrupulous butchers.

They were also suffering regular Comanche ambushes. They lost two more good men while crossing the Llano Estacado ('Staked Plains' in English), between West Texas and New Mexico. John resigned himself to moving his entire operation to Bosque Grande, which he finally achieved in the early 1870s.

Danny interrupted, trying to get everything square in his head. "What became of John's brothers?"

"James stayed in Texas a while longer, while Jeff and Pitser moved to New Mexico with John. Sadly, Jeff did not last too long there. Trouble had dogged that boy like a wolf after a rabbit all his life. He nearly got beat to death back in Paris during the war, over an argument about a hedge."

"A hedge?" Danny quizzed.

"Yep, a Wild West range war over a hedge between his and his neighbors garden. Now that is 'madness', with a civil war going on."

"But he recovered?"

"He did that time. When he was well enough to walk, he went into town with a shotgun, and killed the man who beat him. He was a hothead, but he was let off, as no one liked the fella he shot, and it was witnessed that he was provoked.

"After the first New Mexico drive Jeff headed up to Puerto de Luna to let off steam and got into some kind of fight. I'm not sure if he was beat to death, or if the epilepsy got the better of him, but either way he was dead, at just 37."

"So, the ranch south of Fort Sumner, that was the one in Lincoln County, in the movie?" Danny queried.

"No, it is confusing. He had two ranches in New Mexico, both were in what was Lincoln County back then, but the county was huge in those days, about five times the size of what it is now, so they split the county up, today they would both be in Chaves County. The John Wayne ranch was Chisum's last one, South Spring, which he acquired in the winter of '74. It was forty miles further south, near where Roswell is now, about fifty miles from the town of Lincoln, not the quick gallop in the movie.

"By then his spread ran from Eighteen Mile Bend, just below Fort Sumner, all the way down to near where Carlsbad is now. South Springs was far more central to manage his herds."

McKinley left them chatting in the kitchen and went to watch the TV.

"I've been thinking," Danny revealed.

"Oh, that sounds dangerous," Eugie replied, putting her hand on top of his, to reassure him that she was only joking.

"Would you like to follow his cattle trail to New Mexico?"

"Oh, that's a long drive, and there probably aren't any roads along lots of it."

"No, not drive, I'll fly you, in my crop duster."

"Oh my God, I've never flown," Eugie admitted.

"Never too late," Danny encouraged.

"Will there be anything left to see?"

"I don't know, has McKinley got a cattle digest?"

Eugie fetched the latest copy, of what was the almanac for finding anyone in the livestock business.

Danny thumbed through it, "South Springs Ranch, Roswell, New Mexico, owned by an R.O. Anderson, there is even a phone number."

"McKinley won't approve," she whispered.

"Does he have to?" Danny whispered back.

"Listen to us like a couple of naughty school kids," Eugie admonished; then thought out loud, "I guess he doesn't, we'll do it; next weekend?"

"Next weekend it is, it will take two days to get there, and one to get back, unless we bust a gut, so get you back here on Monday, if that's okay?"

Eugie looked up at her calendar, "So that would get us to the ranch on Sunday? Any chance we could go a day earlier, leave here on Friday?"

"Sure," he replied, not picking up on the significance of the date.

"One more thing, most everyone has heard of the 'Goodnight-Loving Trail', but why wasn't it Chisum's trail, if he blazed it first?" Danny queried.

"I guess that is the way of the Old West, those two fellows thought they were real important, big egos. Some did call it 'The Chisum Trail', but it probably got too confusing, due to that other fella."

CHAPTER 26

HEADING FOR BIG LAKE

The following Friday, Danny turned up at Eugie's for breakfast with a bundle of neatly folded maps and aviation charts under his arm, and an excited schoolboy glint in his eye. He unfolded them on her dinner table, then beckoned Eugie and McKinley to come and join him.

"Okay, I've been back to the library, the lady there was real helpful, I've seen a map of Chisum's trail into New Mexico, and marked my maps and charts to show the route, and ranch locations."

"That's very impressive Danny," Eugie congratulated, "so, what's the plan?"

McKinley interrupted, "Eugie, for God's sake, you're 84 years old woman, are you sure about this?"

Eugie slapped him down, "Mr. Thomas, age is but a number, I'm fitter than most sixty year olds! I'm doing this."

After 44 years of marriage, McKinley had become used to her occasional eccentricities, but few had been as way out as this one. However, he knew better than to stand in her way, so said no more.

Danny was sensitive to McKinley's concern, so continued to explain in some depth, for his benefit.

"My Stearman duster is at the Aero Valley Airport, just outside Roanoke, about twenty minutes' drive from here. To be honest, the toughest thing is getting into her, if Mrs. Thomas is up to that, she'll be fine."

Danny pointed out the airport on the map, and then traced his finger along the route he had plotted, "We'll leave early this afternoon; fly southwest keeping out of the Meacham Field, and Carswell Air Force bases' restricted airspace zones, and head on to the old Concho-Colorado ranch. After that we'll avoid San Angelo, then head west to Big Lake, in Reagan County for the night, it's next to what I think is one of Chisum's old watering holes.

"Tomorrow morning we'll follow his trail west to Horsehead Crossing on the Pecos, and then turn north towards Bosque Grande. We'll swing around over old Lincoln from the movie, then land at the Roswell Industrial Air Centre Airport. In all we'll cover a little over 600 miles, about six hours flying. What we will fly over in an hour would have taken the cattle drive ten days to cover.

"I've spoken to Mr. Anderson who owns South Springs. He says that if I radio ahead to the airport, they'll phone him, and he'll be waiting for us. He sounds like a real nice old-school cowboy."

"And how about coming home?" Eugie queried.

"We'll come straight back, due east, refueling at Lubbock, will make it about 200 miles shorter, we'll be home Sunday afternoon."

He passed a sheet of paper over to McKinley, "Here's a list of all the airfields, so you can phone and check up on us if you feel the need. But I'll make sure Eugie phones home both nights," he reassured with a slightly parental tone.

Danny folded up his maps, finished his breakfast, then gave Eugie a motherly hug, stating, "I'm off to the airport to swap the hopper in the Stearman for a jump seat, and I'll be back at noon, make sure you wrap up warm."

McKinley led Danny to the door, and slipped something in his hand, saying, "This will make your trip more comfortable. Look after my gal!"

Danny looked him square in the eye and stated, "I promise sir," as he walked down the steps he opened his hand to find a roll of ten-dollar bills, which would most certainly make their trip more comfortable.

Despite skipping lunch in favor of a settled stomach, Eugie did not find getting into the jump seat of the Stearman particularly easy, but she did not let on. They were soon airborne, flying southwest towards Eagle Mountain Lake. When they hit their first turbulence her stomach thanked her for her dietary choice.

Danny went into tour guide mode over the intercom in their headsets, explaining where they were every minute or so, more to reassure himself that Eugie was okay than anything else. As they approached cruising altitude over Parker County, Eugie interrupted, "Let me enjoy the view, give me a shout when we get close to the ranch."

He soon recognized the Brazos River snaking below them, but respected Eugie's request for 'radio silence'. He mused that the meandering sliver of water didn't look like such a state-dividing barrier, when cruising over a mile above it.

Eugie found the chill-air passing over her windscreen delightfully refreshing after the heat of a Texan summer; and now out of the turbulence her stomach began to settle. As they headed on towards the hill country, she was pleased to see how much of the state still looked untouched and green, despite decades of a booming oil industry. She wondered how long that balance with nature would last, if things continued like they had throughout her adult life.

They approached the logical location of the Concho-Colorado ranch at the conflux of the two rivers, Danny descended to let Eugie have a better view and take a snap. It turned out that there wasn't much more to see than they had in the last hundred miles, other than the little Concho River flowing into the larger Colorado, and on down towards the Gulf. After two low-level circuits Eugie's disappointed voice came over the two-way, "I've seen enough, let's move on."

As they turned west and crossed Route 83 just north of Paint Rock, what they could not spot from the air was a more relevant, but grammatically challenged, photo opportunity in the form of a plaque designated as State Marker 2808, which had been erected a few years before, stating:

CONFEDERATE BEEF CONTRACTOR.
JOHN S. CHISUM
(1824-1884)
ON THIS SITE DURING THE CIVIL WAR AND LATER, GRAZED BY
TENS OF THOUSANDS THE LONGHORNS OF CATTLE BARON JOHN
S. CHISUM. RANCH HEADQUARTERS WERE 10 MILES EAST. HERE
IN 1863-1865, CHISUM NOT ONLY RANCHED BUT ALSO WAS
BUYER OF CATTLE TO FEED CONFEDERATE ARMIES STATIONED
WEST OF THE MISSISSIPPI RIVER...'

Followed by yet another abridged version of the Chisum life story.

Danny turned south to avoid the restricted airspace around the Goodfellow Air Force Base at San Angelo, a facility very familiar to him, where he and nearly 20,000 others learned to fly in the Air Training Command. He had fond memories of earning his wings in a T-28 Trojan there in the 1950s.

They swung west again to fly low over the virtually unpopulated High Plains oil fields. This would enable them to approach Big Lake from the south for a grandstand view of the Lake. Eugie readdressed her thoughts about the untouched landscape as they flew over endless Pumpjacks, or 'Nodding Donkeys' as they were known locally, sucking up 'Black Gold' or 'Texas Tea', as it was described in the 'Ballad of Jed Clampett', the theme song to Eugie's favorite TV show 'The Beverly Hillbillies'. She felt a very close affinity to the gun-toting Granny Daisy May Moses, despite her white Confederate portrayal.

An hour later, Danny turned north and pressed the radio transmit switch on the top of the Stearman's control stick.

"Reagan County Unicom, Stearman one-eight-eight-two-oscar, ten miles south of Big Lake for landing. Request airport advisory, Reagan County."

A minute or so later, a friendly voice replied, "Stearman eight-two-oscar, no reported traffic at the moment. Wind southeast at about...10 knots. Altimeter three-zero-one-zero."

"Roger, thank you! We'll enter downwind for one-six." Danny replied and adjusted the altimeter with the advised barometric setting.

Danny was about to flip the intercom switch to tell Eugie he was going to set up to land, when the radio crackled to life again, "Hey, Stearman, are you wantin' to go to the movie, it starts in half an hour?"

"Movie? Understand you said movie? Please confirm?" Danny replied. He could see the airstrip appear off the nose of the Stearman. He moved the stick to swing about twenty degrees to port to line up with the downwind leg for landing on runway one-six, the one pointing closest into the wind.

"We have a fly-in theatre just off the field. They're showin' John Wayne's latest, it's really good."

Danny reached to his left and pulled the throttle aft a bit, to reduce power and begin the descent to the airport traffic pattern. As he peered around Eugie's head in the front cockpit, he tried to spot the movie screen near the airport. He had heard of the 'fly-in' theatres, where they reserved the back row of a drive-in's parking lot for rich oil and cattle folk, who would turn up in their light aircraft or helicopters to catch a film, but had never seen one.

He switched to intercom, "Do you want to go for it, I wouldn't mind seeing it again, for research purposes," he joked.

"One life, live it," Eugie replied emphatically, accompanied by a thumbs up as she cautiously raised her hand into the buffeting slipstream.

As they approached the airport, he spotted the movie screen and classic delta shape of the drive-in up ahead. He leveled the aircraft at 900 feet on the downwind leg beside the runway, "There's the drive-in to the right over there, and that'll be your grandpa's lake just before it, looks dry as a bone now, someone must have pulled the plug out."

Eugie's head turned and she looked down at the empty hole in the ground, just as it disappeared beneath their lower wing.

Danny's attention returned to his radio communication "Reagan County Unicom, that's a Roger on the movie. How does this work?"

"Do you need a hotel?"

"That's a Roger too," Danny confirmed, as he moved the stick to the right and rolled the Stearman on to the base leg for runway one-six.

"Okay, after you're off the runway, follow Ed in the Jeep, he'll lead you out of the south exit and spot you across the road. After the movie he'll take you to Big Lake's finest, and tug your aircraft back to the field."

"Roger, got it, thanks for the help." Danny answered, glancing back and forth between the airspeed indicator and the runway.

Danny rolled the Stearman right again until he was lined up for final approach. He reduced the power some more, and the plane descended in a smooth glide, until within a few feet of the runway he raised the nose just a bit and it settled gently onto its wheels, a textbook landing. He rolled the airplane out toward the south exit, and the awaiting Jeep.

They were soon parked in the back row of the theatre, "What do you think of the VIP treatment?" Danny queried over the intercom.

Eugie turned to look back at Danny and laughed, "Ha–ha, only in Texas Danny, only in Texas," as the big prop spun to a stop.

CHAPTER 27

A NIGHT AT THE MOVIES

anny helped Eugie out of her jump seat, for a much needed 'bathroom break'. She never let on that her desperate need was not just for the conventional use of the ladies' room. It was moreover to throw up down the toilet, due to airsickness, which was of some concern to the young ladies queuing outside the cubicle, who wondered if the occupant had been hitting the booze a little early.

She returned more composed, and joined Danny sitting on the Stearman's surprisingly comfortable lower wing.

There was quite a community atmosphere at the drive-in; youngsters were playing on a merry-go-round near the movie screen, while older kids were exploring a teenage rite of passage, sneaking out from car trunks, when they thought no one of authority was looking, to save a buck.

Danny's attention was drawn to a pretty brunette, roller-skating towards his aircraft, sporting a lovely smile. She plugged in, and handed over a crackly speaker, collected $5 off him, and then introduced herself in well-practiced prose, "Welcome to Shooting Stars Theatre. I'm Nita and I'll be your planehop for the evening, if there is anything you need just turn on your position lights, and I'll come a flying along."

Danny had never heard of a 'planehop' before, but was instantly smitten with this one, "I'm sure you hear this all the time, but you have the sweetest West Texan accent I have ever heard."

"Why thank you kind sir, but all us gals sound like this west of the Brazos," she replied modestly.

"I guess so," he responded, trying to come up with something meaningful to keep the conversation going.

Nita helped him out by enquiring, "Where are you heading, this don't look like no oil baron's plane?"

"West 'til we hit the Pecos River, at Horsehead Crossing, then north up to old Lincoln," Danny replied, in a matter-of-fact manner, not expecting that to be of much significance to the young green-eyed beauty.

"Oh right, the old Goodnight-Loving cattle trail," she replied in an equally matter-of-fact manner, catching Danny on the hop.

"Yep... or the Chisum trail," he politely corrected pointing at the movie screen, "you know your Texan history."

"I love history – cattle were king around here, before oil came along."

"So where does this passion come from?" he enquired flirtatiously.

"I'm studying to be a teacher, but got the bug from my grandmother, she was a member of the DRT, I know secrets about the Alamo that would make your toes curl. I'm fifth generation Texan, got an ancestor who fought in the Battle of San Jacinto," she announced proudly.

The DRT, (Daughters of the Republic of Texas), was formed in 1891 as a sisterhood dedicated to perpetuating the memory of Texas' pioneer families, and the soldiers of the Republic. To be a member 'Daughters' must have Texan roots dating back to before it became a state. They are best known for preserving the Alamo, but the DRT's library is considered, by many, to contain the most comprehensive history of the state, anywhere.

"Would you like me to take your order, I'm sure your date could do with a drink?" Nita continued with a playful wink.

"Sure, two hot dogs, a carton of popcorn and cokes, please."

"Sweet or salted?"

"Always sweet, Miss Nita."

Nita smiled, curtsied and skated off to the concession building.

Eugie giggled, "I think she won Danny, and shame on you for flirting with that girl, she's probably young enough to be your daughter!"

"I guess so; but apparently I'm no Jett Rink." Danny acknowledged, referring to a billionaire philanderer from another Texas based movie, 'Giant', filmed over a decade before.

"You may not have a giant fortune, but you sure have a giant heart, Daniel Johnson," she stated, giving him a poke in the ribs with her elbow, "anyways, that movie wasn't true Texan spirit. This fellow's Alamo was the real deal, crossing lines in the sand and fighting for a new future, is what Texan grit is about.

"I would have liked to have joined those DRT ladies, like Nita's grandma did, but daughters of slaves weren't Texan enough for that sorority," Eugie added with a scowl.

Danny pondered that many would think it odd that a black woman would feel a close connection with Wayne's Alamo movie, depicting a time when owning slaves was still deemed a right, and a highly defended one at that, by the Americans in that battle. Or even have pride in being a Texan for that matter.

But he did understand what she meant about the Alamo's defenders fighting for Texas to become a republic. Eugie and her ancestors had fought ongoing adversity and prejudice, to eke out an existence in the eras of Republic, State and the V-n-B of the Great

Depression, she had as much right to consider herself to be a Texan as he did, maybe more so. Unlike Eugie, he had no vision of what his ancestors might have contributed and achieved, or what hurdles they had jumped to do so.

After the seemingly endless commercials, for precisely what Danny had just ordered, the opening credits finally rolled, with William Conrad lyrically narrating the tale of Chisum's route to Lincoln County. Danny pulled out a pad and pen to take notes, but was immediately baffled, and muttered to himself, "Why would he cross the 'River Red' to go from Texas to New Mexico?" as the poetic intro had implied.

A sweet West Texan voice whispered in his ear, "Perhaps he really liked the Indian Territory." It was Nita with their refreshments, showing off her knowledge of what Oklahoma would have been called in the 1870s. She had a young lad in tow carrying a candle.

"Who is this fine fella?" Danny enquired, half-concentrating on the movie.

"This is my little brother, Doug, he makes mosquito candles to sell to the convertible drivers and he was worried that your friend might be troubled by them, they are merciless tonight."

"Doug, that is such a sweet thought, how much do I owe you?" Danny offered.

"Nothing sir, but I'd love to sit in your plane, if that's okay?" Doug asked shyly.

"He's a good boy, he loves planes." Nita assured.

"That'd be no problem young man. I'd feel mighty safe with you looking after her for me, hop on up. If you're around tomorrow morning I'll take you up for a spin, if that is okay with your folks, be at the airfield for seven o'clock."

Doug's eyes widened with delight as he climbed up into the cockpit.

"Thank you sir, that is very kind," Nita stated with a big smile, and then skated off to go about her business.

Danny handed Eugie her hotdog, she took it and gave his hand an affectionate squeeze, rested her head on his arm and said, "You will make a great daddy one day, make sure you don't wait too long!"

He smiled at the thought, and lit Doug's candle.

At the movie's intermission the commercials returned to the screen, accompanied by the purr of a big motorcycle approaching from behind them. Danny looked over his shoulder, to see a rather large policeman pulling up on a Harley Electraglide. He parked his bike behind the wing, and proceeded to wander around, inspecting the Stearman.

Danny was 90% certain that the police had no jurisdiction over airworthiness, but you never know what is in a cop's mind in a strange town, some of his low flying earlier wasn't exactly by the book.

"Can I help you, officer?"

"Well, sir, you have already made the night for my eyes," he replied with an unfathomable straight face.

Then he cracked a big grin, "First time I've seen a Yellow Peril in a while, not fancy enough for the oil folk around these parts, so I'm guessing that you are not an oil man, or from around these parts?"

The 'Yellow Peril' comment was revealing, and a relief to Danny. It was the nickname given to Stearman trainers in the military; the cop was almost certainly a comrade-in-arms.

"Nope, flew down from Fort Worth way today, we're off to New Mexico tomorrow, were you a pilot?" Danny queried.

"I was in the Air Force during World War Two, but doing this pretty much ever since. How about you, any service?"

Danny hesitated, but felt obliged to respond honestly, "I was flying Sabres, caught the tail end of Korea, I went out there with Pete Fernandez, in the 344ᵗʰ."

"Wow, you must have been good to be in that kind of company."

Danny deflected the praise, "Pete was the best, when they sent him home he had fourteen and a half kills to my five, I reckon he would have kept the record if he'd stayed."

The cop's eyes widened, "Five kills, you're an Ace? What's your name?"

"Daniel Johnson, Sir."

"First Lieutenant 'Baby Powder' Johnson?" the policeman questioned with a grin.

"That's what they called me, I was one of the youngest, the name kind of... well stuck."

"I sure remember it; read about you in 'Aviation Week', you were a Texan hero."

He offered up his hand, "I'm Officer Vick Atwood. If you don't mind me asking, how come you are not out in 'Nam, you're still young, and look fit?"

"I was there for a couple of years, but let's say it didn't work out." Danny replied, making a sweeping gesture with his left hand, as confirmation that he did mind Vick asking.

Danny swiftly changed the subject, "Does Big Lake keep you busy?"

"Not overly, Chief Becknell and Sheriff Proffitt run a pretty tight ship. We get the odd shenanigans out at the Dairy King and the occasional drag race down Highway 67. Just kids being kids, they behave when I'm around.

"Though we do keep an eye out for suspicious looking strangers, who might be bringing drugs in from Mexico," he pointed out in a slightly more serious tone, eyeing up the Stearman. Then qualified it with, "but you two would be the oddest pair of dealers I've ever met," and laughed heartily.

"Tell me about the lake, is it always dry now?" Danny asked.

"Mostly, the artesian wells pretty much killed it, comes in handy for the run-off when we get a really big rain though. The kids used to swim in it, but I've never seen it more than a few feet full in the last decade."

They chatted some more about local life, until the interlude's dancing popcorn cartons disappeared in favor of the second half of the movie. Danny politely pointed to the screen and Vick took the hint, "I wouldn't want to interrupt The Duke, it's been real nice talking to you; keep it out of the soup."

'Out of the soup,' being an aviator term for not getting lost in the clouds.

"I'll make sure of that, sir!"

The policeman stepped away giving Danny a courteous salute, which he dutifully reciprocated.

Eugie had been listening intently, she knew that Danny had been overseas with the Air Force a couple of times, and that he had come home 'troubled' the last time, but never realized how distinguished his service had been, or ever heard anyone talk about what had troubled him.

As Vick's bike rumbled away Eugie looked towards the south and could see the faint outline of the dry lake in the moonlight. She could picture her grandfather's men camped out with the herd, and pondered that some of his cattle had probably stood where they were parked. She looked up at the beautiful starry sky to the north, found Polaris and let out a deep sigh.

CHAPTER 28

ROSWELL

Danny was true to his word, and used his remaining fuel to give young Doug the ride of his life, performing a series of rolls and loops above the airfield.

"OH MY GOD!" Nita screamed watching his antics.

"Don't worry girl, he was a fighter Ace in Korea," Eugie reassured, with pride in her newfound knowledge.

He landed to receive a very thankful hug, and a big kiss, from the star struck green-eyed beauty, captured for posterity in Kodacolor. An hour later he was airborne again, with Eugie and a full tank of gas on board.

"Fly as low as you dare 'Baby Powder', so I get a good view," Eugie requested teasingly.

Danny mumbled something undecipherable over the crackly intercom.

With the sun rising behind them, they headed west a few hundred feet above the High Plains, following the line of the Atchison, Topeka and Santa Fe Railway, paralleling Highway 67. Eugie could imagine the cattle and dust that would have dominated the scene below them, a century before.

As they got up to cruising speed, she looked at her watch and timed six minutes, to see the distance that the cowboys would have taken a day to cover. She thought about the stamina and dedication it must have taken to do that every day, for the forty days it took them to get from the Colorado River to Bosque Grande.

As they continued flying west, the road and railroad tracks veered off to the south. Within twenty minutes the Pecos River was winding its way beneath them, "See where that road meets the river, that's Horsehead Crossing. They would have spent all day fording across there; then followed the left bank of the river going north up towards Lincoln County."

Eugie acknowledged, with her familiar thumbs up. An hour later they crossed the state line into New Mexico. Danny climbed to a higher altitude, to avoid the local traffic from the multitude of small airfields that supported the string of towns that had built up along Chisum's old trail.

Their flight path was punctuated by the odd flurry of green, revealing the well-irrigated farming communities on the outskirts of; Loving, Carlsbad, Lakewood, Atoka and Artesia. Looking away from the river, the landscape looked far more inhospitable, ravaged by the summer heat – a reminder of the challenges that the pioneer drovers took on. It was clear why Chisum needed such a massive acreage to support his herd. Compared to the relative lushness of his previous ranches, New Mexico was barren.

As they entered Chaves County, flying over the sprawling dairy farms surrounding Hagerman and Dexter, leading on to Roswell, Eugie opened up the intercom.

"So, how much of this land do you think Chisum would have ranched?"

"Pretty much all of it I reckon, Danny responded, "The book I read said 150 miles along the Pecos River, and 50 miles either side, so I guess everything we have flown over for the past half an hour or so, and everything we will fly over when we swing around over Lincoln and land at Roswell."

Eugie knew that Chisum's operation was big, but this was the first time she could visualize the scale of what he had to protect. You could have hidden entire towns in places.

They were soon flying over the South Springs Ranch, time for Danny to check in with the airport, to get them to call Mr. Anderson.

North of the city, with no further big population centers to fret about, Danny descended to give Eugie a closer look at the terrain. The greenery had all but petered out, roads and buildings had become increasingly sparse, except those supporting the farms and ever-present Pumpjacks, a browner version of their approach to Big Lake the day before.

Forty miles north of South Springs, he located his best guess for where the Bosque Grande ranch would have been. It was similar in many respects to where Chisum had staked his claim at the Concho-Colorado, at the convergence of two rivers. He could only presume that Chisum chose these locations to get a more reliable water supply from two sources. But just like their flyby of the Concho-Colorado, there was nothing left to see.

"Okay Danny, I've seen enough here, show me Lincoln please," Eugie instructed with a frustrated tone.

"No problem," he replied and rolled the Stearman to port, heading southwest.

Danny sympathized with her disappointment, and hoped that she could get a low-level photograph of Lincoln's single street to make up for it. A street referred to by historians as being 'the most dangerous in the West' in its day, but by 1970 it was simply known as Route 380, in what had become a sleepy little rural town.

He approached from the northwest following the course of the Rio Hondo, which would lead them all the way back to Roswell.

They got a grandstand view of the old town and its notorious courthouse. Danny was just about to pull up for the final leg to the airport when he noticed a police car beneath him, he muttered, "Damn," under his breath, but did not reveal to Eugie that he might be in trouble.

The town of Lincoln had remained pretty much unchanged since its Wild West days, to the point that those same historians considered it to be one of the most genuine 'Frontier Towns' surviving anywhere. It was frozen in time when the railroad missed it by thirty miles, causing the county seat to move west in 1909, to the prospering commercial center of Carrizozo. A town built close to a canyon, which would become hallowed ground for Chisum and his men.

Half an hour later, they were making their final approach at Roswell Airport, a large former Air Force base, with a lot of traffic. The very formal nature of the airport controller's dialogue was a far cry from the small laid-back airfields, like Big Lake, that Daniel was more familiar with, but very reminiscent of his days in the military. His instructions were to taxi to a hangar at the edge of the field, and park up next to a Gulfstream executive jet.

As he turned off the engine, a police car pulled up alongside, justifying his earlier concerns.

"What's going on?" Eugie asked.

"I might be in a little trouble, for my low flying."

He helped Eugie out of the jump seat and climbed down to face the music, just as a tatty looking yellow 1949 Oldsmobile convertible pulled up next to the police car.

One of the officers approached Danny, "We have a report of some very ir-re-sponsible flying over Lincoln just now, stampeding horses."

By the way 'ir-re-sponsible' rolled off the cop's lips Danny could tell it was one of his favorite words, and the phrase 'stampeding horses' revealed that he had a colleague prone to exaggeration. As an experienced crop duster, he knew how to behave around livestock. But for a quiet life he was just about to confess, and ask for mercy, when a dusty looking fellow stepped out of the Olds, distracting the cop's attention.

The gentleman might have been scruffy, but he had a certain presence about him. Danny noticed that he was wearing what would have been a very expensive Stetson in its day, in a similar condition to his car, and about the same age. His initial impression was of a man who had been quite wealthy, a while back.

"Mr. Anderson," the policeman greeted, with a tone of humble subservience.

Anderson dived straight in to the conversation, "Low flying you says? Danny was just checking out my fencing for me, up at the Circle Diamond."

"Sorry Mr. Anderson, we didn't know, that's all fine then," the cop stammered. He put his notebook away, then shuffled awkwardly back to his police car, offering a respectful, "have a nice day y'all."

Danny reached out his hand to his newfound guardian angel, "Mr. Anderson?"

"Yes Danny, I hear you were flying damned low, my foreman saw you. I hope you got a good view of Lincoln, but if you did upset any of my brood mares, you might be getting a big bill," Anderson laughed.

Danny was not sure if Anderson was kidding, but being so relieved that he had just dodged a potentially damaging report to the FAA, he was not going to worry about it too much.

Eugie caught up with them with a puzzled look on her face.

"Would you be Mrs. Thomas?" the cowboy queried.

"That I would be. Mr. Anderson?"

"Please call me Bob."

"Happy to Bob... my father's name, a good name, and I'm Eugie."

"We've had all sorts want to nose around South Springs since that damned movie came out, and mostly turned them away. But when Danny called, and said he was going to fly Chisum's granddaughter, 600 miles here, in a Stearman, that I had to see. I have to say you weren't quite what I was expecting, but hell, get in and we'll go over to the ranch for lunch, and I'll be glad to hear your story and show you around."

Fifteen minutes later the Oldsmobile pulled off the Old Dexter Highway into South Springs' driveway, requiring Danny to re-evaluate their host's financial status. In front of the ranch house there was a row of shiny, brand new, Chevy C10 Stepside pickup trucks and two Bell Ranger helicopters.

"Come on in," Anderson beckoned.

They entered the ranch house to be met by the glorious odor of fresh leather and polished timber, the house had been remodeled after Anderson purchased it a couple of years before. A teenage lad came out of a side office to greet them.

"This is my son Jack, he's running this place."

"You don't live here then, Bob?" Eugie enquired.

"Nope, I reside at the Circle Diamond, up near Hondo, just downstream from where this fella was doing aerobatics earlier," Bob replied jovially.

Danny noticed a familiar looking oil painting, hanging above a long button-backed sofa.

"Is that what I think it is?" he asked excitedly.

"Yep, it is one of Russ Vickers' oils from the movie titles. The producers were up here last year checking the place out; they sent that along a few weeks ago, as a thank you. Not really my taste in art, I prefer things a bit more modern, but it fills a space. Jack wishes he had that hill to ride up on Sunday afternoons, like

Chisum did," he joked, pointing at the image of John Wayne, admiring his spread, from the shade of a tree.

"Everything is as flat as a pancake around here. They ended up shooting the ranch scenes in the mountains, down in Durango, Mexico, but that's Hollywood, I guess. It's a shame, I'd have loved to have got to meet Duke Wayne, and tell him how much I liked 'Hellfighters', and of course, let him know what they got wrong," he smiled.

Hearing the Hollywood reference, Eugie gave a knowing smile. While Bob and Danny had been discussing movies, she was distracted by a different sort of picture, on another wall. Bob noticed her interest in his old photo collection, and walked over.

"Most of these were taken after Chisum died, they came with the ranch. Sadly, there weren't too many photographers around these parts, when he lived here. I do find him to be a fascinating man, I've read a bit about him, and have to say I'm a little skeptical about you being his granddaughter. No offense meant Mrs. Thomas, you may well believe that you are, but it just doesn't add up." Bob explained politely, but with distinct directness.

"I can understand that." Eugie acknowledged.

She pointed at one of the older photos of the long white ranch house, "This was taken on August 15, 1882, 88 years ago to the day."

"How can you be so sure?" Bob queried.

Eugie reached into her bag and pulled out an old tintype, and carefully handed it to Bob. It was an image of a mustachioed, middle-aged man and a younger woman. The picket fence in front of them, and a garden frame behind, clearly matched Bob's wider angle photo.

"This was taken the same day, turn it over," Eugie suggested.

He obliged, read the date, and a faded inscription on the back, "Enjoying my birthday with Sallie. Give Harry, Meady and the babies a hug from Grandpa."

"Meady's babies were my eldest brother, Jim, and my sisters, Alice and Virgie, may their souls rest in peace. I had not quite come along yet." Eugie informed.

"My God, Mrs. Thomas!" Bob exclaimed, "I owe you an apology, I really didn't believe you."

"That's fine, you were wise to be cautious, and please call me Eugie," she reminded.

"Come sit with me, and tell me more." The rancher pleaded.

They vacated to the comfort of the sofa, below the Vickers oil painting, where Eugie spent over an hour retelling an abbreviated version of her story, up to where she had got to with Danny. Anderson was amazed by what he was hearing, particularly about Gainesville. He owned a business in the town, was a regular visitor, but just like Danny never knew of the horrors that had gone on there during the Civil War.

Eugie paused from her story, "I hate to be rude, but my stomach's remembering that lunch you offered."

Bob patted his forehead, "My manners," he led them into the dining room where a buffet of New Mexico's finest cuisine was laid out.

"Could you excuse me for a minute please?" Bob requested, "I have a couple of phone calls that I need to make."

He returned a while later with a pixie-like grin on his face, "Here's a plan, would you two like to stay in the guest house tonight?"

"That would be lovely, if it's not an inconvenience to you," Eugie replied courteously.

"No inconvenience at all. I've got a charity luncheon in Dallas tomorrow. Danny, I would love to fly there in your Stearman. I've taken the liberty of asking for her to be refueled. Would you mind taking me at first light, and Eugie can sleep in, and take my Gulfstream, if that's okay?"

"What's a gulf stream?" Eugie whispered to Danny.

"It's a nice plane."

"As nice as yours?"

"You'll be fine," Danny replied, not wishing to spoil the surprise.

"Do you fancy the dime tour?" Bob offered, as they finished lunch.

"That would be lovely," Eugie replied.

Bob took them outside, and a potential situation, which Danny had been fretting about since they arrived, turned out to be more than just potential.

As they were led to one of Bob's helicopters, Danny announced, "Sorry, I don't do choppers."

Bob and Eugie were both taken aback by the announcement, but it was clear from Danny's eyes that this was not a whimsical transportation choice. Recognizing fear had served Bob well in his business dealings, but he was sorry to see it in Danny, who he had taken an instant liking to, but knew better than to push him.

Bob turned on the helicopter's radio, and called in to the house, for Jack to come out and take Danny for a drive.

As Bob and Eugie got airborne, he pitched the question, "What was up with Danny, he looked white as a sheet, but he's a pilot for Christ's sake?"

"I honestly don't know, Bob, I've never seen Daniel afraid of nothing before," Eugie assured with sincerity, and maternal defensiveness.

Hovering at 200ft, Bob pointed out the boundaries of the original 40 acres.

"Chisum bought the ranch from a James Patterson for $2,500 in 1875. He started with a four-room adobe brick house just there," he explained, pointing at what was by then an orchard, "it was quite a fortress, bits of the foundations still pop out of the ground from time to time."

"Do you have roses?" Eugie asked.

"Funny you should say that, wild ones keep popping up all the time in the orchard, I haven't the heart to kill them."

"They are not so wild," Eugie pointed out, "John loved roses; he had about a hundred bushes planted around the house, that trellis in your photo would have been for his prized yellow ones."

Being able to hover over the land certainly gave a different perspective to flying past in the Stearman. Eugie was able to see signs of old buildings in the ground, where they had affected the drainage during the dry summer.

Bob went on to regale her with everything he thought he knew about Chisum's tenure at South Springs. Eugie decided not to correct him on anything just yet, and to be fair, his understanding of that time was closer to reality than the movie had been.

They returned to the ranch house, where Danny was patiently waiting with Jack, sipping cold beers.

"Did you enjoy your drive?" Eugie asked.

"Yep, Jack was very informative, quite a spread they have."

"Okay, let me drive you to the guest house and you can freshen up," Bob suggested, "our housekeeper will serve dinner at seven, and I'll be keen to hear the rest of your story."

CHAPTER 29

BOLDLY GOING

The guesthouse was predictably delightful, reminiscent of an old-style Western hotel, with a large front room, decorated in a similar leather and wood style to the main house, with a hardwood staircase leading up to a gallery of bedrooms and bathrooms.

Eugie pointed to a table in the center of the room, "Is that what I think it is?" in a tone as excited as Danny's had been, when he'd spied the Russ Vickers oil painting.

"What the TV?"

"Color TV?" Eugie specified, "I've only ever seen them in shop windows before."

She turned it on, and while it was warming up Danny took his gear upstairs, to bathe and change. After switching through the channels of the newfound technology, disappointed at finding that most stuff was still in black and white, Eugie did the same.

She appeared on the gallery an hour later to see Danny below, transfixed by the TV. She called down, "How do I look?" and did a twirl.

"Stunning Mrs. Thomas – as always, stunning," he replied courteously.

Eugie emerged at the bottom of the stairs asking, "What you watching?"

"Oh, just a rerun of Star Trek, do you want me to change the channel, we've still got half an hour to kill."

"Don't you dare, I loved this show, such a shame they cancelled it, never seen it in Color before."

Danny laughed.

"What's so funny?" Eugie queried, settling into the sofa next to him.

"Well, I never thought I'd spend this afternoon on the famous South Springs ranch, watching Captain Kirk."

"You never know where a day will take you Danny. Do you think the world will ever be like Star Trek, everyone on the planet at peace with one another?"

"In all honesty, I don't, man is too greedy, I can't ever see us living in a utopia, and how do they build a Starship in a world with no money. But pay no heed to me, I'm just a cynic."

Eugie decided to 'boldly go' where she probably shouldn't, "What happened out there today – the helicopter thing?"

Danny hesitated, "I figured you wouldn't take too long to getting around to interrogating me about that. Trust me, it is history, ain't going to help anybody digging it up now."

"I'm your friend Danny Boy, might help me understand you better... it might help you."

Danny stood up and got himself a beer from the well-stocked refrigerator, then returned to the sofa.

"Well fella?" Eugie pushed.

"You're not going to let this go, are you?" Danny questioned rhetorically.

"Nope, I'm not!" Eugie replied shaking her head, confident that she was one of the few people on the planet who could open this particular can of worms, and be able to put the lid back on it again.

Danny collected his thoughts, and began his story, "It was late in '67, I was flying Hueys in 'Nam, they're similar to Bob Anderson's Bells. We were moving the squadron from Tan Son Nhut, 500 miles north to Nakhon Phanom on the Mekong River. I had my crew, and ten ground crew on board.

"We were about fifty miles short of the base, and then the tail boom was hit by something from the ground."

He paused and took a swig from his beer; Eugie moved closer and held his hand.

"We spun and came down in the jungle like a stone, which at least broke our fall, it saved some of us but my co-pilot and four of the guys were dead. The rest of us were all injured to some degree. I had a broken arm and leg."

"That must have been terrible," Eugie comforted, lost for anything more meaningful to say.

"We did have some luck, the medic was alive and we were transporting a load of guns and a fair amount of ammo, not that the rest had much idea of what to do with them, most had only just come out of basic training," Danny's voice trailed off, his head panned around at the room, but his eyes didn't see it, his mind lost in that crash site in Vietnam, "they were just kids."

Eugie was keen for him to get the rest out of his system, and softly asked, "What did you do?"

"That was just the beginning of it; Charlie found us and kept us pinned down for two hours." Danny continued to stare blankly out at the room, "thankfully one of the kids was a freaking genius and fixed the radio just before he and the medic copped it. I got word out and we got a Napalm strike to fry the bastards."

Eugie let his uncharacteristic expletive ride over her, "Then you were rescued?"

Danny turned to look Eugie in the eyes, "We were... two days later!" He turned his head away again, "they couldn't risk sending a chopper in, for fear of snipers; I lost another kid on the second day."

He paused to take breath.

"I'd seen killing before and killed, but not like that," he slowly shook his head, "Not up close and personal, they were good kids, mostly brave, but they were relying on me to keep them safe," he swallowed hard, felt his scalp tingle, and choked back tears, "and I didn't!"

He stood up to walk away.

Eugie got up and stopped him; she put her arm around his neck and pulled his head into her shoulder. He stood silent for a moment, then quietly sobbed. She cradled his head like a baby's, crying with him. Both were totally oblivious to the fact that the most notorious interracial TV kiss from the 1960s, was being replayed before them.

A while passed, and they sat down again.

"What happened afterwards?"

Danny composed himself, "While we were waiting for rescue, the wind changed and all we could smell was death, Charlie and whatever poor critters had been burned in the forest, it freaked us all out. I was in the MASH for a while, and then they shipped me back to the military hospital in Fort Worth for a couple of months, to be 'mentally assessed' while my bones fixed. They decided on a medical discharge, on the grounds that I was too scared to fly anymore."

"How come I didn't get to hear about this?" Eugie queried with surprise.

"My dad, as ever... he did not want the world knowing his son was a 'nut job'."

"You are no 'nut job' Danny, and you were nearly forty, you were your own man."

"Eugie, I wasn't anyone's man for a while, I was a lost soul and...if I'm honest...I didn't want folks to know either," he looked away, and took a deep breath, "I didn't want to have to deal with the strange looks, and whispers."

"So how did you get back in the air?"

"I had to prove something to myself, and it pays well. Please note, I now fly a plane with a spare set of wings, that you can land deadstick if the noisy part fails." he stated, twiddling his fingers impersonating a propeller.

"I will never fly in a helicopter again, and just in case you ever have any other mad ideas, I don't do parachute jumps either," he stated with a forced smile.

Eugie guessed that there was yet another story there, but did not pursue it. She looked at her watch, "Come on, turn the TV off, or we'll be late for Mr. Anderson."

Danny obliged. Then as they were heading for the door, pointed out, "On the subject of our host, I found out quite a bit about him, while Jack was giving me my 'dime tour', he's very proud of his pa, but he doesn't own two ranches."

"Really?" Eugie replied, sounding disappointed.

Danny paused for dramatic effect, "Nope...he owns eight," flashing a genuine smile, "and if you could bolt them all together his spread would be bigger than the State of Delaware."

"Well I'll be, that would explain the helicopters, and of course the Color TVs," Eugie joked.

"That's just the half of it," Danny continued, "the ranches are just his hobby; his main business is oil and gas. He is a real life 'Giant' a 'Bick Benedict' and some, you've heard of Arco?"

"The gas stations, he owns some of them?"

"All 20,000 of them; he's the boss of the company; gas stations, pipelines, refineries, a skyscraper in Dallas, the whole kit and caboodle. He's one of the richest men in America."

"Oh my, and he's still so nice," Eugie noted with an ironic tone.

CHAPTER 30

LINCOLN COUNTY GOES TO WAR

D anny knocked on the door of the main house, which was answered by a very smart looking Jack.

"Why, you didn't have to dress up for us young man," Eugie stated.

"He's off on a date with a new gal," Bob corrected from the front room.

He strode over and welcomed them in. Introducing a very sophisticated looking lady, who looked about 40, but Eugie guessed was older, in ways that only a woman can tell.

"Mrs. Thomas, Danny, this is my wife Barbara."

"Pleased to meet you Mrs. Anderson, you look so beautiful," Eugie acknowledged.

"The good lord has been kind, but he keeps me humble," Barbara replied modesty.

Eugie turned to Jack, "Who's the lucky girl then?"

"Her name is Margaret," Jack replied shyly.

"What a lovely name, just like the Queen's sister," Eugie observed.

Jack bid them farewell and headed towards the door, hoping to escape before his love life got any further scrutiny.

"My God Eugie, you've been here five minutes, and you got more out of my boy than I have," Bob laughed, "come on into the dining room."

"One moment," Eugie interrupted, "Jack, one more thing before you go."

He paused and cringed.

Eugie pulled out her camera, "Would you mind being in a photograph?"

She gathered the Andersons around Danny and herself in the manner of a much-beloved family reunion, and the housekeeper was summoned to take a snap, "This is what I call a 'Kodak Moment'," Eugie explained.

Bob would remember Eugie's descriptive term some years later, when lunching with an advertising executive friend, who was struggling to come up with a poignant catchphrase, for a commission he was trying to win.

Barbara and Eugie instantly hit it off, chatting about the volunteer work they did during World War Two and after. Meanwhile, Danny and Bob talked about cows, horses and planes, the latter turning out to be another of Bob's passions. Quite an appropriate one considering his middle name was Orville, after one of the pioneering Wright brother aviators.

After three sumptuous courses they headed for the comfort of the front room sofas for coffee. Bob's patience was being tested, "Okay we had got to Bosque Grande, and the demise of poor Mr. Loving."

"That's right, you'll have to bear with me on some of this Bob; some is family stuff for Danny's benefit, let's wait for him to get back from the bathroom."

"That's fine Eugie, you tell it as it comes."

"Oh, and you don't happen to have a bottle of Champagne on hand do you, nothing too fancy, we have a celebration that needs toasting."

Danny returned from the Bathroom and was handed a glass of, what was actually a very fancy and expensive, glass of fizzy wine.

Eugie got everyone standing and announced, "Happy birthday John Simpson Chisum, 146 years young today," to a round of chinking glasses. Eugie's thoughts drifted to the number of birthday parties that would have been thrown, within yards of where they stood, during the decade of Chisum's tenure at South Springs.

They sat down and Eugie picked up where she had left off, "As you know this was Chisum's final ranch, he moved his operation down here in December '74, everything with John always seemed to happen at Christmas time. But he didn't pay $2,500 for it."

"He didn't?" Bob questioned, surprised.

"Nope, it was some kind of complicated deal, as Chisum's tended to be, with James Patterson, and the previous owner, named Hudson. John was cow rich, but cash poor at that time, he'd learned from the war that assets were better than money in the bank. They all owed each other in some fashion or other, so John paid in cows and let the other two fellows sort out the money between themselves. Any bill of sale you might have seen would have just been there to cook... sorry, balance the books."

Danny smiled to himself, listening to Eugie giving the richest man in the State bookkeeping advice.

Chisum was joined at South Springs by the Towerys, their cattle and Sonny, Frances' late brother's son via a slave girl, who was 21 years old by then, and a top wrangler.

Elijah was a tired old man of 48 by then, and appreciated the extra help; he soon became a father figure and mentor to Sonny, who he would turn from being a wrangler to what in later years would have been called a 'horse whisperer'.

Frances took on the role of housekeeper, while Tom took on as little as he could get away with, with his ambitions still set on getting to California.

The 1870s were a decade of mixed fortunes for the family. Meady had met Eugie's father, a wonderful fellow named Bob Jones, but for James it was tragedy upon tragedy. His daughter, Mary, died in '73 aged just 18, followed two years later by the loss of his beloved Josephine.

James tried to carry on making a go of it at Clear Creek, but lost heart. After endless Indian raids, Sallie finally persuaded him to pick up sticks, and take her and her little brothers to New Mexico, to join Uncle John. So, by 1877 all of Claiborne's surviving sons were settled in the 'lawless' Lincoln County.

Sallie was only nineteen, but was a force to be reckoned with. James often noted that 'she so reminded him of his father', all be it with a slightly softer voice and no beard.

"As lawless as Lincoln County may have been, with his army of loyal men protecting him, John had created yet another rural idyll. It was a happy house renowned for its parties and warm welcome. Business was booming, with the Chisum herds reunited, along 150 miles of the Pecos, and 50 miles either side." Eugie detailed, giving Danny a wink, as she poached his research.

Bob interrupted, "I've heard that 150-mile figure bandied around a number of times, I think big, but I still struggle to imagine how he could manage that on horseback."

"They didn't call him 'The cattle King of the Pecos' for nothing." Eugie reassured.

She continued, "As is always the case when you have something good someone else tries to take a slice of it away from you, either by fair or foul means. One of the fouler protagonists was a fella you will have heard of, Lawrence Murphy," stating his name with poison in her voice.

Murphy was a devious Irishman, who had arrived in Lincoln a few years after Chisum had moved to Bosque Grande. He and Chisum could not have been two more different characters. Murphy had served in the Union army during the war, and run his business through fear and intimidation, a man devoid of conscience or moral code.

He had built up a lucrative business by crushing any competition that came on the scene. He employed like-minded villainous souls, such as fellow Union veteran, Republican politician, James Dolan, a young fellow with big ambitions. Having a virtual monopoly, he could charge pretty much what he liked for goods, and folk would have to pay it, or travel hundreds of miles to get a better deal.

At about the time Chisum moved his operation to South Springs, Murphy and Dolan had gone into a partnership known as 'The House', with the backing of a group of corrupt politicians titled the 'Santa Fe Ring'. Their ambition was to put a further stranglehold on the good folk of Lincoln County, by opening the only bank in that part of the New Mexico Territory.

They would sell land that they didn't own, and offer loans that would be difficult to repay, due to Murphy's men obstructing the recipients from having any opportunity to carve out a living. Then when farmers were delinquent on their repayments, the bank would foreclose on their assets, and take their land back.

On the fair side of the entrepreneurial coin, a young English fellow appeared on the scene, named John Tunstall.

"Note I said young," Eugie emphasized, "he was about 24, not an old man like in the movie."

As was their way The House tried to put Tunstall out of business, but he was a shrewd fellow, who had a good lawyer on his payroll, a

Canadian named Alexander McSween, who had arrived in Lincoln from Kansas, with his wife, Susan, a few years before.

McSween was a man of high moral fiber, who had previously been employed by The House, but had parted company with them due to Murphy's lawless approach to business. So, when Tunstall offered McSween a partnership to go into competition with them, he grabbed the opportunity, his experience with Murphy brought some advantageous insight to their business. Tunstall also had the benefit of further financial backing from his friend, John Chisum.

Tensions escalated, with both factions hiring infamous gunmen to protect their interests. The Lincoln County War kicked off in anger during February 1878, with the murder of John Tunstall. He was pursued and shot, by a posse of three Lincoln deputies with allegiances to Murphy, on a trumped-up horse rustling charge, led by the notorious outlaw, Jesse Evans. There were no other witnesses to the shooting, so Evans and his conspirators claimed it was self-defense, but few believed a man like Tunstall would have instigated a gunfight with three supposed lawmen.

Tunstall's most loyal bodyguard, who at the time was going by the name of William Bonney, later known as 'Billy, the kid', led a group of his late boss' friends and allies to petition Lincoln County's justice of the peace, 'Squire' John Wilson, to have the deputies arrested. Wilson agreed and swore in a rancher, Richard Brewer, to lead another posse of special constables, including Bonney and his affiliates, to go in pursuit of Evans' gang of murderers. The group gave themselves the grandiose title of 'The Regulators.'

So, there were then two groups of deputies, both of whom felt that the law, and god for that matter, was on their side. Murphy was a Catholic, from County Wexford in the south of Ireland, whilst the Tunstall allies represented a Protestant front, including the Irishman, Billy Bonney, whose roots were from County Antrim in the north of the homeland, Bonney even spoke Gaelic. The north and south of nineteenth century Ireland were almost as divided as the States had been during the Civil War, but their conflict had over a century left to run.

It is hard to say which group of protagonists was worse than the other, beyond who shot first. The Regulators caught and killed two of the deputies, but Evans escaped. Naturally it was claimed that those killings were also in self-defense, a claim that was a tad more believable than when Tunstall was murdered.

Shootings escalated, and everything came to a head that July, with one of the few real, protracted range war gunfights of the Old West, the five-day 'Battle of Lincoln,' between The Regulators and The House. The battle culminated in the burning of Alexander McSween's home, followed by his murder, along with a few Regulators and a couple of Murphy's men.

Chisum and Murphy were mostly on the sidelines of the war. It was reputed that the Regulators stayed at Chisum's ranch from time to time, and that Bonney got quite close to Sallie. There was also a story that Bonney had rustled some of John's cattle, in revenge for an unpaid bill of $500 for protection services. But there was never any record of John corroborating, or denying any of these stories.

Sallie had noted some level of friendship with Bonney in her diary, but she was known to have a fanciful imagination at times. She was deemed to be one of the prettiest girls in the county in her day, so it is not beyond belief that Bonney would have taken a shine to her. But when you are dealing with a folklore legend like 'Billy, the Kid' it is hard to trust anything you hear second, or third hand.

"But I thought that Murphy was in the thick of it, and didn't Chisum kill him?" Bob asked.

"Hollywood my friend... Hollywood," Eugie replied, echoing Bob's earlier disdain for the movie industry's disregard for historical facts.

"Lawrence Murphy was a very sick man, in more ways than his demeanor. The cancer killed him, very painfully, that October," she added with delight.

"But... there is one more Chisum connection to that episode... have you ever heard of 'The Cattle Queen of New Mexico'?"

"I can't say that I have," Bob admitted, "but as he was the 'Cattle King of the Pecos', I'm guessing you are going to tell me that Chisum found himself a woman out here?"

"Not quite as you might think. She was McSween's wife, Susan, who was not the girly-girl you saw in the movie. She fought hard through the law to get justice for the murder of her husband, but got nowhere other than penniless. She gave up when her lawyer was murdered by Jesse Evans, who also did not die during the Lincoln County War, contrary to what they would have you believe.

"Have you heard of the 'Three Rivers Land and Cattle Company'?" Eugie added.

"That I have, old company name, down in Otero County," Bob confirmed.

"John came to Susan's rescue, and gifted her $400 worth of beeves to make a start of things again. She run Three Rivers, and ended up with 8,000 head of cattle and a fortune.

"She shared your interest in growing fruit. John gave her trees from here. I know he was very fond of her, but I don't know if it ever became anything more than that... but you know men."

"Indeed," Bob replied with a cough, grateful that his wife had fallen asleep, "what became of Susan?"

"I read that she died a penniless old lady about the time Danny was born. I guess she got too used to fine living," she stated, taking a sip of Bob's very fine Champagne.

"So, did the Lincoln County War just go away?" Bob asked.

"That is pretty much the way of it. After the cancer saw off Murphy, 'The House' collapsed, and gunmen don't work where there is no payroll, that is one thing that the movie got right," Eugie begrudgingly added.

When Eugie got tired, her social skills would fall off a cliff. She very abruptly brought the evening's education to a close. "Bob, it has been a delight, but I fear I need to follow your good lady's example and find my bed. If you ever want to talk some more, come visit me in Texas," she invited, handing him one of McKinley's business cards.

Bob hid his disappointment at the sudden termination of their conversation, "I most certainly will Mrs. Thomas, and as you say, 'it has been a delight'. Danny and I will have to head east early tomorrow, but you lay in as long as you like. Barbara will drive you to the airport after breakfast."

"Oh yes to catch that wind... your Jet Stream... Gulf Stream plane, you are so kind."

Footnote: After the Battle of Lincoln, a new governor was appointed to the New Mexico Territory, General Lew Wallace. Something else the movie got right.

Wallace offered a general amnesty to those who had been involved in the war, with a couple of exceptions – William Bonney and Jesse Evans, due to there being outstanding murder warrants on their heads. Bonney tried to negotiate an amnesty for himself by offering to give testimony to a grand jury, regarding another murder, Wallace agreed but went back on his word and kept him in Lincoln jail.

Bonney escaped, and went straight for a while, but the dark side of society was like a drug to him, he would always find trouble. He killed again and got caught again, and shipped back to Lincoln where he was tried, found guilty, and sentenced to hang. He was held at the courthouse and escaped yet again; killing two guards in the process and went on the run. With a $500 bounty on his head, he was hot property, and it did not take long for Lincoln's new Sherriff, Pat Garrett, to track him down near Fort Sumner and shoot him, as is well recorded in history books.

Lew Wallace also had a significant literary career and his own movie connection. While he was the governor of New Mexico, he finished writing a historical adventure manuscript titled, 'Ben-Hur: A Tale of the Christ'. Which would go on to be the best-selling American novel of the 19th century, and be adapted into five motion pictures by 2016. Including; a silent movie in 1907, a couple of years after Wallace's death, and most notably, an epic MGM production in 1959, staring Charlton Heston.

CHAPTER 31

HEADING HOME

Just after 6:00 on Sunday morning, Danny headed down the stairs of the guest house, noting a reassuring deep snore coming from one of the other bedrooms, Eugie had a fine pair of lungs. He would have loved to have been able to see her face, when she discovered how she was getting home.

Jack and Bob were waiting outside by the Oldsmobile ready for the drive to the airport, "Was the room okay?" Bob asked.

"Fantastic, thank you, I slept like a log, and it sounds like Eugie did too."

"It was the first thing we did up after we got here, when Senator Nixon came to stay, to run his western campaign from here. He liked it as well, if only those walls had ears."

Arriving at Bob's jet, Jack skipped up the stairs to deposit his pa's luggage. Danny noticed that it was a brand-new Gulfstream II. He liked to keep up on aviation and knew that it had a range of over 4,000 miles, a ceiling of 45,000 feet and a top speed of about 580 mph, the same as his Sabre in Korea. Eugie was going to love it.

"If it isn't too rude a question Bob, how much did this beauty cost you?"

"To me nothing, the company owns it, it was something like twenty million and some loose change."

"Your Stearman, would you mind if I fly her?" Bob enquired with his pixy grin.

Danny's mind raced for a valid excuse to decline, like insurance or certification, but simply settled on the truth, "Sorry, no, I'm a very bad passenger."

Bob saw a certain look in his eye, and remembered the helicopter incident, so did not push him any further, accepting Danny's need to be in control.

Within an hour they had crossed the border into the High Plains of Texas, in a plane that was not flying as high as its passenger was used to, but Bob was enjoying the view, and the sound of the Stearman's seven-cylinder, eleven-liter rotary engine. They were soon in a descent pattern for the grandly named Lubbock International Airport (an airport that had no direct international flights to anywhere), to refuel for the longer three-hour leg to Roanoke.

"Can I shout you breakfast?" Bob offered.

"That would be nice," Danny accepted.

They were soon in the air-conditioned comfort of the 'VIP Lounge', and Danny was trying his first ever Swiss breakfast, and a chocolate croissant. He could get used to this lifestyle.

Bob opened the conversation in his ever-direct manner, "What ails you, boy?"

"What do you mean?" Danny replied defensively.

"That helicopter malarkey, what devils have you got in your head?"

Bob was even tougher to evade than Eugie Thomas, when he was trying to corral a person, so Danny opened up and shared his story about his time in Vietnam.

Bob could see it was an emotional strain for his new friend, and placed a reassuring brotherly hand on Danny's wrist to console him.

"You know, sometimes the only thing to do, when you fall off a horse, is to get back in the saddle, Son."

"So they say, but I think that horse has bolted," Danny replied, with speedy wit.

"Well here's a thing. Ted Bastian, my pilot, retires at Christmas; his first officer is getting his job. Do you fancy being the new co-pilot? I'll pay for the Gulfstream certification training."

"Are you serious... there are hundreds of ex-military pilots, a lot more current than I am, who would bite your hand off for a chance like that?" Danny replied.

"I never joke when I'm offering a man a job, I don't want hundreds, I just want one, and I don't want my hand bitten off. I like people around me who I can trust, get on with, and who don't suck up to me, you fit the bill."

"The pay is good, and the food is great," Bob added, pointing at Danny's breakfast, in an attempt to seal the deal.

"It's a fantastic opportunity but, back in jets, I don't know." Danny replied reservedly.

"Well, you've got my number, I'll give you a week to decide, and then I'm advertising the job."

With their stomachs, and the aircraft both refueled, at Bob Anderson's expense, they headed back to the Stearman.

"Would you like to take the stick, Bob?" Danny offered.

"Are you sure?"

"Well... I've got to learn to trust someone, it might as well be you, the route is all plotted, heading east – 280."

At about the same time, after an equally hearty breakfast, Eugie and Barbara arrived at Roswell Airport. When she realized what she was flying home in, all Eugie could come up with was, "Oh my."

Barbra laughed, "She sure is pretty, isn't she?"

A distinguished looking gray-haired gentleman framed by the Gulfstream's door beckoned her to walk up the steps to him. She handed her camera to Barbara, and joined the pilot, requesting, "Make sure you get the whole plane in."

The view through the Gulfstream's big windows at 35,000 ft was outstanding. Eugie could really appreciate what a big country she lived in, and felt honored to get to see it from a new perspective. For Barbara Anderson, after spending years jet-setting, it was simply useful time to sort out her makeup for the charity luncheon. No sooner had they got up there, they were descending to Dallas Love Field Airport, where a car was waiting to drive Eugie home.

Not much surprised McKinley those days, but Eugie turning up in a white Rolls Royce Phantom, sitting next to a very glamorous lady, who looked like she had just stepped off a Hollywood movie set, certainly did get into 'surprised' territory, "You're early," was all he could think to say, as the chauffeur held the door for Eugie to elegantly alight from the limousine.

She kissed the young driver on the cheek, to say thank you. He looked just as embarrassed as the two Gulfstream pilots had, half an hour earlier, when receiving the same gratuity.

"Where's Danny?" McKinley questioned.

"He'll be along in a while, then we'll tell you all about our adventure."

As Eugie was landing at DFW, Danny and Bob were two-thirds of the way along their final leg to Roanoke. Danny turned on the two-way, "If you turn a couple of degrees to starboard, and drop to about 200ft, there is something to see."

Bob obliged accordingly, and some old stone buildings appeared ahead of them, "That's Fort Belknap; it was Chisum's first contract out from his Clear Creek ranch, to deliver cattle to the Indian reservations."

"So, about a week and some drive." Bob chipped in to remind Danny that he knew cattle, and that he was good at geography.

Bob landed at Roanoke twice, but the bounce was not too discomforting, and not a bad attempt for someone who had not flown a biplane for years, "Sorry about that," he apologized.

As the two pilots stepped down to the tarmac the Rolls Royce cruised over to them, "Company car?" Danny asked.

"Yes indeed, a bit ostentatious for my taste, but in Dallas you have to play their game, and look the part."

The driver got out to open the door, "Did you get Mrs. Thomas home okay?" Danny queried.

"Oh yes," the chauffeur confirmed, "Eugie is quite the character, I am now an expert on Gulfstreams and Stearmans, and what all the differences are between them," he added with a chuckle.

Bob offered his hand to his new friend to shake goodbye, "One week Son, and then I'm interviewing them 'hand biters'."

"I'll call you one way or the other," Danny promised.

Bob joined his wife in the Rolls, with a parting inspirational quote, which is often incorrectly attributed to John Wayne, "Remember Danny – 'courage is being scared to death, but saddling up anyway'."

CHAPTER 32

BOB JONES

H alf an hour later, Danny's Dodge came barreling up the Thomas' drive, he jumped out and bounced up the veranda steps like it was his own home.

"Lunch?" Eugie offered, just as if it was.

"Oh, yes please."

As they ate, Eugie regaled McKinley with the stories of their trip, the friendly little town named Big Lake, fly-in movie theatres, their new billionaire oilman friend, who would be coming to visit, helicopters and Gulfstream jets. McKinley was suitably impressed by their exploits.

Danny felt obliged to be honest, but waited patiently for his moment. When there was a lull in the conversation he turned to McKinley, who was technically his boss, "Bob Anderson has offered me a job."

"What sort of job?" Eugie interrupted.

"A flying job."

"Crop dusting?" McKinley queried.

"No, his Gulfstream, he wants me to be his new First Officer, the co-pilot."

"Oh my," Eugie exclaimed for the second time that day, in reference to the same aircraft, "that's wonderful."

"But I have a job here; and my crop dusting, I really don't know."

"Well, there is one thing I know Danny, when you look back on life, it is the things that you didn't give a go at that you regret," a regularly quoted Eugie Thomas pearl of worldly wisdom, which seemed more valid than ever, after the exploits of the previous few days.

"I've got a week to decide, I'll think on it some more."

He changed the subject, "What became of Jensie after the war, did she carry on nursing?"

Eugie was tempted to push him on the pilot opportunity, but thought better of it, she had a week to make his mind up for him, so changed tracks with him.

"Well... at the time of the surrender, Harriet was ten and Meady was eight, both had grown up fast during the war. Jensie was a devoted mother; she gave up nursing and worked part-time as a cook and a baker. She made wonderful cakes, and took in sewing work for pin money, or for schooling for the girls. Education has always been important in our family. Ma was really smart, sharp as a nail; she also inherited Grandma's heart and beauty."

"Did Jensie ever meet anyone else after the war, another Charlie Argent?" he pried.

"Nope, John still owned her heart, and I believe she still owned his."

"Last night, you kind of skipped over your ma and pa meeting?"

"So I did, well, that wasn't really for Mr. Anderson's ears. How much do you remember about Daddy?"

"Not much, I was really young when he died; I know everyone looked up to him, my father certainly did. His funeral is one of my earliest memories, I guess I would have been about seven, it was huge."

Eugie walked over to a cabinet and pulled out an old family album, and turned to a page of photos of Bob in his later years.

"He was a very distinguished looking gentleman," Danny confirmed.

"That he was, a handsome man for sure, right to the end."

She turned the page and pulled out a newspaper clipping titled 'Wealthy Negro's Funeral Attended by White Friends,' dated December 28, 1936.

Danny read out the first few paragraphs.

"As many white people as colored gathered in the Baptist church here Sunday to pay final tribute to Bob Jones, 86-year-old Negro citizen and wealthy landowner.

"The crowd of 500 which jammed the white people's church was said to be the largest funeral gathering ever witnessed in the community and the occasion itself unprecedented. Many came from out-of-town.

"A negro preacher from Pilot Point had charge of the services, but the white host pastor, Rev. T. Lynn Stewart, assisted."

"Jesus!" Danny exclaimed, "I can see the writer is trying to be respectful, but the tone is so, so condescending."

"Those were the times. In some ways we were going backwards, it's not that much different now with some folk, they just wouldn't print it like that in a newspaper these days, read the last paragraph."

"Bob Jones, whose full name was John Dolphin Jones, founded the Jones Negro settlement near Roanoke in 1870, several years after he came to Texas from a plantation near Fort Smith, Arkansas. He bought his first 60 acres from his father and at his death his property holdings amounted to about 1,000 acres, including the large two-story house in which he lived."

Eugie spread her hands in the general direction of the corners of the room, "The old Jones Place. That reporter clearly had no idea on acreage, it was twice that size back then, and Dad's full name was John 'Dolford' Jones, not 'Dolphin', no fish in there."

Danny was doing some Math, "Meady would only have been a young teenager in 1870, and how could Bob's father have been a big landowner so soon after the war? Was he already a freeman before emancipation?"

"Leaser Jones was very much a freeman, he was white. Bob's mother, Elizabeth, was a slave, so similar family tree to Meady and me. Leaser had another white wife, Mary Brown, who he left in Fort Smith. He had six children with Mary and then four with Elizabeth, and they all just seemed to get along. My brother, Jinks, was even named after one of Mary's children.

"As it says, Bob bought sixty acres from his father, a little while after the Civil War. He was only just coming out of being a teenager himself, but had a determination to make a go of life; he had a lot in common with Chisum, apart from being a Negro. He was a handsome charmer, the looks of Sidney Poitier, who could dance like Fred Astaire, and boy could daddy dance, that's how he won my mama."

Bob had worked hard building up his spread, but by 1874 he was 24 years old and getting lonely. He had heard that there were pretty girls and great parties to be found in Bonham, a good two days ride away, but no real distance for a virile young man like Bob Jones.

He persuaded a friend to keep him company, and they arrived in town in time for the Saturday night dance. Bob soon noticed Meady, the prettiest girl in town, but played it cool, making a big show of dancing with every other singleton that would oblige him. Which, for such a handsome stranger, was pretty much all of them. Meady noted that he had something of a 'strutting rooster' in his demeanor, and he could raise the roof during the square dances with his hollering.

Eventually there was a slow dance, Bob got Meady in his sights, took a deep breath and asked her to join him on the floor, and naturally she accepted. Afterwards they went outside to cool off, and Meady discovered that her dance partner was a man of many layers. She was impressed that he had land and ambition, she was all but gotten.

They sat and talked until dawn, exchanged addresses and then went their separate ways, but a relationship developed courtesy of the US Post Office Department. There was no postmaster in Roanoke at the time, so each letter took a day's round trip to be delivered or collected from Denton, then more days for it to get to Bonham via Sherman, a very protracted courtship.

The replies became increasingly frequent, and more romantic. Bob plucked up the courage to ride back out to Bonham and propose marriage. Meady accepted and came back as his bride, aged seventeen. They started making babies straight away, with Jim Jones born within the year. They would go on to have ten children by the time Meady was forty.

"Quite a household," Danny noted.

"Yes, a happy healthy household, most of my brothers and sisters lived to a good age. McKinley keeps me young though; did you know that I'm nearly eleven years older than him?" she acknowledged, as her 74-year-old soulmate headed out the door, back to work, nodding in confirmation.

"I've never noticed," Danny replied honestly, as soon as McKinley was out of earshot.

"Yep, this was a happy house, have you ever seen the Henry Fonda movie, Spencer's Mountain? That was pretty much us, except that we were black of course."

He shook his head – he had missed that 1963 motion picture, starring Fonda, Maureen O'Hara and a young James MacArthur.

Footnote: The book that Spencer's Mountain was derived from would be serialized on TV a year later. The TV version centered on a large family, in rural Virginia, surviving the Great Depression and World War Two, titled – 'The Waltons'. Danny would become a big fan, feeling a particular affinity with the mechanically-minded youngest son, Jim-Bob Walton.

CHAPTER 33

BUFFALO SOLDIERS

Engineering and technology had moved on at quite a lick since Chisum moved to New Mexico. The Atchison, Topeka, and Santa Fe railroad had arrived in 1878, making it far easier to get his cattle to market, but bringing in more homesteaders, trying to eke out an existence in the former wilderness.

Instead of single shot carbines, South Springs' gun racks were by then stocked with fifteen-shot, Model 1873 Winchester rifles, which became known as 'The Gun that Won the West'. His top hands had at their disposal, the even more accurate, and desirable 'One of One Thousand' variants. At $100 apiece, the most expensive repeating rifle of the era.

His men's handguns were also loaded with the same .44-40 metal centrefire cartridges as his Winchesters, so no more three-minute reloading times. Killing had become far more efficient in the new Old West.

As the Wild Frontier continued to migrate further west, some of Chisum's old military contracts dried up, but new ones came along to take their place. Early in August 1881, a small detachment of horse soldiers approached the ranch from the west, drawing more attention than was normally devoted to military visitors. They were a rare sight; the senior officer, and all the men were black 'Buffalo Soldiers'. Their insignia identified them as 9th Cavalry, a renowned regiment, which had bravely protected settlers from the Apache since the Civil War.

Danny interrupted, "I was in the 9th Cavalry."

"You were?" Eugie responded, somewhat bewildered.

"In Vietnam, we were called the '1-9 Air Cav', 1st Squadron 9th Cavalry. They nicknamed us 'Headhunters'. The history of the Buffalo Soldiers was held in high esteem in the regiment. Our motto was, 'We Can, We Will', we all had black Stetsons."

"Oh my," Eugie uttered yet again, "it's a very small world... You never did say how come you came out of one war a fighter pilot, and went into another flying a helicopter."

Danny pointed at his eyes, pulled his driving glasses out from his shirt pocket, and shrugged, "These did not go with the skid lid, but I was good enough for choppers, and I'm still good enough for Bob Anderson's Job... And there was a minor incident with an ejection seat," he added, stretching his battle-worn back.

"Carry on," he urged, not wanting further investigation of his aviation career, "the 9th arrived at South Springs, shame Bob isn't around to hear this."

The detachment dismounted, and the officer was taken to see Chisum. He introduced himself as Sergeant George Jordan.

John shook the sergeant's hand, "Welcome to South Springs. I know your name from somewhere."

Jordan had little time, or need, for small talk, so got straight to the point, "I need to buy 200 head of cattle and get them to Fort Tularosa, over Arizona way at your earliest convenience."

"That is rough country, and I remember where I know your name from, you fought the Apache there?"

"I did, but that was just a little skirmish, over a year ago," he replied modestly.

"Why have you had to come 250 miles, for just 200 beeves?" John enquired trying to get to the bottom of the deal.

"Everyone else is too scared of the Indians to supply us, I hear you have more grit than most," Jordan replied, laying down a challenging gauntlet, as he took off his gloves for effect.

"What are you offering?" John replied; equally bluntly, never keen to make the first bid, and risk under-estimating what might be in a buyer's purse.

"$30 a head, $1,000 in advance, me and my men to protect you, there and back, not an offer, fixed price, I've got no authority to negotiate," he stated, not totally honestly.

"Okay, let me meet your men," he sent word for Jimbo to join him.

He addressed the soldiers, "How many of you have worked cattle before?"

The question came as a surprise to the Buffalo Soldiers, who were expecting to guard a herd, not herd it. But John was not going to risk any more men than he had to, on a drive through Apache country, no matter what the price. Four put their hands up. Jimbo walked among them, looking at their hands and demeanor, and held three fingers up. On his way back, he took a closer look at the sergeant, and raised a fourth finger, despite Jordan not claiming any such aptitude.

"Okay, you have your cattle, Sergeant Jordan, make your men comfortable here, we head west in two days."

Later, he gathered his own men together, "We have a drive to a new customer, who I'm keen to make a regular one, but it's through Apache country. We've met Indians before, but they don't come much meaner than the Chiricahua Apache, there is no buying them off with a few cows, so it's volunteers only on this one, with a $50 bonus, I'll lead the drive."

Jimbo and Charlie Argent raised their hands.

"Jimbo you are in, Charlie I need you here while Bungy and Pitser are away, sorry. I need four more."

After some thought about what they could do with $50, Mac Macleod, Kentucky and two other hands signed on for the drive.

The first day wasn't quite what the soldiers were expecting, something was missing, namely cattle. The second day was spent rounding them up from John's north-western pasture, thirty miles from the ranch house.

By the third day they were out of Chisum territory, pushing the beeves along the Hondo valley, they camped near San Patricio that night, about five miles south of Lincoln.

Jimbo was both foreman and cook on the Fort Tularosa drive. The lamb stew, which he served up for the first few nights, got no complaints from the hands or soldiers, who would have to suffer the monotony of beefsteak and beans for the rest of the three-week drive.

George Jordan opened the campfire conversation, "Those Winchesters that your men carry – are they what I'm thinking they are?"

"Possibly," John replied, motioning for Jimbo to go fetch his rifle.

Jimbo obliged, handing it over like it was a newborn baby.

"One of One Thousand, ain't she a thing of beauty," Jordan complimented, "that would be half a year's pay for me," he mused, while stroking the Winchester's delicate engraving.

John wasn't one for bragging, either on behalf of himself or his men, and always looked for a positive in another man's position, "Well, at least you can fit a bayonet to your Springfield if you run out of bullets."

"Or when it jams, I can use it as a club," Jordan replied with a chuckle. Jamming was an infamous problem with the army issue

Springfields, especially when loaded with cheap copper-cased cartridges.

John's mind drifted back to memories of listening to firearms banter on his Eagle Lake drive with William Wallace, nearly three decades before. He never imagined that he would become the subject of gun-envy, the world had surely turned. The thought struck him that he would have enjoyed the company of his old mentor on this drive.

He took the opportunity to probe into Sergeant Jordan's notorious Indian battle, "I take it you did not get too many jams at Fort Tularosa, fighting with the Apache."

"Thankfully not... Victorio, he was a nasty piece of work, in truth we got lucky," Jordan replied with his usual innate modesty.

In early May, the previous year, Sergeant Jordan's commander had received a tip-off regarding a potential attack by Chiricahua Apache, and ordered Jordan to lead a detachment of 25 soldiers from K-Troop, to protect the settlers near the abandoned Fort Tularosa. On arrival his men worked around the clock to reinforce the fort, and build a stockade for the townsfolk to secure their livestock in.

A day later Victorio turned up with 100 warriors, but they were spotted in time to get the settlers safely within the confines of the fort. George's detachment killed a number of Victorio's men, and managed to hold off the onslaught, until reinforcements arrived to run the Apache off, with no casualties among the cavalry or settlers.

"What happened to Victorio?" John asked.

"He got away, but the damned Mexicans murdered him a few months later."

"You sound sad about that?"

"Not sad," Jordan replied, "just respectful, he was a brave chief, just trying to protect his way of life, it just happened that it got in the way of your way of life."

John was curious why Jordan would use the word 'your' rather than 'our'. Clearly, he was referring to the pioneers' belief in 'Manifest destiny', but wondered why Jordan had excluded himself from that concept. He decided to let the subject ride.

"Well, at least we won't have to worry about meeting up with him," John observed.

"Nope, Nana is chief now. He is at least eighty years old and half-blind.

"But, he's the cruelest Apache you could ever cross sabers with. He's spent a long time learning how to hate – nothing for you to worry about at all, Mr. Chisum."

CHAPTER 34

CARRIZO CANYON

John, his men, and the soldiers continued pushing the herd northwest, avoiding the new settlements that had sprung up over the previous decade. The Buffalo Soldiers had soon picked up how to herd beeves, a skill which would keep some of them in full employment when they left the army. Late that afternoon John and Sergeant Jordan broke off from the herd to check in at Fort Stanton, one of John's regular customers, since Murphy had been out of the picture, to get any updates on the Apache situation.

They rejoined the herd in the morning, with a further detachment of Buffalo Soldiers from the 10th Cavalry in tow, led by a white officer, Captain Charles Parker, to offer added protection ahead of the herd. They had got word that Nana's band had raided a settlement, on one of the late Lawrence Murphy's old ranches, near Carrizo Springs, too close to the drive's route to Fort Tularosa for comfort.

A couple of days later they approached the area in question. The soldiers and hands were on heightened alert, looking out and listening for trouble, which wasn't long on coming. That afternoon faint gunshots could be heard in the distance ahead.

The source was almost certainly Parker's detachment. The cavalry and hands abandoned the herd to gallop west. The shots got louder as they approached a deep canyon, where Jordan spotted Parker and his men, pinned down behind some rocks on the first bend, with their dead horses scattered along the canyon floor, clearly an ambush.

Jordan turned to Chisum, "You and your men wait here; me and my men are taking to the high ground. Shoot anything that comes out of that canyon, that isn't wearing blue."

"Take Jimbo, and his Winchester with you," Chisum offered.

Jordan nodded and cantered off.

After a while, the pace of firing accelerated for about fifteen minutes, then abruptly stopped, followed by a shout of, "Chisum!" echoing out of the canyon, followed by a chorus of galloping hooves.

About forty Apaches emerged from the canyon, Ken shot one and Mac got another, there were too many of them to pursue, so Chisum instructed, "Let 'em go."

They trotted into the canyon to find a very grateful Captain Parker, but with two dead men, an equal number of dead Apache and nine dead horses.

John was distracted from the carnage by a call from the ridge, "Mr. Chisum, you need to get up here."

John galloped around and up to where Jordan was calling from, with Mac following.

"NO!" was all he could utter at the sight before him.

Jimbo was laying with his head resting on a rock; a medic was doing his best to stem the flow of a gushing stomach wound.

Chisum jumped off his horse and knelt by his dear friend, holding his hand.

"Sorry Mr. Chisum, I was too big a target."

He was clearly in agony, the medic administered morphine to ease the big man's pain.

An hour later he spoke again, "I think I'll be signing off now boss. There is something in my pockets that I'd like you to keep, and something else that I'd like to keep with me, you'll know," his last words as he passed away, without yelling out once to acknowledge his pain, or his anger.

John sat for a while, just looking at his old friend, in disbelief that he was gone. Then, as instructed went through his pockets, and found two envelopes. The older looking one had the crusty remains of an important looking wax seal. He took out the letter inside, read it, sighed and smiled, then returned it from whence it came. While no one was watching he took out his Barlow knife, and stole a lock of Jimbo's graying hair.

John found the only two shovels they had between them and started digging. Jordan picked up the other one to help. A peculiar unspoken bond developed between the two men as they quietly spent a couple of hours digging a suitable grave, in hard ground for a big, big man. Neither would let anyone give them a break, an understandable commitment from Chisum, but puzzling behavior from a man who hardly knew his friend.

Eight men lay Jimbo to rest in his grave. Chisum said some kind words over him and then pulled Jimbo's other envelope from his pocket. Choked back his tears, and read.

"A Soldier's Lament by Edward James Thomas Brown.

"From England to New Mexico the road has been so long. Through wars and droughts and gunfights, I have soldiered on.

Cows and horses break your bones, but only people break your heart.

For most I've shared my trails with, I've sweet memories, so where to start.

"I never saw a black man until I got off the Galveston boat. I couldn't understand them being treated worse than dogs. I hope that you remember me as a man who was fair with folk.

I don't care about riches or color so long as you work hard, and can take a joke.

"Most I fought and worked aside I remember with respect. I may not have said much in life, but know I gave a heck. I must be dead for this to be read, but please don't be too sad.

If I've lived my life as well as hoped, I'll be watching you from the other side."

The soldiers, who did not know Jimbo, nodded their heads in appreciation of his sweet words. Those who knew him better shook their heads in amazement that he would have poetry in him, questioning how little they knew of their friend. John kept his own thoughts to himself.

"So, he was a military man?" Jordan queried softly.

"Yes, he was, Mexican war and before," John replied.

Jordan called out commands, "'tension... Bugler, Taps for a brother."

Cavalry and cattlemen alike, be they veterans or not, stood to attention in two smart lines next to the grave. A soldier slow-marched away from the detachment, turned, wet his lips and played 'Lights Out' or 'Taps' as it was known among the ranks. The haunting melody echoed around the canyon, as a beautiful sunset descended in the west.

As the bugler lowered his instrument Chisum turned to Jordan and said, "Thank you," while his men proceeded to gently cover their lost comrade in dirt and rocks.

"No problem sir, he deserved no less. Parker's fallen will get the same respect when we get them back to Fort Stanton."

"What happened?" John had to ask.

"We were close on losing the battle; Nana's band had killed two of Parker's men. Jimbo changed position to get a better shot but was too slow, was left exposed and got shot himself. He threw me his gun and I got those two," pointing at the Indians, still dead, on the canyon floor, "that changed the tide. I'm so sorry, Mr. Chisum, I let you down, I was here to protect you and your men, not the other way around."

"What happens, happens, it was me who sent him up there with you... I think he would have wanted to die with his boots on... It would have been his birthday next month, we will throw a party for him when we get home," John added affectionately.

He picked up Jimbo's Winchester and passed it to the sergeant, "I'm guessing you could make good use of this, Sir."

When Captain Parker got around to writing his report on the 'incident', the civilian contribution to the Battle of Carrizo Canyon would be somewhat brushed over. Probably because losing one of the people the cavalry were supposed to be protecting, in a battle he had got them in to, would not have sounded too good in dispatches, or have inspired much faith among the settlers.

Eugie passed Jimbo's poem to Danny, the writing was scratchy but still readable.

"Damn it Jimbo!" Danny exclaimed, "I liked him."

It struck her as curious that Danny had developed such affection for a man who he had not known of a couple of weeks before, was not family, and who had been dead for nearly a century. She resolved that it must mean that she told the story well, Grandma would be proud.

"What was in the letter from Queen Victoria, it had to have come from her?"

"It was addressed to 'Teddy' and signed 'Drina', but I don't know what she wrote, no one will ever know, that did go to their graves."

"Damn... did they finish the drive?"

"They had to, Chisum never backed out of a deal. They had to get Parker, his horseless cavalry, and dead back to Fort Stanton first, which slowed them down by a couple of days. Then they rounded up the herd, and rode on to Fort Tularosa without any more trouble, worth speaking of."

"And the cavalry got them home?"

"Oh yes indeed, Sergeant Jordan insisted on leading the detachment himself. He wasn't letting Chisum, or the hands, out of his sight until he deposited them safely back at South Springs."

There was one extra soldier on that return trip, a stonemason named Corporal Augustus Giles. Jordan seconded him, with the excuse that work needed doing at Fort Stanton, but first he had work in mind at Carrizo Canyon. A suitable rough stone was picked out, which would not attract too much attention from thieves, and an afternoon was devoted to its dressing and carving.

On it was inscribed:

LIEUTENANT

EDWARD JAMES THOMAS 'JIMBO' BROWN

1816 – 1881

BELOVED FRIEND

A week later, there was a big party at South Springs to celebrate their safe return and Jimbo's life, but John's toast, "To Teddy Brown, God save the Queen," went safely over the heads of all present, as it should have.

Later, John sat at his desk to write a very formal letter, to a very important lady in London. In which he offered his heart-felt condolences regarding the loss of her former bodyguard, and assured her that he had died a hero, was buried with military

227

honors, and had remained an English patriot to the last. He carefully inserted the letter into a handmade envelope, along with the memento he had retrieved with his Barlow knife in Carrizo Canyon.

John's letter arrived at Buckingham Palace a month or so later. The recipient was pleasantly surprised to learn that her old 'friend' had not died nearly four decades before, as she had been informed, but shed tears to learn of his recent heroic demise.

She tied Edward's lock of hair to one of her own, lit a candle, cuddled a pillow tight, and explored fond memories from what felt like a lifetime ago, and mostly was.

Losing Jimbo had a profound effect on John. He had viewed him in the same manner that he had his father, as indestructible, and then he was gone. He could not shake the guilt that his friend had died following his orders. The Fort Tularosa drive would be the last one that Chisum would ever lead personally. The following spring, he decided he needed to get away for a while, so left his brothers in charge, while he headed east to explore a long-overdue, latest indulgence of the wealthy – a vacation.

Footnote: Sergeant Jordan did eventually get acknowledged for his valor at Tularosa and Carrizo, nearly a decade later, when the Indian wars had pretty much ended, and the Wild Frontier was no more. He was awarded the Medal of Honor, making him the most decorated Buffalo Soldier of his era.

His citation read: 'While commanding a detachment of 25 men at Fort Tularosa, N. Mex., repulsed a force of more than 100 Indians. At Carrizo Canyon, N. Mex., while commanding the right of a detachment of 19 men, on 12 August 1881, he stubbornly held his ground in an extremely exposed position and gallantly forced back a much superior number of the enemy, preventing them from surrounding the command.'

CHAPTER 35

A MAN ABOUT THE HOUSE

Each time John stepped off the train at Bonham, the town was noticeably busier, and more sophisticated. The population had quadrupled, to nearly 2,000 souls, since he'd moved Jensie back there, over eighteen years before.

He normally rented a horse while in town, but was planning to stay for a while, so went for a pretty one-horse buggy. Jensie was out when he arrived at her place, he let himself in, noting how tidy she kept the rambling house, for someone living on her own, not expecting guests.

Harriet had married four years earlier and moved out, she was now Mrs. Cloud, and had a three-year-old daughter named Margaret, who John had never met. Harriet was an independent soul, who was always away somewhere when he visited.

He deposited his luggage in Jensie's bedroom, put the red roses that he had bought in town in a vase, found a comfortable chair, and fell asleep.

He was woken by a kiss on his forehead, followed by a fond cuddle, as Jensie fell into his lap. The smell of her skin was still as intoxicating as the first time they had held each other. She was 48 by then, but still looked like a young woman, and a beautiful young woman at that.

She stroked his hair, "Hey, you're starting to go gray."

"Could you still love an old man?"

Jensie decided that actions would speak louder than words, so led him to the stairs.

She stopped at the staircase and turned, "There is one thing you should know, I can't make babies anymore."

"Oh good," John replied, with a wink, and chased her up to her bedroom.

As they lay in a post-coital embrace John brought Jensie up to date. She was mortified to hear of the loss of Jimbo, but John did bring brighter family news with him. Sallie was finally a mother. She had married John's German bookkeeper, William Robert, early in 1880 and became pregnant almost immediately, but sadly their son died at birth. However, being the tough pioneer woman that she was, Sallie got straight back in the saddle, and now had a bouncing baby boy, named John Ernest.

"I do miss the sound of children," Jensie admitted, "this house has got lonely since the girls have gone, I rattle around it, and spend half my life either cleaning it, or walking backwards and forwards from town to it."

"I've had thoughts on that, get dressed," John requested.

He drove her into the centre of town, and pointed at a brick-built town house, with a bay-fronted shop on the ground floor, and a 'French Flat' above it. It had a sign up, advertising that the building was available to rent.

"How about I set you up in business here, flower shop, clothes shop, bakery, anything you like, you can live above, and it's just four blocks to the railroad station. I'll sell the old house, and bank the money for you to rent this place, or buy it if they are willing."

Jensie did not hesitate, "Yes, yes, yes," she replied, giving him a big hug and a kiss.

It turned out that the owner was up for selling, 'at the right price', so the townhouse and shop were Jensie's. She had grown tired of the cruel hours required of a baker, and did not want to upset her old boss by going into competition, so settled on what else she knew; flowers, clothes, haberdashery, and taking in repairs. She hoped that Harriet might agree to work for her, and keep it all in the family, so the shop was named 'Miss Chisums'.

It appeared that Miss Chisum had acquired some of John's business acumen, she had chosen a good all-seasons mix of trades, rather than put all her eggs in one basket; he was impressed, and very proud.

While the shop was being remodeled, and Jensie's furniture was moved across town, they needed somewhere to stay. Yet again Harriet and her husband were out of town, so they decided to visit Meady and Bob. They got a train to Sherman, and then took the new southerly leg of the Texas and Pacific down to Roanoke.

"They stayed here?" Danny interrupted.

Eugie had to get her bearings, the house had been rebuilt after a fire in the 1940s, "Yes, they would have stayed in the bedroom that would have been above here," she calculated pointing at the ceiling.

"Talking of bedrooms, do you want to stay for dinner, and sleep-over tonight; I have a job for you tomorrow morning."

"Can I give that room a go," Danny almost begged, pointing at the ceiling.

"Sure, let me know if there are any ghosts, a couple of people have died in that bed."

Eugie picked up the story, "In the end they stayed here for two whole weeks, and it turned out to be one of the happiest fortnights of Jensie's life."

She had her man with her, and got to play with her grandchildren every day. Meady even taught John the skill he had failed to learn as her father, how to change Virgie's cotton napkins, all thanks to possibly the greatest technological advance of the 19th century – the safety pin. John loved the simplicity of the Jones' lifestyle and the bustling family home. It turned out that he was good grandpa material; he delighted in getting down on his knees to play horsey with Jim and Alice, Eugie's eldest siblings.

John and Bob became firm friends, John would help him on the farm during the day, and they would spend their evenings before supper sitting on the veranda, smoking and putting the world to rights. Bob was still a relatively young man, but John admired the wisdom, beyond his years, which he revealed, his daughter had chosen well.

John's stories of New Mexico, the Apache and massive herds were like a different world to Bob, the Wild Frontier had pretty much moved on when he'd arrived in Texas, from Arkansas, but he loved hearing the stories from those who came before him.

All good things must come to an end, and on a Monday in April, Bob drove them to the station for the trip back to Bonham. But Jensie was as excited as ever, she was going on a train, then she had her new home to look forward to. John, despite being widely travelled, was also still in awe of the railroads. Being able to travel 25 miles in comfort in an hour, instead of a day in the saddle, remained a mind-blowing achievement to him. He loved to look out of the window, and time how far they had travelled with his pocket watch.

By mid-afternoon they were stepping off the train for the short walk to Jensie's new abode. As they arrived, she noticed two naked papier-mâché mannequins in the bay window.

"Oh my lord," she uttered, "this could be in Paris, France," Not that she had any idea what a Parisian boutique would look like.

They went inside, and she found the freshly painted 'Miss Chisums' sign, that John had secretly ordered, Jensie burst into tears.

"What's wrong?" John asked.

"Nothing, absolutely nothing, I'm so happy John, thank you," she hugged him.

They dived into homemaking the flat, like a seasoned married couple, enjoying each other's company, with love and laughter filling their rooms. John wore a mask of anonymity while in Bonham, at last Jensie did not have to fain dispassion when they were out together. No one knew who her man was, though John did introduce himself as the notorious 'Pat Garrett' to one overly-inquisitive neighbor.

Back in New Mexico, after the Lincoln County War, people who did not know them well often mistook Chisum for Garrett. They both had an air of authority about them, and a taste for sharp suits, long moustaches and nice cigars. Needless to say, the neighbor kept his nose out of their affairs thereafter.

Later that month, while they were eating lunch, there was a knock on the door. Jensie answered and returned to the table, with a troubled look on her face.

"What's wrong?" John asked.

She handed him a Western Union telegram addressed as 'Care of Jensie Chisum', they seldom brought good news.

John opened it with trepidation, read it and handed it to Jensie.

She did not need to read it; the look on his face said everything. As was always inevitable, their exquisite bubble had just burst.

"I guess you've got the telegram," Danny enquired rhetorically.

"Of course," Eugie passed him an envelope.

Danny opened it with equal trepidation, and read it.

'John,

'Rustling is out of hand you need to find a new way to deal with it.

'Get home soonest.

'James.'

"Damn!" Danny stated, "couldn't they work it out without him, was she never going to get a break?"

CHAPTER 36

CATTLE RUSTLERS

Another thing about 25 miles per hour trains is that they gave lots of relaxed thinking time when crossing a state. When John got off at Pecos the following afternoon, to be met by Mac leading his favorite mare, which he had bred from the long-departed Jennie, he had a plan. It was time for him to get back in the saddle again.

After the cozy home comforts of Fannin County, the five day ride up to South Springs felt like going back in time. John loved the wildness of New Mexico, but was chronically missing Jensie. But, by the time he got to the ranch he was mostly reacclimatized and ready for business. Bonham seemed like a distant, but very happy memory from a different world.

The influx of migrants to New Mexico weren't all hard-working farmers and ranchers. There was a notable increase in the criminal element coming into the territory. Rustling was almost as bad as the last days of the Concho-Colorado, but John had no plans to move on this time.

One rustler, who John suspected had sympathies with the old Murphy-Dolan faction from the Lincoln County War, was so bold that he regularly posted Jinglebob ears through the post box at his store. It was the final straw in persuading him that he needed a 24-hour guard at his premises.

When John arrived at the ranch house, he found James sitting at his desk. He jumped up to relinquish the throne to his brother. John got comfortable and asked for numbers.

"While you've been away, I reckon we've lost 150 calves, getting on for fifty cows and steers, and two bulls."

John interrupted, "Not the ones from Kentucky?"

"Afraid so, we're not catching anyone at it, so I'm guessing they are working at night. Whoever they are, they are covering their tracks well."

The quantity of cattle they were losing, as a percentage of his herd, wasn't as bad as John had expected, but did add up to a lot of money. Having his bulls rustled was a painful affront to his breeding program, almost certainly taken out of spite, as they could not be sold on. More significantly there was a principle at stake, 'you don't steal from a Chisum!' It had to stop.

John's plan was ridiculously simple, but as his father had taught him, 'sometimes you need to be away from the coalface to see the coal'.

"Okay, if we are going to catch rustlers, we need to think like them, if they are stealing at night, we need to be out at night. I want our best nighthawks out on patrol, I want every man to mark up on a map where they have ridden, and put a groove in their horseshoes so we know what tracks are ours, and what aren't.

"Everyone is banned from town until we nail this, if we have a spy, they aren't going to get the chance to let on what we are doing, but don't tell the men that we might have one. Any tracks leaving our land will be the ones to follow. Tell the hands that they 'just need to bring 'em back alive and I'll make sure they never rustle again'."

James was surprised by the phrase, 'I'll make sure they never rustle again.' It wasn't in John's nature to exercise vindictive Frontier Justice, and since the Lincoln County War the judge, Warren Bristol, had adopted a no tolerance attitude to cattle and horse thieves. If John simply let the sheriff deal with anyone they caught, they would almost certainly hang.

The hands were not overly enamored by the going to town ban, but John had nurtured a culture among his men, whereby they felt that stealing from him was stealing from them, so they accepted it.

In reality John thought it unlikely that there was an insider involved in the rustling, but he had learned not to take anything for granted. His top hands had weeded out a few bad apples over the years, mostly waddies passing through, and he had not hesitated in firing them.

John's approach was successful; within the week a couple of rustlers were caught red-handed, and brought to the ranch. The hands gathered to see how the boss was going to 'make sure that they never did it again'.

John appeared from his office.

"So, you have been stealing my beeves."

"We had no choice, we needed the money," one stated.

"Men always have choices; you just made the wrong ones. But I'm going to give you another choice. I can let Judge Bristol decide what to do with you, or I can deal with it here, and let you go."

The question didn't need much consideration, "Here Mr. Chisum," one replied.

"Sir," the other added.

John walked into the barn, and appeared with a whip in one hand, and some rags in the other.

"Okay, strip and bend over that hitching rail."

The rustlers preferred a whipping over a hanging, so did as they were told without complaint, but the hands, particularly the former slaves, were shocked that their mild-mannered boss would inflict such a barbaric, brutal punishment.

"Blindfold and hold 'em," John instructed.

The suspense, waiting for the first lash, was torture for the summarily convicted men. But they could not see John going back to the barn, or what he returned with. The laughter from the ranch hands seemed mercilessly cruel.

John cracked the whip in the air, and the thief on the left heard his partner-in-crime scream out in agony, he sobbed at the certainty that his back was also about to be peeled open. But instead, he felt the lesser pain of his butt burning, accompanied by a smell familiar to any cattleman.

"Throw some cold water on 'em," John commanded.

Their blindfolds were removed, so that they could see the method of their punishment, a small horse-branding iron.

"Those brands mean I own your souls now, you can explain how you got 'em to your wives or boyfriends any way you wish, but if you are caught rustling again, or any of my men find you in town, you'll be undressing again, and explaining it to the sheriff."

The icing on the cake of John's unique form of summary justice, was watching the two rustlers trying to find some comfortable way of getting back on their horses.

John only had to repeat this ritual humiliation once more, and the torrent of rustling eased to a trickle. After a couple of weeks, he lifted the going to town ban, but he kept up the night patrols, a decision that he would come to deeply regret.

Kentucky and Mac rode back into the ranch a week later, leading four horses with bodies tied across them.

Chisum was called.

Ken untied the first body, and laid it gently on the ground.

"NO!" John exclaimed, for the second time in just under a year, it was Elijah.

"Someone go and get Sonny... and get Frances."

Frances appeared from the house, saw Elijah and burst into tears. Sonny came running over, but Frances stopped him in his tracks and held him tight.

"What happened?" Chisum asked.

"We were creeping up on three men," Mac explained, "turned out there was a fourth we'd missed, and he got Elijah, sorry Mr. Chisum."

Ken picked up the story, "I got two with my Winchester, Mac got the third."

"You did well to stay alive, any way of identifying the one that got away."

"It was pretty dark, but he's got dark hair, a big moustache, a scar on his face and a lame hand," Mac replied.

"How did you spot a lame hand in the dark?"

"I shot him in it, it was holding this," he pulled a blood-stained Colt Army out of his saddle bag.

Elijah was buried that afternoon in the family plot. John was grateful that there were no family members in there yet, but some of the men in there felt like they were, including the one he had just lain to rest.

After the funeral he gathered Mac and Ken together, "We'll set off for Lincoln in the morning, and talk to Garrett".

By the second day they were grateful that the wind was ahead of them, and that they had a long rope to lead the rustlers' horses with, as their cargo was getting a mite odorous, even their horses were snorting in objection.

Garrett identified one of the men as 'Sanders', a member of outlaw John Kinney's gang. Kinney was a name that John remembered from the Lincoln County Wars.

Sanders had a $100 bounty on his head, which Ken reluctantly accepted, seeing it as being close to blood money for a lost friend.

Mac described the man he shot.

"Yep, that would be Kinney. When he's not rustling around here, he operates with Selman's mob down Las Cruces way in Doña Ana County. He got that scar when Billy Bonney shot him in the face in the battle at McSween's. There's $200 on him, any of you want to be deputized, and see if you can get him?"

Mac and Ken put their hands up.

John interrupted the deputizing, "No, there's been enough killing, my men chase cattle, not outlaws, but I will raise that bounty by $1000."

Mac did wonder what the difference was between shooting rustlers on the ranch, and going after them, but the boss was the boss.

The rustling immediately stopped. Anyone who would take on the Kinney gang, or strip you, then horse-brand your ass, was not to be meddled with.

"Did they ever catch him?" Danny asked.

"Yep, John got a visit from a bounty hunter the following year, collecting his $1,000. He had a letter from the Sheriff in La Mesilla, Doña Ana County, stating that Kinney was in custody, and being tried for the murder of two soldiers, as well as rustling."

Footnote: There wasn't enough evidence to proceed with the murder charges, but Kinney was found guilty of rustling. He either had a good lawyer or a soft judge, as he wasn't hung. But he was fined $500, and sentenced to five years in the Kansas State Penitentiary.

John Kinney was lauded as a fine example of the correctional system doing its job. He was released after three years, turned his back on his outlaw ways, and joined the army, to fight in Cuba during the Spanish-American War. But his epiphany wasn't going to bring those he murdered back to life.

CHAPTER 37

A LUMP IN THE NIGHT

After the visit from the bounty hunter, John decided it was time to pick up where he had left off, and get back to Bonham.

Getting on the train at Pecos he recognized an old friend, John Horton Slaughter, playing poker with a couple of other smart looking gentlemen. The two Johns had done business prior to the Lincoln County War, and used to seal their deals with a poker game, often well into the night, Slaughter was a mean bluffer. He spotted John and invited him to join them. It turned out that the other two were also cattlemen, who John knew of by name and reputation, but not as well as they knew his.

Such chance encounters were always useful to keep abreast of what was going on in the wider world of their business, a business that was changing rapidly and dramatically. The old Texas cattle trails had pretty much died out, due to barbed wire enclosures and the very mode of transportation that they were riding. There was no need to push cows north to Kansas, when there was a stockyard in Fort Worth. With a few exceptions the open ranges had been relegated to history, the golden age of the epic cattle drive was all but at an end.

In the conversation between poker rounds, it turned out that one of the men wouldn't be getting off the train with him and Slaughter at Fort Worth, he had another day ahead of him getting all the way up to Kansas City, Missouri. He pulled up his sleeve to reveal a huge lump which he was going to have removed by the 'brilliant surgeons' at the modern, new St. Luke's hospital. His deformity was a disgusting sight, but at least John knew that there were no cards hidden up his sleeve, at least not that one.

By the time they went their separate ways, Slaughter was nearly $400 ahead, $150 of it from John. He chastised himself for his stupidity, as he always lost to his old friend, and never did work out if he was a cheat, or simply a good card player. Poker never was one of Chisum's skills.

John liked to sit on the left side of the train from Fort Worth up to Sherman, so that when they got north of Denton, he could look northwest, across the flatlands of the North Central Plains, and see all the way to his old Clear Creek ranch, twelve miles away. After his conversation with Slaughter and associates, it struck him how far they had come from the days of Comanche raids and the 'bird table'. He considered how different his business could have been if the railroad had come along thirty years earlier, but then thought about all the undesirables it would have brought with it. He concluded that everything had its time and place, and that the world was no doubt unfolding as it most likely should.

At Sherman he changed trains again to head east for the three short stops to Bonham. He could not wait to be back in Jensie's arms, and was soon enjoying her fond embrace, catching up on the latest news.

Jensie's life was busy again, Harriet had agreed to go into business with her, and Miss Chisums was doing really well, bolstered by Bonham's ongoing growth and popularity. The biggest irony was that where Jensie used to work to get tutoring for her girls, folk were by then coming to her to learn handicrafts and pattern making. She even taught at the town's Masonic Female Institute from time to time. Miss Chisum was a pillar of the Fannin County community.

As they lay together under the gaslight that night, Jensie teased him that he was getting even grayer. She gently put her hand around his neck to pull him towards her for a kiss, then paused and whispered, "Oh."

"Oh, what?" John queried.

"You have a lump."

"Oh, that's just a spot, not eating the right food; I need some healthy Jensie Chisum cooking."

"No John, that is a lump, we're going to the doctor in the morning!" she commanded.

He did as he was told, and the doctor prodded and poked, "Umm, it could be something, could be nothing. Have you had lumps anywhere before?"

"Not that I've noticed."

"Well, keep an eye on it; if it's just fat it'll go away, if it gets any bigger find someone smarter than an old sawbones like me to cut it out."

"Like the surgeons at St. Luke's in Kansas City?" John queried exercising his recently acquired knowledge.

"That would be the place for sure, full of Eastern geniuses."

"John agreed to the plan, but was not overly concerned."

His time in Bonham flew too fast; as fall was turning to winter it was time to get back on the Texas and Pacific heading back west. But at least he had got to catch up with Harriet and meet her daughter for the first time.

Jensie walked him to the station, they were early despite knowing that the train was always late, but it gave a chance to sit and play their favorite game of people-watching.

Jensie pointed at a man, "Banker."

John nodded towards the coy woman next to the 'Banker', "His lover?"

Jensie pointed out another, "He's a gambler."

"Not too good at it, looking at those shoes."

They could play the game for hours from their bubble, but as ever it always burst. The train arrived, disappointingly only an hour late.

"All aboard!" was called by the conductor.

"Try to come back sooner," Jensie begged.

They shared the fondest embrace that they felt they could get away with, against the background of the prevailing Victorian morality that was 'civilizing' the town. John stepped up into the carriage and reluctantly waved goodbye, blowing Jensie a kiss.

This time, by the time he got to South Springs re-acclimatization had failed, he was homesick for another place.

By spring his lump had not gone away, it had grown to the size of an egg and it hurt, by July it was twice the size and really hurt, Kansas City beckoned. The quickest route from South Springs to Missouri was north to Las Vegas, New Mexico, and on to the Atchison, Topeka and Santa Fe railroad, eastbound through Colorado and Kansas.

On the third morning of his train journey, they pulled into the infamous Dodge City. John got off the train to buy a newspaper. On his return two marshals were bustling their handcuffed charge onto his carriage. One of them, a black man, with a fine moustache, dropped his bag. John picked it up, and returned it to its owner.

When the lawmen had got their prisoner settled and secured, the recipient of the returned luggage walked up the carriage and sat opposite John. He rubbed his moustache and chin in a thoughtful manner, then looked deep into John's eyes.

John was getting uncomfortable with the silent invasion of his personal space, "If you are looking for a criminal, I'm not your man," he assured.

"Do you still play a good game of chess, Mr. Chisum?"

"Do I know you?"

"You know me, could be safe to say that you inspired me. Paris, Texas, thirty years ago, shooting contest won by Bigfoot Wallace, can you place me yet?"

"Bass Reeves?"

"Yes'um, Sir."

"My God it's good to see you, you've kind of all grown up."

"Well, you've kind of all grown old."

"So, you are a Marshal now?"

"Deputy US Marshal, for Judge Parker in Fort Smith."

"The 'Hanging Judge'?"

"That's the one."

"I thought you fellows were cleaning up the Indian Territory badlands?"

"That we are, but sometimes I have to clean up a bit further, when the dirt hears I'm coming, and runs. Been chasing that murderer for six months on and off," he stated, pointing over his shoulder.

Chisum attempted to bring Bass up to date with his own life, over the previous three decades, but it turned out that Reeves pretty much knew of all of it. Including his Brother Jeff's altercation in Paris, which he had been witness to, "The other fella had it coming," was Bass' take on that incident, an interesting perspective for a lawman.

Bass picked up the bag that John had retrieved for him and pulled out a small travel chess set, "Would you like a game, for old time's sake?"

"I sure would!" John replied enthusiastically.

As they approached Halstead, Bass' colleague pointed out that it was their stop, to change trains for Fort Smith, "Sit down, we'll get the train at Emporia," Bass instructed with authority, determined to finish the game, which he won, with equal authority.

As they approached Emporia, Bass stood up and offered John his hand to shake.

"You truly did inspire me John Chisum, not just that day with the gun, but by the way you lived your life, your kindness and your honesty. And I know you never betrayed the trust I placed in you, with the things I told you. Good luck in Kansas with that lump, I'm sure you can afford the best doctors, and rightly so."

"Thank you Baasaewi; that is music to an old man's ears. Please try to stay safe my friend."

"Just call me 'Bass', I'm a proud American now."

Bass stepped off the train, and John was left with an overwhelming sense of pride, that in some small way he had contributed towards the nurturing, of the incredible fellow, who he had spent the previous few hours with.

Kansas City was the biggest metropolis that John had ever visited, with a sprawling population of nearly 100,000 souls. He could not begin to imagine what New York must have been like with over two million. He found St. Luke's and it was just as described, 'modern' and staffed by brilliant geniuses.

The surgeon was pretty sure that the lump was cancerous and scheduled an operation within the week. It was removed, and John was soon pain-free again. The surgeon suggested spending some time at Eureka Springs, a getaway town for the rich down in Arkansas. The waters were reputed to be 'invigorating and health restoring'.

To John that sounded like the advice you would expect from a snake oil salesman, rather than a top modern medical practitioner. If he was going to go anywhere to recuperate it would be to his personal oasis in Bonham, but he had far too much to be doing in New Mexico to consider another vacation, whatever the justification.

Footnote: Bass Reeves had escaped from slavery during the Civil War, and took Wallace's advice, headed north and lived with friendly Indians. He never learned to read or write but had a talent for picking up native languages, an invaluable gift in the Indian Territory.

After the war he settled down as a farmer in Arkansas, married and went on to have 11 children. When Isaac Parker became the federal judge for the Indian Territory, he appointed James Fagan as his Marshal, who recruited 200 deputies, who became the stuff of legends, in both fact and fiction. Including the Rooster Cogburn character Charles Portis created in his book, 'True Grit', who John Wayne went on to play in his award-winning movie of the same name.

Over a 32-year career as a Marshal Reeves was reputed to have arrested over 3,000 felons, in the Indian/Oklahoma Territory. Including one of his own sons, Bennie, who had murdered his wife. Bass was a master of disguise, including dressing up as a woman on occasions, which helped him avoid ever getting injured, though he did have his hat and belt shot off in separate incidents.

He could not read, but Bass did benefit from an eidetic (photographic) memory. He would get someone to read warrants and wanted posters out to him, and remember every minute detail, an ability which gave him an edge over other marshals, if he unexpectedly chanced upon a member of the criminal fraternity.

During his career, he was responsible for putting 14 outlaws into the ground, a modest figure considering how many he apprehended. He retired from being a Marshal when the territory became the state of Oklahoma in 1907, but carried on working as a policeman in Muskogee until his death, from Acute Nephritis three years later, aged 72.

CHAPTER 38

EUREKA SPRINGS

Early one late-fall morning, there was loud, demanding knocking on Jensie's door. She ran downstairs in her nightdress, bleary-eyed, and could see someone through the opaque glass door, holding a parcel. She opened the door, just enough to reach out an arm to take the delivery, whilst protecting her modesty, thanked who she assumed to be an early-rising postman, put the parcel to one side, and went to shut the door.

"Wake up Jensie!" a woman shouted, barging the door open.

"Sallie?"

"You've got five minutes to get dressed, and pack for a week. I've bribed a train conductor to wait, but he won't wait long."

A smidgen over Sallie's allotted time, and still half-asleep, Jensie left a note for Harriet, and was outside with her bags. They boarded a buggy, driven by an equally bewildered gentleman, who she faintly recognized, who had been a willing recipient of Sallie's greenback arsenal, when she arrived at the station. They headed south at a fast trot, to catch a train that was heading east, the very second they were on board.

They took a moment to catch their breath, but Sallie could not put off what had to be said, which could not be sugar-coated, "It's John... he's dying."

"Oh no, please God no."

"I'm so sorry," Sallie consoled, holding Jensie's hand.

"I need to go to him... where is he?"

"You do, and you are. He's in Eureka Springs, Arkansas."

"Arkansas?" Jensie looked confused, having assumed that the reason they were heading east was to get to Paris.

"It's a healing spring water town, up north in the Ozarks, near Missouri."

After his surgery, John had got all the way back to Las Vegas to be met by James, who told him that he looked a mess. John admitted that he felt like one, and explained what had been done in Kansas. James had heard of Eureka Springs, and reassured him that it wasn't such bad advice. Pitser and the men could run the ranch, he'd stick their horses in livery and go back east with him.

They got there a few days later, and John could already feel the lump returning. But he also had an ache deep inside, the cancer had spread. A couple of weeks later he was coughing up blood, had resigned himself to his likely fate, and sent word that he needed the rest of his family around him.

Eureka Springs was well-placed for vacationers to get there from the distant east or west, but from Texas Jensie and Sallie had a long and frustrating dogleg journey, via Little Rock, Fort Smith and finally Seligman, where they walked out into the chilled mountain air, to get on the town's private railroad train, for the last, even more frustratingly slow, eighteen miles.

They arrived at the Grand Central Hotel, where John had taken rooms. James met them in the foyer and hugged them both, "It's been a long time Jensie; it's good to see you. You are just the tonic he needs... but you need to know, he is not in a good way."

"I was a nurse, I've seen the worst. Take me to him."

"Of course, but he really isn't himself, he asked for a gun two days ago, we've had to hide them."

"I understand," she replied, remembering the desperation of some of her patients during the war.

John's room was on the ground floor, in preparation for a dignified exit, in future presumed inevitabilities. She entered nervously, to find Pitser sitting by his bedside. He offered her his seat and went outside.

John sat up in bed, and composed himself, "My love."

His voice was croaky, and the growth on his neck was enormous.

Jensie held his hand, not knowing what to say, and let out the first trivial thing that popped into her head, "Nice hotel... smells of fresh paint."

"Yes... they just finished building it."

She collected her thoughts, "Why didn't you write and tell me?"

"I didn't want to scare you... I hoped it would go away, but that 'old sawbones' was right. But while I was well in your mind, I was well somewhere. Until I sent for you, and the family, I really thought I might get better."

Jensie sat on the bed to cuddle her man.

"Any news for me?" he asked, trying to get off the subject of his predicted demise.

"Well, Meady has had another baby boy, she's called him June, strange name for a boy, but he is real pretty."

"And the business?"

"We're fine; Harriet will keep it going while I'm here?"

"How long are you staying for?"

"For," she hesitated, "...for the rest of your life."

Her literal statement was both comforting and disturbing. He would never spend a day without her again. But her words were revealing, his loved ones had accepted, with certainty, that it really was his end.

The four of them would take six-hour shifts, to sit and talk with him when he was up to it, or read to him when he wasn't. Jensie chose the night shift, so that she could cuddle up to her man, and no one objected. It meant that he was asleep most of the time she was with him, but in his final days he pretty much slept all the time anyway.

A doctor would come to the hotel twice a day to check on him, and Jensie would always make sure she was in the room as his 'nurse'. The doctor was a kind and gentle man; he soon worked out the situation between Jensie and John and did his best to comfort her as well.

As he left one day John mustered up the strength to speak, "Off to chase a nurse."

"Or perhaps a doctor," Jensie whispered, "he has soft girly hands."

Both their minds drifted back to people-watching on Bonham station the year before, when the world was almost perfect.

A few days later, in the morning, the doctor called for James, "It's soon, you should gather your family."

John never got to see the afternoon of December 22, 1884.

Danny sat and looked at Eugie, feeling emotionally drained. These people had become like friends over the previous couple of weeks, his grief was real. Eugie walked over to McKinley's drinks cabinet and returned with two large whiskeys. Danny had never seen her take a drink before.

He looked at his watch; it was nearly one in the morning, "I ought to let you get to your bed. You said you had a job for me tomorrow... today?"

"Yes, would you take me to Paris, to find his grave?"

"Yes, I would love to," Danny answered with total sincerity.

As Danny headed upstairs to explore the mysteries of the Chisum bedroom, Eugie stepped outside to explore the stars, she looked up at Polaris and spoke to her grandma, "It is time."

CHAPTER 39

PARIS

A t noon they pulled off Route 82, into Paris' downtown Plaza, and parked up opposite its Art Deco theatre, it was still showing Chisum, but they didn't need to see it a third time. The Plaza had a perimeter of old-style brick-built town houses, reminiscent of Jensie's love nest back down the road in Bonham, but sadly most were covered up by modern store frontages. The Plaza was dominated by a central marble fountain, which struck Eugie as a tad ostentatious for the sleepy little city.

The plan was to find the public library or courthouse, to ask for directions to Chisum's grave, but noticing a pleasant looking café, boasting air conditioning, Danny suggested lunch first, to get them out of the energy-sapping midday heat.

They ordered and waited for their food, Danny was very quiet and subdued, worried that after their long journey Chisum's grave might be an anticlimax for his friend, assuming that they could even find it.

Lunch arrived, Eugie watched him listlessly chomping into his burger, and thought about their exciting journey to New Mexico, it had truly been an adventure, but she felt tired, it was time to get back to her simple life.

The waiter brought Danny the check, but Eugie grabbed it exclaiming, "My last treat!" Danny nodded acceptance.

"If you want to wait here and have another coffee, I'll find the library and where his grave is," he offered.

The waiter overheard, "We don't give free coffee here, the public library is three blocks south, opposite Bywaters Park, but which graveyard are you looking for, mister?"

Eugie sensed her traveling companion ruffling his feathers, so discretely raised her hand to him, accompanied by a stern look.

"Not sure, are there many around town?" Danny replied through gritted teeth.

"Who are looking for? If it's 'Jesus in Cowboy Boots' he's down at the Evergreen Cemetery, just head south out of town on Church Street." He could see from Danny's puzzled look that he was on the wrong track.

The waiter looked down his nose at Eugie, "If it's for her, there is a Negro graveyard at Hickory Grove, south of Perry, about fifteen miles west of town, or there is an Odd Fellows cemetery on Pine Bluff St."

Eugie interrupted, "Yes, Chisum was an Odd Fellow, that'll be the one."

The waiter blanked Eugie, as if she wasn't there. Directing his response to Danny he burst into out of tune song, emulating the theme from the movie, which he'd watched at the Plaza theatre that weekend, "Chisum, John Chisum".

He ushered Danny to the window, and pointed to the north west corner of the plaza, "Go four blocks west on Bonham, then turn left on to 7th Street, head south as far as you can, turn right into Washington and keep going 'til just before the railroad tracks, and pull up on the left. It is quite a tomb, you can't miss it."

Eugie retained the moral high ground, left the waiter a tip, bade him farewell and thanked him for his help, despite his rudeness. He did not deign to reply. She sighed as he begrudgingly picked the gratuity up with two fingers, as if it was dirty, thinking to herself, 'We have still got a long way to go, for sure'.

They stepped outside, and it felt like they were walking into an oven. Fortunately, the waiter's directions were better than his manners. Five minutes later they pulled off the road, to where a substantial monument stood before them, just as described. It was constructed from three stone pillars, with the Odd Fellows brand at their junction.

The memorial was not only conspicuous by its size, but also by the quantity of flowers that had been left there; presumably by movie fans, unless there were lots of folk celebrating his birthday. Eugie looked down at the yellow rose tribute she had brought along, and wondered whether that particular perennial had any meaning to the others who had visited the grave.

Thankfully none of the movie fans were around to interrupt Eugie's moment. She got out of the car, and a wave of emotion ebbed over her. She turned around a full circle to try to imagine where the Chisum homestead would have been, but all signs of it were long gone, in favor of a stark industrialized landscape of railroad tracks, warehouses and power lines.

A horn blew, as a train approached from the north, Eugie took Danny's hand and motioned him to sit with her on a rusty bench next to the grave. She covered her ears from the onslaught of the seemingly endless freight cars that rattled past. The breeze it created was cooling, but not appreciated, just twenty yards from such a hallowed place.

The racket subsided into the distance, Eugie's mind drifted to the scene on December 25, 1884, which had been retold to her every Christmas for years, by either her grandmother or mother. She could picture James and Pitser Chisum, along with the new Sheriff, William Gunn, the County Clerk, Charles Pegues, and two other representatives of Paris' great and good, whose names had long been forgotten, but had been deemed appropriate pallbearers for this great man, on his last journey.

They carried John's coffin to his parents' freshly re-opened grave, its dark depth in stark contrast to the snow that had fallen overnight, and slowly lowered him into the ground. Two hundred or so mourners sang along solemnly to Amazing Grace, accompanied by a rousing, tartan clad, lone piper, as was the Chisum family tradition.

The Parisians departed, wishing their best to the surviving Chisums, and the grave diggers prepared to go about their business. The Jones family emerged from the shelter of the neighboring trees into a fresh flurry of snow, which had symbolically started to fall the moment the piper released his last note.

Sallie stomped towards Meady exclaiming, "You give me that boy!" she lifted baby June high up in the air, "he is growing so fast!" she lowered him down to smother him in her best Aunt Sallie kisses and hugs.

As the rest of the family exchanged more hugs, kisses and tears, Jensie slipped away from the huddle and approached John's grave, "Would you mind waiting and giving me a moment?" she asked the diggers, flashing her beautiful radiant smile.

Having seen rich whites hugging blacks, and kissing their babies, the puzzled grave diggers were not going to argue about anything that day, particularly not with this smartly dressed Mulatto beauty. They doffed their hats and removed themselves to a polite distance.

Jensie patted her pretty red dress under her knees, to keep them warm as she knelt in the snow.

"Well John Chisum, look how far you've come, and our family too. I don't know how you expected it all to turn out... I'm guessing not quite like this, you should have been around longer, to enjoy it all my love.

"I wish you could have found a way to take me as your wife, but you will always be my husband. Just know you always have been, and always will be loved."

She opened her bible and read aloud from Corinthians thirteen, but from her own perspective.

"Though I speak with the tongues of men and of angels, and have not LOVE, I am become as sounding brass, or a tinkling cymbal.

"And though I have the gift of prophecy, and understand all mysteries, and all knowledge; and though I have all faith, so that I could remove mountains, and have not LOVE, I am nothing...

"...When I was a child, I spake as a child, I understood as a child, I thought as a child: but when I became a WOMAN, I put away childish things.

"For now we see through a glass, darkly; but then face to face: now I know in part; but then shall I know even as also I am known.

"And now abideth faith, hope, LOVE, these three; but the greatest of these is LOVE."

As Jensie gently closed the precious book, which John had given her for Christmas, thirty years before, her tears flowed. She unpicked the yellow rose from her hair, and let it tumble down to lie on John's coffin.

"Sleep in peace, my love."

Eugie closed the very same bible, which she had been paraphrasing.

Danny had become somewhat immune to being in awe of the antiquities which kept emerging from Eugie's apparently bottomless bag, and could only come up with, "Well that's that then," feeling somewhat deflated that their journey had apparently come to its end.

"Pretty much, but aren't you curious what the parcel was that Sallie left at the apartment?"

"Oh yes, I forgot about that, what was in it?"

"Jensie forgot about it too, it sat in the corner for days. She was so bound up in grief that she did not remember Sallie leaving it, and thought it was stock for the shop or something. When she finally got around to opening it, she found a beautiful oil painting of him."

"Would that have been the one I saw in your house?"

"Yes, it would be, he was a handsome devil, almost as pretty as you."

"Isn't it a bit self-effacing, sending someone a painting of yourself?"

"I think you mean 'self-serving'... maybe, but not on that occasion; on the back of it there was a package."

She passed him a small jewelry box, inside was a tiny folded note. He unfolded it and read, "With this ring, I thee wed."

"Oh wow, he finally committed... what happened to the ring?"

Eugie held up her left hand and pointed at her wedding ring, "When you take me home take a closer look at John's hand in that painting."

Danny smiled, "Wonderful... okay, one more question, you told me before that you were, 'almost at his funeral'?"

"That's right I almost was. After the Texan and Pacific got them back home, Meady and Bob set about making me," she revealed with a sly old wink.

Danny smiled, and suggested, "Are you ready to head home?"

"That I am Daniel," she stood up and looked at the Chisum monument for the final time, and then at her modest bunch of roses, "these will look lost here, do you mind going by the Medlin Cemetery on the way, so I can pay my respects to the rest of the family?"

"No problem."

"One more thing," Eugie rummaged through the bottomless bag to drag out her beloved camera. In the absence of any potential photographer to recruit, she passed it to Danny, and stood dutifully next to her grandfather's dwarfing monument, for the penultimate 'Kodak Moment' of their adventure.

"Say cheese," he instructed.

CHAPTER 40

MEDLIN

The 20th century was steadily encroaching upon the once remote Medlin Cemetery, but it endured as a quiet, pleasant and well-maintained place to visit. Not least of all because of the Jones' patronage, their graves were in a neat row, sheltered by the eastern tree line, in what used to be known as 'The Negro section.'

Eugie worked her way along them, with Danny following, carrying her flowers, handing her a rose to lay for each family member. They ended up at Meady and Bob's where she laid four, to also acknowledge her aunt and grandmother. She popped the last one into a buttonhole in her blouse.

"Where are Jensie and Harriet buried?" Danny queried.

"When Jensie died Harriet sold the business, and moved away, we lost touch, that woman had gypsy in her blood from somewhere, but she will surely be in the ground by now, she'd be 115.

"Grandma is a sore point. She was buried with honors, for services rendered in her nursing days, in the Confederate cemetery off Highway 78. Some of those young men she saved had long memories. But through the Depression it wasn't looked after, it became a ruin. A few years ago, they built over it."

"That is outrageous."

"I used stronger words than 'outrageous' at the courthouse, I can assure you."

"You still take great comfort from them though?"

"Well, at the end of the day family and God are mostly all we've got."

"And the occasional good friend," Danny added.

"Sure, them as well," Eugie responded, somewhat dismissively.

He pondered out loud, "Maybe all this talk of death brings you closer to your God, and your family, I guess we all need something to hang on to."

"Danny, my God is your God... my family is your family."

"Thank you," Danny replied softly, acknowledging her generous inclusion.

Eugie exhaled a deep tired sigh, "It's time."

Danny turned towards the car, assuming she meant 'time to go home', but Eugie did not follow. She looked perplexed and uncertain, almost fearful, a look that Danny did not associate with his ever-confident friend. She chewed on her bottom lip then beckoned him over, put her arm in his, held his hand tight, and walked him to another old grave.

She pointed at the stone, the inscription was barely readable. Danny knelt down for a closer look, then exclaimed, "What the..."

"Read it out, Danny."

He obliged, "Daniel Johnson, August seven, 1853 to..." He wetted his hand and rubbed the stone beneath the birth date in the hope of revealing more information, but there was none, "there's no date of death."

"Read on," Eugie encouraged.

He looked at the other half of the stone, "Delilah J Johnson 1854 to 1923, 'Delilah,' I know that name."

"Yep, they are your grandparents, except your granddaddy is not buried here. No one knows for sure where he ended up."

"Why did I not know about this?"

"It was your father's wish, if he'd told you that, he would have needed to tell you more."

"I need to go talk to him."

"You do for sure, but wait, there is more that you should know first. It might not be my place to tell it, but I have no doubt that you need to hear it, and you need to hear it right."

She continued with a question, "Do you and your pa ever talk to each other at all?"

"We have nothing in common... well... it's ironic considering the last couple of weeks, nothing in common except Westerns, Pa is a big fan of Harry Carey. Danny clasped his left hand over his right elbow, impersonating Carey's classic pose, which John Wayne emulated in the closing scene of 'The Searchers', to honor Carey as one of his own heroes.

"Pa grew up in the silent movie era, and then used to take me to all the old B-movies when I was a kid. A penny dropped, yes that is one thing he used to tell me, Delilah would take him to the theatre when he was young. I thought Delilah was like a child minder or something, so she was his ma."

"Danny, your father is not a dishonest man by nature, but he has not been completely straight with you, 'some Mexican from way back,' my black ass, you've got as much Mexican in you as I have. You remember Sonny, the slave who became a wrangler?"

"Yes, Frances' brother's son with a slave girl, who Elijah sort of adopted," Danny replied, confirming that he had been listening.

"He was your grandfather, Daniel 'Sonny' Johnson," she explained, pointing at the grave, "Daniel, you are as black as I am. You really were a Buffalo Soldier in the 9th Cavalry."

Danny released his elbow exclaiming, "I can't be!"

"The Johnsons and Chisums were entwined for over a century, like tumbling tumbleweeds. The Johnsons were the cousins who spent three days crossing the Red River with the Chisums into Texas in 1837, Frances was Frances Johnson Towery. If you go back to the Clear Creek ranch there is an old graveyard, about half a mile down the hill from where we sat, you will find Josephine Chisum and her daughter Mary resting there, next to most of the Johnsons. You and I are family, real family."

Danny paused for his mind to process what his ears were telling it, and then slowly and angrily enunciated, "Why did no one ever tell me?"

Eugie ignored Danny's angry tone and drew a breath, "As ever, it's a long story," for the second time that day she motioned for him to sit down on a graveyard bench next to her.

"1892 is as good a place as any to start. The South Springs ranch had been sold to a fellow named Hagerman. Sonny was one of the best wranglers in the state, maybe the whole of the West, but Hagerman already had his own top hands, so there was no job for him, at least that was the reason the foreman gave, couldn't have been because he was black.

"Sonny came back to Texas, with his wife Delilah. He turned up here, with a letter of recommendation from Sallie, Bob gave him work, and your father, Samuel, was born a year or two later, a few months before my brother, Jinks, he grew up with us Joneses.

"Farming never really suited Sonny, but he stuck at it for nearly ten years out of loyalty to the family, in fact to the day that news came out that Queen Victoria had died. In that same newspaper there was an advertisement for wranglers to work in the rodeo. He decided he wanted to give it a go.

"From then on the news was patchy. Sonny sent money home for a good few years, but then it suddenly stopped. Bob went to Fort Worth, when the rodeo came to town, to try to find out what had happened to him. There was talk that he had gone over to Europe with a Wild West show, and there was another rumor that he had moved to New Jersey, to work in motion pictures.

"That was why Delilah used to take your pa to the theatre every Saturday, in the hope of seeing him, Jinks and I used to go with them. There weren't many black men in Westerns, so he wouldn't have been hard to spot. Sam was a very angry young man, he would tell me that he was going to find where his pa was one day, so that he could 'go and sort him out,' whatever he meant by that."

Daniel interrupted, "But that does not explain why no one has ever told me any of this!"

Eugie put her hand up to silence him, "Patience... America joined the Great War in 1917 your father and Jinks decided to enlist. But the only option for men of color was to join the Buffalo Soldiers, protecting the Mexican border. Sam was a virile young man, who wanted to cross the ocean and see Europe. He looked white enough to get away with joining the regular army, so he went down to Fort Sam Houston in San Antonio, signed up in the cavalry, and sailed to France."

"I still can't see how this never slipped out: this is one hell of a conspiracy!"

"When Claudine got pregnant with you, they decided that America was a better place to bring you up, but Sam had been living his lie for a decade, Claudine had no idea who she was really married to.

"Delilah had passed away, and pretty well all of the old-timers had either died or moved on. Only my family knew the whole story and agreed to keep quiet. But your pa could not have picked a worse time to come home, by the time you were a few months old the 'Great Depression' hit us, and times were hard. But my brothers helped keep your father on his feet, and to be fair, having 'white' friends did not do them any harm either."

"With all due respect, Mrs. Thomas, why have you taken it upon yourself to tell me all this now?"

"Danny, look at my family, I mean the Jones family, we all look different, we all got a different dose of the tar brush, I'm nearly as black as Harriet Tubman, but Jinks looks white. I know you want to have kids some day. There is no telling how they will come out. How would you feel in the delivery room if a Negro pops out of your white woman? Who would you have believed?"

"Is that really likely?"

"The color can skip generations, I've even heard of twins coming out black and white, I decided it isn't fair on you to take the chance, everyone should know what their roots are."

"But why would you be concerned about me having a black baby, in all honesty I'm not?"

Eugie paused... "It is still a cruel world out there that your children will have to grow up in. There are a thousand waiters out there, like that one in Paris, who would look down their nose at them. You need to know so that you can make choices, with all the cards on the table. And it isn't just for you, whoever you end up hooked up with needs to know the truth. I love you like a son, Danny Boy, I needed you to know," she started crying.

Danny put an arm around her, and a faint childhood memory came drifting into his head, an Irish song that someone used to sing to him.

He recited the first line in tune, with tears welling up in his eyes, "Oh, Danny Boy, the pipes, the pipes are calling... was that you?"

Eugie nodded and smiled, "When Claudine got sick, I would mind you, and sing to you, you were such a sweet baby, and we really do have some Celtic in us from way back."

Danny paused for thought, and then backtracked, "'If a Negro pops out of your white woman,' are you suggesting that I should play it safe, and find a black woman, so there will be no pointed fingers at my wife, or our children? I'm not going to choose someone because of their color. Not the color of their eyes, their hair, or their skin. I'm in my forties and still single, I'm single because I've not found her yet, when I do it will be for love. I'm not John Chisum, when I find her; black, white, brown, red or yellow, I'll commit with everything, one-hundred-percent everything. Chisum learned it the hard way, life is too short to let true love slip through your fingers, and at the end I reckon he knew it. He was so rich, but he was so poor."

Eugie turned to him and held his hand tight, "I'm proud of you son."

"I really do need to go, and talk to my father, let me take you home."

She hugged him fondly, and he felt something being slipped into his hand. He looked down at the raggedy edged notebook he had glimpsed, and then forgotten about, at the start of their journey.

"It's Chisum's journal, the first entry was the day he joined the Odd Fellows; he gave it to Jensie just before he died. You and your pa should read it together, remind him of where he came from, but make sure I get it back."

The historical and monetary value of the small tomb-like 120-year-old notebook was not lost on Danny, the thought that he ought to buy some white gloves to read it crossed his mind.

"I promise, and I'll take good care of it."

"You will", Eugie acknowledged, without doubt.

Danny took a last look at the grave, "What became of my Grandma?"

"Without Harriet around, she became like a sister to Meady, Bob made sure she was looked after, after all she was family, it was him who buried her here, and had the stone carved."

As they walked back to the car, arm in arm, Eugie whispered, "Don't be too hard on Sam. He must have found peace with his father somewhere along the road, to name you after him, find your peace with him... and send him my love."

On the drive back to the Jones Place, Danny had time to compose his thoughts. They arrived at the old homestead to find McKinley on the veranda, sitting in his rocking chair, smoking his pipe, reading the newspaper.

Danny opened the car door for his special friend, and held his hand out to her; she gracefully exited and looked up at him.

"What you going to do, Son?"

"Well, I think I want to find me a beautiful woman, fall in love, make a baby and see what comes out."

"Anyone in mind?"

Danny slipped a piece of paper out of his wallet and waved it tantalizingly, "There is always that green-eyed girl in Reagan County."

Eugie laughed, "You ol' dawg."

"And I may be taking that pilot job, babies are expensive. I'll make sure I'm here for your birthday though, cuz!" he added.

McKinley stepped down from the comfort of his chair, put his arm around Eugie's shoulder and led her up the veranda steps, he acknowledged Danny with a nod, "Thank you for bringing her home safe."

As they entered the house Eugie turned to look at Danny, framed by the doorway, and held her hand up for him to wait. He smiled, looked up at her and clasped his right elbow with his left hand, Harry Carey style. After a click from Eugie's camera, and a second, 'one for luck', he winked and turned away.

The wind-blown red Texan dust gradually obscured Danny's exaggerated impersonation of a John Wayne swagger, as he walked off into his future.

A puzzled McKinley turned to Eugie and asked, "Is everything okay, that boy looks drunk?"

She patted his chest reassuringly, "Yes, he's fine – everything is going to be just fine."

THE END

ABOUT THE AUTHOR

Russ is an English photojournalist and magazine columnist. Who has a life-long passion for the Western genre, particularly the movies of Duke Wayne. This passion ramped up a notch after spending a week with Duke's youngest daughter, Marisa, raising money for his favorite charity, Macmillan Cancer Support, on a 4x4 rally.

While researching this book he spent a week in Texas visiting graveyards and the library of the Daughters of the Republic of Texas in San Antonio. He describes his out-of-hours personal tour of The Alamo as one of the most humbling days of his life.

You can follow Russ at –
facebook.com/RussBrownPhotojournalist

SPECIAL THANKS

Members of the Wayne family:
For their supportive encouragement.

Richard Bastian:
For teaching me about flying and Englishisms.

Liam F. Rooney:
For his insight into the true West.

Perry Giles:
For his homespun Texan wisdom.

Garrett Roberts & Kenneth L. James:
For teaching me more about firearms.

Michael Philpot:
Cover Photo.

Hayley Brown:
For her editing skills.

And especially to Clifford R. Caldwell:
For reminding me that you can't mess with history, and generously
sharing his research. Read his history books, they are great!

Printed in Great Britain
by Amazon